RENDITIONS
of My Soul

The story of a Balinese woman

DESAK YONI & SARITA NEWSON

Renditions of My Soul - The story of a Balinese woman
by *Desak Yoni and Sarita Newson*
Copyright © 2013

Design and layout: Sarita and Kadek Ludra, Saritaksu Editions

ISBN 978-979-1173-23-0

Published by:

Jl. Padanggalak 101, Kesiman Kertalangu,
Denpasar, Bali 80237, Indonesia.
Tel. 0361-287816 Fax. 0361-289621
Email: books@saritaksu.com   www.saritaksu.com

RENDITIONS

of My Soul

I would like to thank all those dear friends who showed patience and kindness to me when I was going through my [own personal process of] rendition. The unconditional love you showed me was like a light at the end of a tunnel, a place of peace where I was finally able to rest and find myself.

Desak Yoni

A note for the reader:

I started out to write a memoir, and ended up writing a novel. In hindsight, I think all memoir must be fiction, as our memories are subjective in what they recall, especially after times of great stress. I have discovered, however, that "the ambiguity of memoir, its shifting planes of truth and memory, can take us somewhere important in discovering ourselves" (Mimi Schwartz). Having changed all the names to protect the privacy of those who inspired my story, I would like to assure anyone who feels any part of a character reflects their real lives, it is not intentional. In using memory, fact and imagination to recreate the complexity of real moments, I now know that the border between memoir and fiction is never clear.

D.Y.

Contents

"Everything will be all right in the end... If it is not all right, then it is not the end"

— from the film

The Best Exotic Marigold Hotel, 2011

1

Out there in the dark

Black Magic Powers

"Who is that out there in the dark?" the old lady called.

I was scared to death. It was Dadong Tublen. I thought she would kill me with her infamous black magic.

She was one of the two 'black magic' ladies in our village who were sisters, and they were both around my grandfather's age. *Dadong* means 'grandma' in Balinese. Dadong Tublen lived near our *Pura Dalem*, the temple for after-death ceremonies, which is close to our local cemetery. People in our village were always busy sharing scary stories about her; it was said that she and her sister were shape-shifters and could turn themselves into all kinds of frightening creatures. Farmers on the way to their rice paddies at night saw fireballs surrounding their house, and there were rumors of other strange apparitions.

She was standing there with her sarong scrunched up on either side in her hands, her legs apart, about to pee right in front of me. She peered out into the dark, only about half a meter away from me.

"Who's there?" she repeated.

"It's me, Madé Angel," I said, took a deep breath, and turned my torch on, aiming it directly at her face. In the dim torchlight I could see Dadong's face, but to my disappointment it hadn't changed at all. It was the same wrinkled face I saw every day when I climbed her fruit trees to spy on her.

I was both disappointed and relieved to see she looked just the same as in the daytime. She took a few steps away and got on with her pee; I could hear the splashing as it hit the banana palms. Her back was to me. She did a little jiggle and let down her sarong, turning back towards me.

"Please don't tell my mum and dad you caught me peeping, Dadong," I said.

I thought I heard her chuckling, but it turned into a cough, or perhaps she was just clearing her throat.

I knew I wasn't the only one to spy on her. Sometimes as many as six men would hang around in the neighborhood of Dadong Tublen's house, pretending to clean the drain or redirect the flow of the irrigation water to their fields. They were waiting for the moment when, just after midnight, she was reputed to change into *Celuluk*, an evil witch with long saggy breasts. I was always fascinated by their scary stories. Often after midnight I would sneak out. Stealing my dad's torch, I would walk to the bottom of my lane and hide in the corner behind Dadong's room to whet my curiosity. This was I had done on the night that Dadong caught me standing there, when she went out to wee under her banana palms.

Dadong Tublin lived next door to us; she always sold peanuts at Ubud market, Payangan market and Sukawati.

I used to sneak to her house to help her peel her peanuts, and then she would give me lots to take home to eat. At first my mum used to get angry with me when she found out I was helping Dadong to peel peanuts. Then my mum made an exception.

"You can bring some home, as long as you don't eat them raw," she said. She was sure that the God of fire, *Bhatara Brahma*, could get rid of any evil black magic from Dadong's peanuts. So my mum made sure any of those peanuts I brought home were boiled for a long time, or deep-fried over our kitchen fire before we ate them. What she didn't know was that I loved eating raw peanuts, so I was always eating them at Dadong's house, just as fast as I could, while peeling them. I figured a little bit of black magic in a peanut couldn't do me any harm back then, but now I wonder.

Kajeng Kliwon is a special date on which we Balinese make special offerings to protect our homes and villages from evil spirits and people practicing black magic who hold their meetings at our cemetery. Apparently these old ladies with black magic powers would meet at *Pura Prajapati* temple. It was said that they would dig the remains of dead children from the graves, and share the parts of the dead bodies around. I was keen to witness this. Being a very bold and fearless kid, I waited for the right day to sneak out at midnight, not forgetting to grab my father's torch before I left. Quivering with anticipation I sat under a banyan tree, waiting for something to happen. But nothing ever did. The only things I ever saw were a number of mangy old dogs, bats and other night animals. Either the old ladies were better at changing form than I imagined, or perhaps they were purposely keeping me in the dark.

When my brother died as a baby I was told that he had passed away after Dadong Tublen came over to my house at midday. In those days midday was also considered a very sacred moment, especially for innocent and vulnerable souls. My mum told me Dadong came over to borrow our *saab barak*—a *saab* is a round shaped lid used to cover offerings, and *barak* means red, but it also is a word used to describe a baby that is still too young for the early protective and naming ceremony that happens at 210 days.

My mum automatically interpreted it as if Dadong was asking for my brother's soul. She shrieked with anger.

"Go away, get out of our house immediately, before my husband comes home and kills you on the spot!" she shouted.

Apparently my brother, who was nearly six months old at the time, got really sick that day and died the same night of a high fever. My grandmother also told me that she thought my brother had been killed by black magic.

I gather from my mum's stories that her baby son was so young she panicked when he came down with a high fever. She piled many layers of clothing on him, covering him with thick blankets, trying to warm his shivering body.

She also covered my brother's head with a thick knitted hat. I wouldn't dare to even attempt to explain it to my mum, but perhaps her baby died from a small stroke in the brain when his fever rose too high. As he was all covered up, there would have been no way for his little body to cool down. There was no doctor available at midnight in those days, and no phone with which to call even a nurse, so all mum could do was pray to the Gods in our family temple that her baby would get better.

My mum's pain from losing her baby boy still scars her to this day. She is still angry with the old lady even though Dadong died long ago. I will never be able to comfort my mum for her loss, as a baby boy has always been much more important than a baby girl in Balinese society.

Apparently, when I was born my mum was really sad that I was born as a girl. My grandmother used to tell me this, without realizing how it hurt my feelings. I also could see my mum's sadness when my little sister was born. She wanted her little boy back, because she wanted my dad to be happy. She used to blame us when dad had an affair with another woman. She said that if only she had a little boy, my dad would be so happy he would never leave her to see another woman.

I grew up feeling the resentment from my own mother, so full of regrets that I was born as a girl. She assumed I was going to be useless and anyway I would eventually be married off into someone else's family compound.

The Battle of the Sexes

My mum and my grandfather never got along. It was really weird and so hurtful to see the two of them always fighting like children. My grandfather would always hurt my mum's feelings.

"Only a bad woman cannot produce a boy," he would say.

She would defend herself by saying "Yes, well I did produce a boy. If it wasn't for that old lady's black magic my little boy would have grown up to be the best looking boy in the whole village."

Then my mum would go on "He had the most beautiful curls, and fair skin just like mine. He would have been so smart and he would have taken care of me when I get old."

Grandfather was always smoking cigars to irritate my mum, as my mother hated the smell of cigars. He loved to drink whiskey, vodka and gin—whenever he had alcohol in the house he was so drunk all the time. He got all the best classic brands given to him by an English anthropologist. My grandfather was assisting him with his research on *wayang kulit*—the shadow puppets and their plays. They were the main source of entertainment, and education, before we had TV or schools—the shadows on a flickering screen were like magic, and that was how we learned all the old stories and deep philosophy from the Mahabharata and Ramayana. The puppeteer spoke in the ancient *kawi* language, but then he converted it into our local dialect and context, with funny stories we could relate to, so everybody in the village could understand.

Even in those days there was a limitation on how much alcohol you could bring into Indonesia, but my grandfather's English friend knew how to find Malt Whiskey on the black market, and he made a good home brew. Unfortunately whenever my grandfather drank he would become full of regrets and argumentative, and that was when he would pick a fight with the nearest person. Of course my mother was the only one stuck at home with him, so she took the brunt of his bad behavior.

The fights between my mother and my grandfather apparently continued after I left home until one day my grandfather got really ill. He was only sick for one or two weeks and died in his bed. My sister was there to witness his death as my mum still refused to go anywhere near him. My sister said that my grandfather asked where I was and told her to tell me that he missed me and loved me; his last word was my name. I was in Australia at the time, seven months pregnant with my first child back in 1995.

I think my father inherited his anger and his charisma from his father, but he never had as much charm, or the ability to make such good jokes as my grandfather. It was said that my grandfather had walked from Ubud to Bedugul as a young man, at the time when there was no food to eat, in search of some distant relations who had a farm. It took him three days to find them, and nothing to eat but insects along the way. Things were grim in those days as the Japanese had taken all the food from the island, and only a few isolated villages had managed to hide supplies. The Japanese even took the woven sarongs and batik, so all there was to wear was old sacks. My grandfather ended up living near Bedugul for a long time and that was where he met my grandmother.

When he got angry with me my father used to get very violent. He nearly drowned me several times. He would drag me across the yard to the catfish pond at the back of our house where the creek used to run all the way to the temple of the dead. It was a huge hole in the ground— probably around five to six meters deep. He dug the hole because he needed the mud to make his own bricks for building. In that particular spot the mud was clay and it was next to a creek, so my father didn't have to carry water to make his muddy dough for his bricks. When my father had already made enough bricks to build our house he filled up the hole with water and used it to farm catfish.

The water was really dirty and smelt bad from all the catfish waste. Once my father got me to the pond he would start taunting me, pushing me in and out of the water, saying "*enceb-angkid*" (in you go—out you come) and then push me in as deep as he could, holding me under the water till I was about to burst from lack of air. He would lift me up just in time to catch my breath. Many times I thought I would one day die of this kind of punishment, as often he left me too long under the water. I often ended up swallowing a lot of dirty water. The trauma of this experience made me so afraid of water and it is probably the reason why I can't swim, even until now.

I was always scared when my dad's mood changed from happy to angry—it would happen so suddenly. He would drag me across the yard, or smack me until his finger-marks swelling on my leg would turn black and blue. But at other times he was someone I could feel proud of, such a smart man and an inspiration to everyone in our village. He built houses, he voiced his opinion at the village *banjar* community meetings, and for a few years he was even the head of the *banjar*.

My father was also deeply involved in politics. I used to go campaigning with him for the *Golkar* political party. We would travel to another village in a truck. Sometimes I missed school so I could go with my dad to attend *Golkar* meetings, representing our village in Denpasar. There were no women to be seen attending these meetings. I used to be spoiled with cakes and Coca-Cola by all my father's friends. I have such good memories of Indonesian politics at the time. It seemed to me like one big picnic. For a poor girl from a small village eating cake and drinking

Coke was an unheard of luxury.

My father also had affairs with young married women around the village. This hurt my mother's feelings tremendously. It didn't only hurt all of our feelings, it also made our family much worse off financially, as dad was all too happy to help himself to our little hard-earned income from harvesting rice and working on someone else's land. In my experience a third person is never good for any marriage, let alone in a poor and disadvantaged family like mine—it can result in hungry and starving children who for a bonus get beaten up for no particular reason.

At times like that I would run to my grandmother's to hide, and see if she had anything extra to eat in her kitchen. My grandmother was very nice to all of her grandchildren but of course she had her favorites. I was very lucky to be one of her favored *cucu*, as she always felt sorry for my misfortune or rather my mum's misfortune in marrying my dad.

Grandmother was always saving from any little thing she could manage to sell in our local market. She would sell banana leaves, bananas, mangos, flowers, coconuts and rice. My grandmother had ten children, and my first aunty had eight—so I have many cousins in my village. And some of my cousins from one side of the family married my cousins on the other side, in fact it was encouraged to do this, so most people in my village are probably related to me.

When my mum had nothing for us to eat in the house I always knew where to go, but mum was too embarrassed to let me stay at my grandmother's in case I told her the true situation. My mum always tried to hide her misfortune. She always told our grandmother that everything was ok.

"All good!" she would say, when my grandmother asked her how she was. She didn't want to be seen as a failure, no one does. My mum worked very hard with the most basic skills and know-how. She used to sell steamed rice-cakes called *ketupat* made from rice wrapped in coconut leaves and she had her own roadside *warung* where she sold food when I was little. She was always getting things to sell at the local market just like her own mum. Grandmother knew better than to trust my mother to let her know if anything was wrong, so every a few days she would come to check on us. She would bring us food and often a little pocket money.

Purification ceremony

Another fascinating old lady lived next door to my parents' house, on the west side, and she was known as Dadong Tinggal. Our *banjar* community had officially declared her insane. She loved to sing, and she would start early each morning, waking up the whole neighborhood, around 1 a.m. Then we would hear her again at 2 a.m. and then every hour from then on—she sang with the roosters each hour of the morning. And she was not a bad singer!

Something about Dadong Tinggal always fascinated me. I think she actually liked being declared insane. She seemed to enjoy her life, in spite of what all the villagers said. She sang every day and she was able to go wherever she wanted, including places that were forbidden or even haunted by ghosts. Then at night she seemed to rather enjoy drinking *arak*, a local brew made from rice, with a very strong alcohol content. "Hmm… she's not so badly off," I thought.

In other ways she still functioned more or less as normally, just like all the other old people in my village. She worked for local traders, cheerfully carrying their goods to the market each morning, fetching clean water and cleaning up people's yards for money. Dadong Tinggal was always rather extraordinary in my mind; she seemed to always be so happy and never judged me like the other villagers. She always seemed to be pleased if I said I wanted to join her in her daily adventures. She didn't talk to anyone else other than her own daughter and me.

One Sunday, I set off with Dadong Tinggal for an adventure. We went to explore our local cemetery. The idea was to collect firewood, and also to seek young fern fronds for vegetables. Inside the cemetery I caught lots of dragonflies, which my mother could fry up and make a delicious snack. Normally no one was allowed to go into the graveyard, especially children, unless it was the day of a cremation or a special day on which we are allowed to bring offerings for the dead.

In those days our cemetery was full of dark, overgrown plants that covered all the ground and it was hard to get from one part to another. Since no one would dare to go inside there were lots of fresh ferns for us to collect. I was so looking forward to yummy blanched ferns mixed with spices and coconut for lunch.

On that particular day Dadong was happy and playful; we were both so overjoyed with what we had collected in such a short time and it was barely even midday. I spent some time playing, swinging from one low banyan tree branch to another, but I slipped and fell. Fortunately I managed to land on an old burial mound, which had been dug out for a cremation ceremony. At that stage they were no longer taking the whole body out of the grave, instead they were only doing it symbolically, opening the grave and calling the spirit of the dead person, so all the aging skeletons were simply being left underground.

I was so excited when I found a human skull, Dadong and I danced with it for a while. Then we got tired, so we set out on our way to go home. We had to carry our firewood, our bundles of fresh fern fronds, and plastic bags of dragonflies, and as well as that, concealed in my fern fronds, I carried the human skull I had found. I was planning to scare my friends with it the next day at school or I thought maybe we could keep it at the front of my classroom instead of our plastic model. I didn't really think much of it all. I was in year four at school—around 10 years old at the time—the same age as my second son right now.

My mum was so overjoyed to see me; she had been looking for me for hours and had checked with all my friends to find out where I was. No one knew where I was, so everyone was in state of panic! However, my mum was not very amused when she saw the human skull. She asked me where I been, interrogating me about every detail. Nothing that I had brought home was any use, she told me, as we are not allowed to bring anything home with cemetery dirt on it, not fern fronds, not firewood, and especially not a human skull.

When he heard what I had done my angry dad pushed me violently towards a banana tree and tied me up. I could have easily escaped, but before I had the chance to get away he began to belt me black and blue. That wasn't enough to satisfy him. He then went on to attempt to drown me in the muddy pond at the back. In the meantime my mum was busy preparing a ceremonial basket filled with rice, eggs and coconut. She set off with this to see our local priest to ask for a good day to do a purification ceremony called *Mecaru*. Lots of animals would be sacrificed to pay for my misbehaving, being so naughty to bring home dead things from the cemetery.

"How could you be so careless?" they all asked.

My mum and dad were threatening to declare me insane just like Dadong Tinggal. Deep in my heart I had a crazy and rebellious thought: "I would actually love that, as long as I am still allowed to attend school and play with my friends."

Seasons of my life

The seasons we had when I was a child in Bali were nothing like those of children in other countries. Now I know how in the west children always look forward to the changing of the seasons. When it passes from cold winter to sunny spring and the warm weather arrives the flowers bloom and they can go outside to play. Then when spring is gone they anticipate summer, a time when they will enjoy lying around on the beach, swimming, picnicking and camping. Then, after summer, it's back to autumn when the weather is getting cooler and they can look forward to snow, or for some there will be ski trips if they are from a well-to-do family. Or to simply enjoy staying at home by the fireplace at night, with warm winter soups, roast dinners and parents happily chatting with their glasses of red wine by the fire.

My childhood was not even remotely similar to this scenario. The seasons we had to get through were sometimes even life threatening. There was 'head-lice season', which was not so bad, as there was always some elder woman in the family ready to pick the nasty *kutu* and their eggs out of our hair and reduce the itching. But then there was 'skin-rash season' which could be completely disfiguring, and 'dysentery season' that coincided with mango season, but it was a time when many of the little ones in our families died. We did have a harvest season, but that was not so exciting either, as although it was a chance to earn some money, it was such hard work. During the harvest season I would have to go out in the heat to collect leftover grain after the harvest from amongst the stubble in the rice fields. It took ages to fill up a woven basket and then I had to carry the heavy load on my head, sometimes for a distance of more than six kilometers.

Some of the most vivid images of my childhood are of these seasons. In 'head-lice season' lots of my friends would need to have their hair cut very short to make it easier to get rid of the *kutu*. Mari had the worst case I had ever seen—she was filthy—she didn't like washing her hair and she barely showered unless her mom forced her. One afternoon Mari, Jelih and I were playing *mecingklak*, a kind of hopscotch, when all of a sudden I saw head-lice dropping from Mari's head to the floor. She was scratching like mad and it still makes my head feel itchy today, just thinking about it. I remember I told her mum. It wasn't good to 'dob' her in, I have to admit that much, but I felt so sorry for my friend.

When her mum checked on her head it was too late to do the usual trim. Her mum had to completely shave her and it looked like her scalp was full of holes that had been dug by the lice. Her mum shaved Mari's head very clean then she put wet tobacco in every hole and covered Mari's head with a white cloth. I remember she cried so much from the embarrassment of having a shaved head—there were no secrets in a village like mine.

Skin disease season played havoc with the more sensitive of my friends, especially Rosi. We used to tease her by chanting *Rosi kerek dongkrek* and then repeating it over and over again. Her entire body would be covered with blisters, and a thick fluid the same colour as condensed milk would seep from her skin. Some days she could not move out of bed and even if she could she would be too embarrassed to attend school. Her mom took her to the holy spring once a week to have her purified, and she was also treated at the local health centre. My mom and her friends would tell me not to visit her because they thought that the *kerek* rash was the result of her own mom's actions. People in my village believed that Ibu Rosi could do black magic, and they said she had lots of enemies in the black magic world and that was what made her little girl sick.

I will never forget the time I got a leech in between my legs. I was very young, just in year two at school. I vaguely remember playing in the river, swimming around as usual, waiting for my dad to finish his bath and then we went home together. On the way home I walked in front of my dad so he could watch out for me better in the torchlight. My father was shocked to see blood dripping down my legs.

"There's no way you could have your period yet," he

said, "you are only eight years old!" And he rushed me home to my mother.

I remember how worried he was. He kept on saying… "What if it is her period? What a horror to have our child having her period at this age!"

Then my mum undressed me, and checked my private parts, and, she reckoned there was a leech in there. So my father took my baby sister's plastic baby-bath, filled it up with warm water, then added lots of salt and some eggs that were just about to hatch out. He said the leeches would sniff the blood inside the eggs. Luckily in those days it was easy to get fertilized eggs as everyone used to keep at least 10 chickens in their compound for breeding purposes.

My mum soaked me in this round bath while my father rushed off in a panic to get the local male nurse, Pak Kota. I was so scared of Pak Kota because he always gave us an injection that hurt like hell and most of the times his needles looked as if they were rusty.

News spread all over the village so quickly and lots of my friends gathered by my side including the boys. I was so ashamed of myself being naked and lots of curious boys from my class were there. Then a huge leach fell out from between my legs just as my father got back with Pak Kota. So I didn't have to have the injection but I still had to lie down and drink lots of coconut juice as I had lost a lot of blood. For years people in my village used to tease me by joking that my virginity had been taken away by a leech. I was so embarrassed! I thought I would not be able to find a husband, as I was no longer a virgin from that day. I carried that uncomfortable thought in my head for a long time.

Playing Adult games

Another childhood story I haven't ever told anyone, was the 'taboo' experiments I did with the girl from the other side of the river. This girl's dad was infamous for his sexual arousals and he had been caught many times masturbating in public. People in my village just put him down as crazy and over-sexed and they thought there was nothing they could do about it. His daughter Wati was my best childhood friend. Our secret remained with her forever, she swore she would not tell anyone and I believed her. She died at the age of twenty-two from a bad fever stroke and took our secret with her. Nobody knows why she died so young.

"Perhaps it was black magic," they said.

Wati was around 4 years older than I. She was rather slow at school and repeated her primary class every second year. It took her nine years to finish Primary School. Even though her dad owned a large parcel of rice paddies she wasn't allowed to continue her schooling after that, because it would be just a waste of time her dad said. This didn't worry Wati one bit, as she hated school and could still barely read after finishing year six.

Wati and I used to sleep over in each other's houses but it was more convenient for me to sleep over at her house as she had her own room and I was still sharing a room with my parents and a bed with my sister. Poor Wati was the only child and her mom died when she was around six. Her house was a building with cement floor and cement rendering, so it was a luxury for me to stay in her room instead of mine.

Wati told me she often watched her dad masturbate alone under a tree, and she had been trying it, touching herself. She told me how good it felt. I was only nine years old at the time and I didn't believe a word she said. Then she started touching me. First she touched me from the outside of my underwear. Then she said "It is much better if you take these off."

I did not say a word. Slowly and gently she took my pants off, and she rubbed me with her finger. It felt very good, and got better and better, making little aching bursts of electric warmth travel through my body. She then asked me if I would do the same for her. "It's better if you do it," she said.

We played our little game on and off for a couple of years, sometimes we would rub each other with our fingers, and other times we rubbed against each other, like two pairs of scissors. And then one day I fell in love with a handsome boy from my class in year six. I told Wati I thought I was in love with him. She responded maturely.

"Our secret game has nothing to do with love," she said. "We're just having fun, as we do when we play with rocks, hide-and-seek or any other game." I agreed.

All I could think of now was how I would win the attention of the handsome looking boy in my class, and my visits to Wati's house became less and less frequent. He was smart, good looking, nicely dressed. He even had nice shoes and was nothing like the rest of my friends. We were a rather grubby, untidy bunch, and my shoes were full of holes. I have kept none of my pictures from my days at Primary School, as I hated myself so much in those days. I burned them all.

My father's daughter

From a very early age I was expected to do all the things boys do, and although he was very hard on me, my father liked to take me along when he went campaigning for his political party *Golkar*—short for Golongan Karya, the Workers Party, and *SOKSI,* Sentral Organisasi Karyawan Swadiri Indonesia—the Central Organization of Self Employed Indonesian Workers.

Together we attended political conferences, and I was such a cute little "fellow" I think his friends thought I was his son, as he encouraged me to have my hair cut short like a boy. He even sent me to karate training, something very few girls did in those days. I was used to hard physical labour, as every day I cut grass for the family's cows, helping my mom to bundle it into big bamboo baskets, and together we would carry the heavy load home on our heads. Often I would be the only girl out in the fields in the evening, cutting grass and climbing tall trees with the other boys.

I always tried to fulfill my father's expectations and generally felt more comfortable in the company of boys and men. We remained close as I was growing up, until I hit puberty and suddenly my world changed and I was relegated back to the world of women, a rejection I have never quite forgiven him for. From then on he didn't like me playing with the boys any more, and started to tell me to be very picky, wanting to know who the boys were in my class, and what families they came from.

My father considered the Balinese caste system to be very important for us to maintain. He didn't care that it was a replica of the Indian caste system except that it does not include the 'untouchable' caste. But any friends of mine who were in a lower caste might have been considered untouchable, as far as he was concerned.

Our family had originated from the *ksatrya* or warrior caste, second only to royalty and priests, so he did not like me having anything to do with boys from the lowly *sudra* caste, in case I lost my standing in society by falling in love and marrying someone of a lower status.

My father always angrily chased away any boys who wanted to see me, unless he was sure they were the same caste as us or higher. When I got interested in dating I was only allowed to go out with a distant second cousin, Dé Tu, because he was the same caste as we were—his family shared the same '*merajan kawitan*' family clan temple of origin. The fact that he was also rich and his family had lots of productive land around the lake in Bedugul, in the highlands of central Bali, was another strong point in his favour as far as my father was concerned.

I must admit that Dé Tu was very good to me, to my sister and my entire family in the beginning. He was staying at his auntie's house in my village so he could continue his High School education without having to go all the way to the old capital town of Singaraja in the north, which was where the children in his district were sent. I went to High School in Gianyar, so I usually went home at weekends and sometimes I was allowed to accompany Dé Tu to Bedugul. I really loved the Bedugul area, as it is the cold part of Bali, lots of mountains, lakes, the landscape very lush and green and all vegetables fresh. I used to go and stay there almost twice a month. Dé Tu's stepmother really loved me. She was wife number two. Each morning she would heat water in a big pot for my shower. She looked after me so well each time I went there. I thought it must be because she didn't have any children of her own.

Dé Tu's father had two wives when I started dating him. Wife number one (Dé Tu's mother) lived at the top of the mountain with her two daughters. The houses were built on a steep plot, with rooms staggered at various levels from top to bottom and lots of steps to climb up and down each morning. It was so hard for Dé Tu's mum to carry buckets of water to the bathroom for me, she would be exhausted by the time the concrete tank was full, but she insisted.

Six months after we had been dating I noticed that Dé Tu was making excuses not to visit me—he would say he was busy with ceremonies, then he would be sick, and so on. And then one day, my friend in Gianyar saw him with a girl two years younger than me (Dewi was in year 10, while I was in year 12). I defended my beloved Dé Tu.

"Don't spread rumours it's not a good thing to do," I said.

And then one day I saw a girl riding Dé Tu's motorbike, and when she stopped at the little *warung* street-stall in front of my *kost* room in Gianyar I noticed she was wearing gold jewelry similar to the necklace and bracelet which Dé Tu usually wore—it belonged to his stepmother, and she had promised to lend it to me to wear at my village temple ceremony the following week. How bizarre!

"This is not right!" I thought to myself. I let her go, but I continued to keep an eye out for her from afar each day, as her school was just across from my place. My friend also followed her one afternoon to find out where she lived for me.

My distant cousin was by no means a handsome boy but he was reasonably good looking by my standards. It was very convenient for me to date him; he was a nice guy, my father approved and his family approved of our relationship. This is perhaps the ideal situation for a Balinese girl like me, from a village like mine. What does love have to do with it?

"Love grows by itself once you spend time together," my dad said. And it had for me after getting to know Dé Tu better. He was staying so close by to my house, and I got to enjoy lots of weekend trips to the mountains of Bali in cooler weather and spent time with the friendly farming families up there.

I was very nervous the following Saturday.

"What if it is true he is dating another girl?" I worried. "What would I tell my father?"

I waited until very late that day and finally Dé Tu turned up at my house. His expression was not happy and he was unusually quiet.

To break the ice I asked him: "Hey do you know this young girl in Gianyar?" I described her. "I think she is part of our family's 'kawitan' temple." I pretended it was a coincidence that someone in my family had mentioned her.

Dé Tu denied any knowledge of her, and then he said he had to go home to Bedugul and he didn't want me to come this time, because his friend was having a special ceremony.

"I just want to hang out with my male buddies for the weekend," he said.

"OK!" I replied, and pretended it didn't matter.

But the very next day I asked my friend to take me for a long ride on her motorbike all the way to Bedugul in the morning, and sure enough I saw the very same girl in the front yard of his house. I didn't go in to confront him or her. We carried on up the road, and I asked my friend to take me for a ride around the lake to enjoy the scenery for the day.

We went home with a big pile of vegetables from the Bedugul market. The following week when Dé Tu came to my house again he had no idea I had been by his house in Bedugul on Sunday morning the week before. He pretended everything was normal between us.

"No way," I thought to myself, "I have to break up with this cheating cousin of mine." And I told him I didn't want to have anything more to do with him.

Dé Tu asked me why I wanted to break up when he hadn't done anything wrong. My father took his side and told me to listen to what Dé Tu had to say for himself. He went on and on about having nobody else special in his life, but it all sounded like a big lie to me.

"You should swear you are telling the truth!" I said. "And if you lie something bad will happen to you."

In front of my father Dé Tu swore that he was telling me no lies.

"I swear this is the truth," he said, "I will have a big accident on my motorbike and die if its not."

"Well, you can go home to Bedugul on your own," I told him. "I need to think about your story and I will follow you to Bedugul once I calm down." But I didn't go.

One Sunday afternoon several weeks later I decided to go to back to my room in Gianyar early, instead of waiting till Monday morning as usual. I asked one of my school friends to take me to visit the girl's house that afternoon, and I found Dé Tu there at her house.

"I have a quick message—for Dé Tu only—I said, when they opened the gate. Dé Tu came over to me with a red face.

"You will die soon" I whispered into his ear, "as you swore to me but you lied." He laughed. "It was just a made-up vow," he said. "It will never happen."

I took a deep breath and left without another word.

Two months later, someone from Bedugul came to our house wearing traditional clothes, so we thought he must have been coming to invite us to a ceremony. It was his uncle. He had come to let us know that Dé Tu's cremation was to be held in a certain number of days. Dé Tu had died in a motorbike accident on a very sharp bend; he had a head-on collision with a truck. My father and I went straight away to Bedugul and we stayed at Dé Tu's house for several weeks until the cremation was over. I met Dewi, the new girlfriend, at the ceremony. She was crying uncontrollably, but I had no tears.

I was angry, but it wasn't with her. I was feeling guilty for my whisper and feeling so angry with myself. On the day his body was being given its ritual bath, naked as custom decrees, in front of all our family relations and the community, I joined them all and touched him for the last time, asking for his forgiveness. His head was badly broken, his face unrecognizable and his arms were all smashed up. He was put into a coffin and burned that day.

"Goodbye and I'm sorry..." I whispered into the

cremation pyre. I didn't want to ever remember this moment of sorrow again.

"He didn't deserve to die just for lying to me," I thought.

No one knew what I felt, except perhaps for my father who stared deep into my sad eyes, acknowledging that Dé Tu had gone to a better place; a place where he could not lie again.

When I saw the flames burning his head I started to cry and put my head on his stepmother's lap.

"This will be the last day that you and I will be in Bedugul together," she told me. "Dé Tu's dad has remarried again. I didn't want to stay here on my own." She had already moved back to her own village.

"I only came here today for the cremation," she said, "I am so pleased to see you here. I am so sorry that Dé Tu was not honest to you," she went on.

"All will be forgotten now he has gone," I told her. "All that is left is to say goodbye."

And I have never been back to see the family in Bedugul since that day, but I have often wondered if I had refrained from cursing him perhaps he would not have had that terrible accident. I still remembered the peanuts I had eaten at Dadong Tublin's house... so many of them... whenever she wasn't looking. Maybe my mother was right. And then there was my fear of karma, after all the stories my grandmother and grandfather had told me.

"What kind of karma will I earn from this?" I asked myself, and I felt really scared. Dé Tu hadn't deserved to die just for cheating on me. I made up my mind never to curse anybody ever again, no matter how angry or hurt I might feel.

* * *

My first real boyfriend, Kadek, was from Sebatu village. He was not a bad looking boy, and quite shy, but his smiles really got to me when I peeped at him from the corner of my eyes during lessons in the classroom.

One Sunday we planned to meet at the market. He brought a spare helmet with him and I hopped on his motorbike. After a quick drive around Gianyar we went up to the top of Bukit Jati hill and back down, and then he bought me my favorite *babi guling* lunch at Gianyar market. He wanted to buy me a skirt, but I refused. When he insisted I told him: "If you really want to buy me something, then buy a skirt for my little sister, not me."

"Sure," he said. So he bought a denim skirt for my sister. Of course I hadn't thought what I would tell my parents if they asked who had bought it. I was so excited and very happy that Kadek had bought a denim skirt for my little sister. When I got home I gave it to my sister and I told her she had to lie about who had given it to her. We had a rich lady friend, a coffee-trader who often gave us gifts as a reward for helping her with bits and pieces during the day. So, my sister had to tell my mum, our lady friend had given her the gift. We didn't think that my mother would go and thank her for it and "bang!" in a flash our lies were exposed. I realized I hadn't planned that very well.

I could tell that my friendship with Kadek was about to get complicated from then on as my parents were bound to find out, especially as he was from a 'Sudra' caste family and I'm from the 'Ksatria' caste. So, it was much easier to never invite him again.

My High School years were full of unfulfilled desire. I got no satisfaction until I was in year 11 at High School. I learned from my first real love affair that curiosity kills. Kelin and I started dating, first just casually, then it become more intimate by the day. Until one day he asked if I would stay for the night at his *kost*, the room that he rented nearby our school.

"Of course," I said, as I was so in love with him.

Kelin and I had no protection and we kept on doing it again and again. He promised that he would use a condom next time. It was my first time and the worst part was that he didn't believe me that I was a virgin because he said I was supposed to bleed.

"I don't know why I'm not bleeding," I told him, "am I really supposed to?"

"Yes," he said, "yes, all virgins bleed when they first have sex."

I didn't tell him about my childhood adventure with the leech, and we continued to see each other. I would sneak out from my own *kost* room at night to visit him, as my landlord did not allow us to invite boys around. I was falling more and more in love with Kelin and in retrospect I think he took advantage of me because he seemed to be so experienced. He was in year twelve already and I was worried at the end of the year I might never see him again. I began to spend more time with him and less time at school. I didn't care any more about school, although I thought that was weird, and then I realized it must be because I was in love. I would sneak out from my classroom when I saw Kelin's motorbike parked at the front gate of my school. I could see him signalling to me from the gate. I took my bag and went off with him wherever he wanted to take me on his motorbike. He came from a wealthier family than mine and he was able to buy me *nasi goreng* from a warung. To me that was absolute luxury.

The teacher was threatening to tell my parents about my many absences from school. I even missed my class test and one day of the end of year exams. Kelin and I had been indulging in the pleasures of sex and spending more and more time at his place. We had been dating for months now. And then… I missed my period.

"I'm pregnant," I told Kelin in panic.

He hugged me.

"I will take the good news to my parents at the

weekend" he said, "and we can make arrangements to get married."

"Hey" I said … "No…no, no, no!"

All of a sudden I had remembered my purpose for being in that town. I had gone there to continue my education because I didn't want to be stuck in the village making offerings for the rest of my life. Why was this happening to me now, while I was in the middle of my year-eleven end of year exam period?

"No. You must help me to get rid of it while it's only in the early weeks."

But he wasn't going to have anything to do with abortion. "It is sin to do that. I must marry you."

At that moment I decided to never see him again.

I caught a bus to Klungkung, and went to a hospital there where no one would recognize me. I asked for a specialist. "*Kandungan*—Maternity," I said. A doctor came to talk to me and asked me where my husband was. I told him my story off the record, and then he gave me details where I could get it done. I cried—it was such a relief. I rang the number he gave me from a public phone and they told me what to do, how much it would cost etc.

Where was I supposed to get the money? Then with anger and feeling such a loser and all alone, I sold my gold earrings and gold necklace, determined to simply tell my mum I had lost them. It all worked out. I didn't give myself time to think about it, and studied very hard the very next day, right after the abortion. Luckily my teachers were happy to give me a repeat exam at the Principal's office.

During the rest of my high school years I dated all types of Balinese guys but each time when I saw in their eyes they were just about to ask to sleep with me, I managed to come up with a scenario to break up with them. Until finally, in year twelve, my childhood sweetheart—my dream boy from Primary school—came to visit me at my *kost* room. I almost died of excitement but it turned out he wanted unprotected sex as well and I wasn't going to allow it.

Then another *ganteng* (gorgeous) guy, also rich, named Agus, came into my life. We were dating for a little bit, until one day he took me to his house in Denpasar and tried to get into my pants without a condom. Again, I asked: "Why you won't use condom?"

But as with every Balinese guy I had ever been with his answer was the same.

"I love you. If you get pregnant we'll just have to get married."

"What about your studies, and mine?"

"We can always quit school."

"No way." I said.

So that was an end of another relationship. After that I decided to focus on finishing my school and then get a job as soon as possible so I could study more. I wasn't going to end up in the same situation as my mother, dependent upon a man, with no choice but to accept everything that happened. I had much bigger and better plans for my future.

The "*tonyo*" ghost in my bonsai

I noticed my nice potted banyan tree was missing from the middle of our yard. I thought my dad probably moved it somewhere we couldn't bump into it.

"Bapak, where is my bonsai?" I cried.

"I already chopped it up and threw away the bits, we can use them for firewood" he replied.

"Bapak, what did you just say to me? Why on earth would you do a stupid thing like that?"

He was becoming so offended and I was too familiar with the mean look on his face.

"Your bonsai had a ghost in it and it has been disturbing our family every day."

This accusation was bizarre and absurd — my Bapak's needless destruction of my beautiful, green blooming bonsai hurt me so much.

"How could you come up with so much crap?" I accused him.

Arguments between my Bapak and I at that time often lasted for days. I wasn't going to agree with his way and he wasn't going to let me have it my way. Perhaps on that day of destroying my bonsai tree my father realized that I was not going to be just the average Balinese girl who is going to grow up to be a normal Balinese woman.

"How dare you question your parents' belief in ghosts, black magic and even God?" my father shouted. "You are a bad daughter! You will never find a good husband!"

I felt it in my bones that he was right. I already knew in my heart that I would never find the right Balinese person to marry me. An argument ran through my head but I kept my thoughts to myself as I pondered the double insult: "First he destroys my beautiful bonsai and then I have to listen to him cursing me so I will not find a Balinese husband? How can he make any sense — if he mixes up two such different things in one sentence? Better I ignore him altogether!"

When my parents could not answer my questions they would either curse me for asking too many questions or simply tell me I should believe what they were telling me because it was part of our tradition, culture and religion that had been passed down from our ancestors

"If you don't believe it" they would say, "You will have bad karma and for sure you will go to hell."

Black Lava – to hell and back

Now I know for sure they were right, as I have been to hell and back.

Most Balinese people believe in the 'cause and effect' that we know as *karma*; when you do good things you will go to heaven and on the other hand if you do bad things you will go to hell or suffer in some other way. My mum has always drilled this idea into my head since the days when I first learned how to talk.

The way my mum pictures hell is quite bizarre and doesn't really make any sense to me. She would say the god of hell has a huge pot of boiling water and fire to throw bad people into, and according to her, first our spirit will be tortured, then we will be reborn again deformed or reincarnated as an animal or even as a cockroach.

This is why some uneducated Balinese people have such a low opinion of disabled people; they assume they must have been bad in a past lifetime so they must deserve their punishment—perhaps they could even be a cursed soul from hell. Although lately as more people become educated, this attitude is changing, especially as many westerners are now paying attention to physically and mentally challenged people in Bali. I was involved at one stage with a foundation that supported such people, located in Tampaksiring, and I could see how hard it was for them to be accepted by their families, who felt ashamed of them.

In my imagination hell would look like a black lava field—dark, pitch-black rocks as far as your eyes can see. No life, absolute loneliness, and it would be a great struggle to get from one rock to the other. As for heaven, I picture it as if I am high up in an airplane. On top of white clouds, where it is bright like in the snow but yet very quiet, everything so soft and peaceful, everyone floating as if without any weight, a place where you cannot fall, as there is no gravity!

On our graduation day from High School, my school friend Wayan Muliani and I were very sad, because we knew our friendship might have to end there. From then on we would lead different lives, and none of us had any clue what would be ahead of us. We decided to go for a ride together on her motorbike. We rode all the way from Gianyar up to Kintamani. She was not bad on the motorbike, although she had once had a bad accident in which she had broken her leg and that was why she walked with a limp. Anyway, she was no longer worried about her accident; she had put it behind her. We drove down the steep and windy road all the way to Lake Batur and all the way around the edge of the lake to the black lava. In those days only motorbikes could get down to the lake, and even then with lots of difficulties as it was a narrow and dangerous path, but we were determined to have an adventure on that day.

We got to a spot where there was some high ground, dark lava rocks and empty space. There was no sign of life as far as the eyes could see. I told her this is how I imagined hell would look.

"Wow… we must be in hell," we agreed, laughing. "Ok, now we've been to hell together, we had better make sure we make it back somehow."

We decided to sit side by side in that desolate place to reflect upon our uncertain futures. We were both despondent. Neither of our parents would be able to pay for our university studies, so there was little doubt that we would be going back to our villages and perhaps we would be expected to get married to one of our first or second cousins so as to be less of a burden to our families. We were hoping some sort of whisper would be heard from behind a huge rock, or at least a voice that could guide us in what to do next with our life.

But there were no voices except our own to be heard in that large empty space, where we sat with black rock and black sand all around us. And then I spotted a small cactus, all alone—a tiny green, healthy looking baby plant, hanging on a rock and barely any dirt underneath, just a little sand for its roots to hang on to. I could not imagine how this cactus could be looking so good or even survive here in this desolate place. All of a sudden I realized this was the sign that I had been looking for, a sign of survival against all odds. This small cactus was the inspiration I was seeking, and it gave me hope and the courage to know that I could survive life too. In spite of all the darkness in my soul, my unsupportive environment, the pressure of my culture and all the negativity surrounding me I felt sure I would somehow survive and find my own way.

2

For better or for worse...

A Hard Lesson in Life

My life was about to change for better or for worse. I had no idea. It was the eve of our six-monthly Galungan and Kuningan festivals, celebrations of the victory of 'Good' over 'Evil' in which we welcomed our ancestral spirits to our family temples with decorations, cakes, offerings and prayers. This was a time that we young people all loved, as the Village Youth Association would celebrate the occasion by having a charity "Bazaar" event to raise funds for our village and temples. It was one of those rare opportunities for the youth of the village to get out together at night with their parents' blessings and enjoy each other's company.

I was only eighteen and just beginning to enjoy my life as a young adult. I had just finished High School and got my first job in Ubud as a waitress in a small place called *Sriwijaya Café*. My boss came from Surabaya, a city on the nearby island of Java. His name was Pak Ismael. I recently heard he had passed away, which makes it a bit easier for me to tell this story.

Pak Ismael was a very unique character; a big guy with grey hair that he kept tied back in ponytail. He owned the café, a gallery with a bungalow at the back that was usually occupied by his second wife Patricia, from Australia. Pak

Ismael had three wives. His first wife had already left him and re-married to someone else in Surabaya, his second wife lived at the back bungalow on her own and he had set his third wife up in luxury in Banyuwangi, east Java.

My boss Pak Ismael liked to tell stories. When it was quiet in the restaurant he would sit and drink beer and ramble on to whoever was willing to listen. He told me about his life and his multiple offspring. I remember the story about how he was caught drug dealing in Perth and spent a few years in jail there. That was where he met his third wife—Ibu Indah. She was a taxi driver in Perth. Pak Ismael had two children from his first wife, Rini and Adi (they both lived in Melbourne), one from his second wife Patricia named Seth, and none from his third wife. However, the first wife Ibu Ani had two children from her second husband. Patricia already had two children from her first marriage and Ibu Indah had three children from her first marriage but two of her children had remained in Perth. Only one little girl about nine years old lived with her in her mega mansion in Banyuwangi, but she had a nanny, a cook, a gardener and a driver to take care of their every need.

During the 'Bazaar' fundraiser everyone was supposed to invite all of their friends and acquaintances to attend this charity occasion and spend on food and drinks. In that way, we would raise as much money as possible during the event, and the proceeds were to be used to fix our temple, to enhance our community hall, and so on.

Pak Ismael's son Adi had just come back from Melbourne to visit his father in Bali. He was a very short, typically shy Javanese guy of a similar height to me, with a round face, curly hair and moustache. So, I thought, hey I can invite him, as he seemed he might be the kind to spend a lot of money and have lots of friends who would join him to drink beers at our village 'Bazaar'.

On the night when I was doing my work as a waitress at the Bazaar event when Adi showed up with four of his Javanese buddies. They were buying more large Bintang Beers by the minute. It was such a competition to see who could display the most 'big' Bintang bottles on their tables. Sure enough, drinking warm Bintang beer would make anyone feel sick in the stomach and perhaps mixing it with ice covered in germ-laden dust made it so much worse, for after consuming copious quantities of beer, Adi became very ill, and threw up all over the place. His other friends were still in good enough shape to travel back to Ubud. So I suggested Adi leave his bike next to the Bale Banjar and rest at my house. He agreed, so around midnight I took him to my house where the lights had all been turned off, as my family was already fast asleep. I told Adi where to wash and suggested he use my room for the night.

I left him there in my room, as my shift wasn't yet over at the Bazaar, and went back to my duties as a waitress. Around 2 a.m. when the last guests had left I went home and slept in the east pavilion, the one that we call the *Bale dangin*. In the morning, awaking at 6 a.m., I went to my room to check how Adi was doing. He seemed to still be in a deep sleep and I didn't want to disturb him. As I was walking out from my room my father passed on his way to the kitchen. He said "Hi" and glanced at my room. And then he paused in mid-step.

A look of shock and surprise flashed across his face—followed by a look I knew so well—it was the mean expression of pure anger that I had often seen when he glared at me as he belted me, beating me black and blue. He had always seemed to be determined to make my life miserable, ever since I was a little girl. It was as if he had never forgiven me for being born the wrong sex, when he had wanted so much to have a son.

"Why is that man in your room?" he demanded, the anger in his eyes looking more and more dangerous, as if he were about to explode. I shut the door behind me quietly, not wanting to wake up Adi. Pulling my father to our kitchen I tried to explain what had happened. But he was not willing to listen to a word.

"No! No, no… no… daughter of mine is going to have a guy sleeping with her without marrying her first," he shouted, as if he had heard nothing.

I knew worse trouble was coming but I was helpless. There was nothing I could do. I barely knew Adi but I knew he really liked me. This would put him off forever.

My father stormed off in anger and I breathed a bit more freely for a while, but it wasn't long before he came back with a group of men in tow. I peeped out my window and saw a bunch of confused looking men that included our local priest, the *kelian Banjar* (chief of the community affairs), *kelian adat* (chief of village traditions), and the *Sekehe Teruna-teruni* (head of the youth association) all gathered around my father. Even our local family priest, *Mangku* Desa, was there.

"What the hell is going on?" I screamed at my father from my verandah in outrage, ignoring the guests.

"These people are here to talk to Adi to make sure he marries you," he shouted back.

I felt as if I had been struck by lightning. I ran into my little sister's room and locked the door from inside. In the meantime, Adi was still sound asleep on the bed in my room, completely oblivious of everything that was going on.

As I watched in horror from a tiny window of my sisters' room, I saw my life disappearing into the dark mists of future uncertainty. My father had taken charge and in a matter of a few minutes my life would be irrevocably changed. My feelings and my innocence were totally irrelevant, it seemed.

It was his 'tradition', his 'people' and his 'commitment to village *adat*' that he had to maintain—and he had to keep his reputation—or so he told me afterwards. He had no idea that he was ruining his daughter's life.

The men went to my room to wake Adi up and tell him to marry me. I could tell by the tone of their voices that they were threatening him, but I could not hear what they were saying clearly.... all I could hear was Adi, who kept on saying "Yes. Yes. Yes!" in a scared-sounding, hung-over voice.

Adi was taken out and seated on the floor of my *Bale dangin* pavilion, and then my father ordered me to come out of my sister's room so he could discuss everything in a formal manner. But I yelled and swore at my father, using every swear word I had ever learnt in the Balinese language.

Most likely embarrassed by my tirade, the village officials decided to leave my compound, giving my father and I some personal space in which to talk.

"How could you force me to marry someone who I don't even know!" I wailed at my father.

To my surprise he said "Sorry," and lowered his head.

"But it is too late now. We have so many witnesses here and there is no way to back out. Our family reputation must be saved, this is our culture, our tradition!" my father explained.

"What reputation are you talking about?" I asked my father bluntly. "We're poor and nobody gives a shit about us in this whole damn village! Culture and tradition should not be allowed to steal my youth and change my life to some unknown fate. I will never forgive you for this!"

"One day you will understand," he said.

I wanted to make it clear to my father then, right there—perhaps one day I would find it in my heart to forgive him—but I would never forget this day, the day when for the sake of conforming to his culture and tradition he had to ruin my life and steal my freedom.

Adi tried his best to calm me down.

"I want you to know that I fell in love with you the first moment I saw you working at my father's restaurant," he said. "Maybe it's not so bad, lets just follow your father's wishes. Lets just take our time... give me time to get to know you. You can keep on working with my father in the restaurant and gallery. Instead of being a worker there you will be Papa Ismael's daughter-in-law. It will be better."

I tried hard to calm down and then we both went to Ubud together to talk to Pak Ismael. Adi explained our situation to his father and described how he was going to be adopted as a son, a process known in Bali as *Nyentana*, to become a part of my family.

When he heard this Ismael roared with laughter—as if it was a huge joke. He kept on laughing, and went on for a long time, at the same time insulting my family—saying how poor we were, and how the chairs in my house were full of mites, how chicken pooped all over my yard and that Adi would have to get used to the stink of pigs' shit. He clearly didn't understand that I was not in love with his son Adi or that I barely knew him. Being a Javanese man, Ismael had no clue of the actual situation or the traditional *adat* laws of my village.

"Anyway, it's up to you!" he said. "You two can work it out." And he dismissed us with a wave of his hand.

Adi and I set off on his motorbike to find a restaurant or a private place to talk about how exactly we were going to do this. According to Adi, he was happy to marry me in the Balinese way to keep my father's reputation, even if it was a figment of my father's imagination as far as I was concerned.

That evening Adi and I went back to my village and told my father we would do what he asked. We would have a Balinese wedding but I would not be living in the village or taking over all my duties as a Hindu immediately. My father agreed. Off he went to tell the priest and to announce our wedding day to all of our relatives and neighbors and friends.

As far as my family were concerned the wedding went well; Adi went through all the ceremonies of becoming a Balinese Hindu, he even accepted having his name changed to 'Jero Lumut'. The wedding party also seemed to be a big success—some of Adi's family and friends had come all the way from Surabaya to witness his wedding. We invited my fellow members of the youth club and all the members of our local banjar community and I did my best to play the role of a happily married bride.

Two weeks went by quickly, filled with the mundane

things of moving house and setting up a kitchen and getting into a new work routine. And then one night Adi said to me: "Come on, it is time!"

At first I didn't know what he was talking about, and then he started grabbing my breasts and poking his fingers between my legs and I realized he had decided it was time for him to claim his marital rights over my body, now I was his wife.

I was feeling very uncomfortable about it all as I was not attracted to him and had no tender feelings towards him at all.

"You are officially my wife now and everyone in your village has witnessed it," he said. Then, angered by my passive reaction, he savagely tore off all my clothes and forced himself upon me. I closed my eyes and let my body go limp, but he would not cease. He kept on doing it over and over again all night until my body felt like it had been trampled and torn apart.

I felt a deep pain inside, and a feeling of sickening insult was brewing in the depths of my heart like an angry volcano, but I said nothing and gave in to every demand he made. To me he was like a wild rutting animal, I hated everything about my first experience of these so-called "marital rights" that he claimed in such an insensitive fashion.

To add insult to injury, each time he ejaculated, he would roll a marijuana joint and smoke it. Then his eyes became red and swollen and he showed me the effect it had on his hard weapon, ready to savage every part of my body once again.

From the very beginning, the moment his intentions became clear, I had begged him to not make me pregnant. "You can do whatever you want to my body but please make sure you wear a condom and don't make me pregnant." Fortunately he agreed to my request, so at least that was one small victory for me.

To Java to see new things

After Adi and I had spent our first month together in the village I asked him if he could show me Surabaya where his mother lived, on the island of Java. He agreed, and we eventually set off on our trip several weeks later. We caught a public van, known as a *bemo*, from Tegal Pisang market all the way down to Batubulan bus station, and then we took another from Batubulan to Ubung, the bus station on the northwest side of Denpasar, where we bought our bus tickets to Java.

I had never before left my island home of Bali, and in spite of my inner misery, which had reduced over time to a dull ache that I had almost begun to consider normal, it was exciting to be taking my first journey to Java to see new things. Perhaps seeing something new and meeting people with a different culture would enable me to be more optimistic about my marriage to a man I did not love, and help me to resign myself to a future with him.

At Gilimanuk port, on the northwest tip of Bali, the bus was driven onto the ferry. Once on board we walked around on the deck and my husband bought me a bowl of *bakso* on the ferry. It was the best meatball soup I had tasted in a long time. I thanked him with a smile and he smiled back. We chatted and before we know it we had arrived in Java on the other side of the ocean strait. Our long trip continued into the night from Banyuwangi, heading for the port city of Surabaya. Adi told me that the bus always had a stopover in a half way restaurant so their passengers could have dinner. I was ready for the stop, and it was a nice dinner, I thoroughly enjoyed it.

We arrived in Surabaya at Bungorase station early in the morning and caught a *becak* to his house. That was my first experience of riding on a pedicab in my entire life. I figured that this kind of transportation would be impossible in Bali due to our steep landscape, which is either downhill or uphill, with not many flatlands in between. Surely it would take too much time and energy for a becak driver to pedal north, although it might be fun for him on the way back down.

Finally we arrived at my mother-in-law's house around 10 a.m. It was quite a large house, with many rooms and nooks and crannies but not nearly enough windows. The house was rather dark and it felt damp in every room. His mom got us some towels so we could clean ourselves up after the journey and his grandmother provided us with the best Javanese cooking I had ever tasted. I would say the best as this was my first exposure to a full Javanese lunch buffet, and after the long journey and the lack of sleep it tasted great to me.

Another 'surprise' wedding

Adi had invited a few of his friends over to meet me and some neighbors also came by to introduce themselves. I had no idea up until that time that Adi's family was actually preparing for our Javanese wedding.

Actually our Javanese wedding was much more fun than the Balinese one, as it involved a party where people actually danced together and had fun. Adi's family was very gentle towards me, especially his little stepsister Esti, who was only eleven years old at the time; she was an angel and my best company. She was so keen to ask me about my Balinese culture and the Hindu religion. And she was very aware and understanding of my discomfort at becoming a Muslim wife to her stepbrother. The wedding preparations only took around three days. My mother in-law booked a salon near the house for my big day, and I bought special Javanese headwear, a traditional lace *kebaya* blouse and a very nice new batik sarong—a present from Adi's big sister Rini. She had come home to Surabaya for our wedding all the way from Melbourne, Australia. Their entire stepfather's family also arrived from Jepara in central Java. They came bearing lots of presents and also hired a special performing troupe from their hometown as entertainment for the day. All Adi's family seemed to be very nice people and very accommodating, including his third stepmother who came from Banyuwangi to Surabaya with a driver and a carload of presents. I actually felt quite special in spite of my feelings of reluctance at having to become a Muslim. The people in the neighborhood also were very nice and welcomed me into their community and mosque.

I still wished they had told me in advance that this was going to happen. Perhaps I would have had a chance to say no. But Adi said I had no choice in the matter as he had gone through a Bali Hindu wedding and now it was my turn to go through a Muslim one. I said "Ok", but I asked him to promise not to make me undergo female circumcision, as is still the tradition in Java.

The wedding went relatively well; at least all the family seemed to enjoy it. I still felt like a big fraud as I couldn't reconcile myself to spending the rest of my life to this rather shallow, selfish man, even though he had moments of kindness towards me.

Since Adi's step-dad was the *Kepala RT*—head of the neighborhood organization, we were able to close the road for our wedding. There was a temporary stage built for dancing and a concert for the night after the wedding, right in front of Adi's mother's house.

The very next day after our Javanese wedding Adi called me. "Now you are my Muslim wife," he said, "I want to give you our wedding present!"

He handed me an oblong package, wrapped tightly in green wrapping paper. You can imagine my surprise when I opened it and found a Muslim *Quran* written in a strange language that I didn't recognize. Adi told me it was Arabic.

"Now you must learn the Arabic alphabet," he told me. "You must start reading it every day—5 times a day. Then you can start memorizing the *Quran!*"

Adi proceeded to ask his grandmother to take me to the mosque each morning and teach me how to memorize passages from the holy book. She showed me how to put on the appropriate clothing, and how to wash, and together with a group of women dressed from top to tail in white drapes we prostrated ourselves and chanted in an area of the mosque reserved for women.

By this time I had decided that my Surabaya trip was a huge mistake. I had no money and now I was trapped, at the mercy of Adi. Being forced to learn a new language and a new religion that meant nothing to me was like rubbing salt in my wounds and for the first time in my life I felt completely bereft of power to make any of my own decisions.

Sex, Drugs and Rock'n Roll

The hypocrisy of my new life in Java did not cease to amaze me. It wasn't long before Adi showed me the darker side of his personality. During the day, Adi wanted me to be a nice Muslim wife, who attended the local mosque, cooked and stayed at home. But then, in stark contrast to this foreign creature he wished me to become, as if to really confuse me, at night he began taking me out and exposing me to the full-blown underbelly of Surabaya's nightlife.

It was only after dark that the other side of the man I had been forced to marry emerged. He started to take me to hang out with his friends at karaoke bars full of prostitutes. On these occasions he would make sure I wore the clothes he chose for me. He dressed me up in tight, short skirts and high heels just like the rest of the naughty girls in the neighborhood.

Then Adi began to take me along to join his friends—mostly Javanese guys who had exposure to working and earning big money in Australia. They would have huge parties, serving lobsters, crabs and the "best of the best" to all their friends. There was lots of alcohol, and by the end of the night everyone was drunk and some of them were having sex in the open. They even sniffed cocaine and injected drugs into each other, in a back room.

I kept well back from these scenes, watching in amazement what was happening around me. I was uncertain to what to do, how to behave, and what to think, and after a while I would start to panic, desperate to find a way to get out of the frightening situation. Then just when I couldn't stand it any more, all of Adi's men friends would head for the infamous red light district known as Kampong Dolly and pay for each other to have sex with prostitutes. Adi dragged me along there too, and to my absolute disgust he even made me watch him having sex with three prostitutes on one night.

I was forbidden to say anything about this to his family, especially his grandmother. Adi had noticed that I was becoming close to his grandmother. The old lady fascinated me. She was capable of creating so many delicious dishes of food within her simple kitchen, all of which she cooked on one tiny kerosene stove.

Adi insisted on showing me more and more of Surabaya's nightlife. Together we caught a taxi to the renowned *Jembatan Merah* where cross-dressers have sex under the bridge, behind trees and dark walls. There were cops everywhere tracking them and attempting to arrest those involved in street prostitution. Adi threatened me if I dared to say anything to his family or mine he would turn me out into the street as a prostitute. He was holding my Bali ID card, to make sure I could have only one identity in Surabaya—that of his wife, securely bound to do her duty, in fear of his retribution.

One day when I was changing the bed sheets and cleaning the bedroom I found a huge bag of dried leaves that looked like *ganja*. I wasn't sure at first, but I had seen Adi rolling cigarettes with something similar. When I opened it up it had a musty smell, and as I kept on cleaning I found more and more similar bags under the bed. This discovery made me so scared I thought it would be the end of me. I wasn't ready to spend the rest of my precious life behind bars. There was no doubt in my mind that I would end up going to jail if Adi got caught.

I now realised that while I was being expected to be learning to be such a good Muslim wife by all of Adi's family, he was busily dealing drugs with his friends and connections. I started to listen in, and overheard their conversations on how they got it from Sumatra to Surabaya and how they were going to transport it to Bali for a huge profit. It turned out that Adi's father Ismael was behind all this, organizing finance, transportation, and sales to his wealthy expat connections and artists who needed the drugs to enhance their creativity.

I decided to confront him about it to see what he would say.

"I know what's in those bags," I said, pointing out the obvious.

"So? What are you going to do about it? Report me to

the police?" he replied. "Go ahead because you are going to be a witness in the case and your life will be miserable," he said. "If you dare to do that then I will have no choice but to make your life unimaginably unbearable." There was nothing I could say or do but to give in to his demands and do as I was told. I realised my life could be in danger, whatever I did.

Adi had got all the drugs stashed in one place now, so he was waiting for his dad to come to Surabaya to make the pickup in his car. Pak Ismael had a big station wagon at the time. By then I was feeling completely helpless. I now knew I was married to an alcoholic, drug-using, drug-dealer. Hanging on for my dear life, I traveled back to Bali from Surabaya fully aware that our vehicle was loaded with bags of marijuana. Now I was also witness to a drug dealing syndicate, a criminal by fact of my knowledge.

All through the journey sweat kept on pouring down my face, even though the air conditioning was on. I tried to take my mind back to happy memories of childhood when I was chasing dragonflies in rice paddies with my friends, and after a while I fell into a deep sleep that lasted all the way until the ferry crossing from Banyuwangi to Gilimanuk. My father-in-law Pak Ismael drove his car onto the ferry and he stayed in the car while Adi and I wandered around on the upper level.

I could not wait to get back to Ubud where I could find a way to stay away from my father-in-law and perhaps my husband as well. They were working out plans on how they were going to distribute the drugs, who would be involved in this deal, what percentage they were going to earn and who would carry out each transaction. Everything was planned carefully and it seemed that they already had lists of orders to fulfill.

Instead of heading back to Sriwijaya Café where Ismael had his restaurant and gallery with the bungalows at the back, I chose to catch a local *bemo*—a small covered pickup truck—back to my own village. I used the excuse that I missed my family too much after the long Surabaya trip. Adi didn't seem to even notice, and he didn't come to find me in the village for a few days. I was full of trepidation, and could not pluck up enough courage to go and look for him back at his father's place in Ubud.

When he finally came back to my village he showed me a huge pile of cash in his bag. I didn't know whether I should be proud or scared and really had no idea what to say.

"We now have enough money to live on for at least a year" he told me.

After a few weeks of not doing anything in the village Adi said he was so bored he was thinking of going to Australia to find some laboring work in a factory in Sydney. I felt so relieved that he would go away at last and leave me alone.

As soon as he was gone I decided to work in a

restaurant again, preferably back in Ubud, but this time not at my father-in-law's restaurant. Once I was back working, and separated from Adi, I managed to slowly regain my independence and self-respect and started once more to develop my confidence.

Six months went by and then one day Adi came back, determined to take me to Australia with him.

I was reluctant to go with him after my awful Surabaya experiences, but he told my boss that I was not allowed to work there any longer.

Consequently, I found myself without a job, and I had no choice but to go with him to Denpasar to organize my passport and purchase my ticket. Now, in retrospect, I'm actually grateful he did that, but at that time I felt really scared. Would my life be any safer in a foreign country? What if my husband reverted to his former evil self and put me out on the street to earn money as he had threatened to do many times?

My first trip down-under

Adi left for Australia before me with the intention of finding a room for us to rent so I would have a place to stay when I arrived.

When the day came for me to leave Bali for my first journey to Australia I had no idea what to do at the airport although Adi had explained it all to me via a collect call the day before my trip. I caught a *bemo* from my village to Ubud and then a shuttle bus to the airport, following the instructions Adi had given me the day before. I was wearing a pair of Levi jeans, a white t-shirt, a backpack and a pair of sandals. I had never caught a plane before and I had the feeling that this was going to change my life forever. It was 1992 and I was about to embark on a journey to a new country, to a place of the unknown.

Adi had told me the day before over the phone that he had to work so he couldn't pick me up at the airport. I managed to get through Immigration without a problem, but going out of the airport was somewhat of a dilemma. The automatic doors at the airport looked really scary, they seemed to open and close on their own and I was worried I could get myself jammed in the door if caught when they closed. I waited until someone was next to me and then I held my breath and I went out at the same time. Oooh… I breathed a sigh of relief! What a stupid girl! The feeling of clean air suddenly brushed my skin, welcoming me to Kangaroo country, and I took a deep breath, allowing myself time to realise where I was.

Holding a piece of paper with an address on it, I went to find a taxi. There was a queue so I took my turn. The taxi smelt of clean carpet and perfume, and the driver kept on talking all through the trip but I had no clue what he was saying, as my English was very limited. The road from the airport to Surry Hill was so large, almost like our Bypass in Bali, but four times larger, just for one-way traffic, and hardly a motorbike in sight, except for one big Harley Davidson driven by a scary looking man wearing black leather. We passed a train along the way and I was amazed at how streamlined and flash it looked —nothing like the train I had caught back in East Java from Surabaya to Banyuwangi, which looked so old and decrepit and seemed to be carrying a load of live animals.

I had my mouth open and my head glued to the window, staring out at all the amazing tall buildings of historic and modern Sydney. It was just like those places I had seen in the movies and on TV, the largest city I had ever seen, with wide avenues and lots of old English architecture built of stone.

The taxi driver dropped me off in Surry Hill, which seemed to be the same address that Adi had written on paper for me. But I was shocked when an Arab woman wearing a veil answered the door. The place looked old and large—a six-storey building with narrow steps all the way up. I showed her the name and address on my piece of paper and she took me up all the way to level six. There was no one there; all I could see was a large room with only one door leading to a balcony. There were six single beds scattered around the room divided by curtain cloth and six microwaves lined up on a long bench. I stared at the room for quite some time, looking at the mess. Every surface was covered with filth—there were dirty cups and cigarette butts everywhere. A classic bachelor pad.

I saw a familiar bag, a blue bag that looked like one belonging to Adi. I went to the bag and opened it up and saw his jeans and t-shirts in it, so I felt a bit better knowing that he had left something in the room.

"Yes, he must definitely live here!" I thought.

An hour later a man turned up—he came into the room and introduced himself directly. He was very friendly—he knew immediately who I was as Adi had shown him my picture before and everyone staying there had been told about my arrival. I asked this guy if he could give me the address of my husband's work, as I didn't want to wait all day there on my own.

"Maybe you can call my husband where he works and find out what time can I meet him outside?" I suggested. This guy was very helpful. He called a taxi for me and he even made sure to tell the taxi driver exactly where to take me. I was very grateful.

My husband worked in a warehouse near Darling Harbour, so I was happy to walk around sightseeing while waiting for him to finish work. I still could not believe that I was actually in Sydney, almost six thousand kilometres away from the people I knew—with no family and friends. I was anxious. On one hand I felt as if I was walking in a dream, but on the other I had a sinking feeling of being so far away from everything and everyone I knew.

During my walk I saw a row of restaurants in Chinatown. I went into one where I saw an Indonesian & Malaysian Takeaway Restaurant sign flashing and asked if they had any jobs going. The boss was a small and wizened Indo-Chinese man with slit eyes and a nervous twitch.

"Yes," he said, "We are looking for someone to help out. *Berapa lama miss disini?*…. how long have you been living in Sydney?"

"*Ini hari pertama.* It's my first day," I said, looking him straight in the eye. His dodgy eye twitched, but he looked impressed, and he took me aside and interviewed me. He explained to me that because I didn't have a working permit all he could pay me was $5 an hour and I must make sure to hide or *pura-pura jadi tamu*…. pretend to be a guest… should there be any inspection from custom officials or cops.

"Just say that you're my relative from Jakarta and only visiting" he said.

I agreed to his terms and he said I could start working there in two days time. I was over the moon with happiness at my good luck, and thanked the boss with a big smile. Then I started walking back to the entrance of the warehouse where Adi was working, determined to buy some black t-shirts, a few more pairs of jeans and a pair of sneakers as I saw other waitresses were wearing that type of clothing.

Adi was so surprised to find me there. He was really happy to see me and showed me off to his co-workers. He called out to them. "Hey you guys, come here, meet my beautiful wife."

At that moment, for the first time, I actually felt connected to him. He was the only person I knew in Australia.

That warm feeling did not last for long. Adi treated me to a pizza at Pizza Hut nearby and then without any more questions or consideration for how tired I might be after flying all night the night before, he walked me all the way home—a long walk through the city to the suburbs— all the way to Surry Hills. Once we arrived there I met his roommates. I was kind of embarrassed to be living with six other people in one room knowing full well what my husband usually wanted to do to my body during the night, but I was too tired by then to even ask him what had happened to the accommodation he had promised he was going to find for us.

"This place is only temporary until I have enough money for a bond for a private unit for us," he told me. Then it was my turn to surprise him. I gave him my news. "I've already found myself a job in a Chinatown takeaway, so I can help you to pay the rent."

"Wow!" he said... "I'm impressed!"

We spent two weeks in the shared bachelor pad and when Adi got paid I got my wages too, but it wasn't quite enough for the bond to a new place. So I put my gold necklace in a pawnbroker as well, and then we were able to pay for a bond and the stipulated two weeks rent up front for a unit in Canterbury, rather far from the city. I didn't mind the distance at all. At least it was new, nice, and private. It even had a lounge area, a modern kitchen, and a large bedroom with a door—I thought this was heaven, after our last accommodation. The bathroom had a bathtub and we shared a laundry at the back.

I thought to myself maybe life wasn't going to be too bad in Sydney after all. Adi showed me the way to get to work on public transport on my first day, which I thought was very nice of him, taking a day off from his own work to take care of me. And it wasn't long before I got into a routine of traveling from the unit to work and back, starting out mid-morning and then getting back late at night when my shift was over. I had realized by now that my pay was not very good, but at least it was something, and I was able to supplement it with tips from my favorite customers.

On weekends we usually had Sundays off, so Adi would take me for a train ride showing me different parts of Sydney; it was fun riding the gleaming new trains that seemed to slide, slither and sway their way through the city at remarkable speed. He told me that they had just discontinued the old "Red Rattler" and I had no idea what he was talking about.

I loved the contrast between busy weekdays and more restful weekends, when most people tended to dress more casually and moved slower, taking their families out to play sports. It seemed games were on everywhere at the weekend. Saturday night was the 'big night out' and Sydney offered a full range of entertainment, from dining out, to movies, pubs and parties. To me this culture was one of freedom—nowhere in this new lifestyle could I see any particular commitment to community or temple or even family, as we had in Bali.

I really loved Sundays in Sydney, when I would go to Paddy's Market to pick up the week's supply of fruit, vegies and meat. At first I couldn't understand why fruit was cheaper when it said 'special'. I looked up the word 'special' in my English-Indonesian dictionary, and it didn't make sense. Then Adi explained to me that the 'special' referred to the price, as that fruit was generally over-ripe and the seller was trying to get rid of it at a cut price. Often bread was put on special towards the end of the day as well! I couldn't help laughing at my misunderstanding.

Then one weekend we got a call from his older sister. She was having a fight with her husband and wanted to move to Sydney to be near us. Adi's sister Rini turned out to be a very strong woman, bossy and loud. She yelled all the time. When she came to Sydney she moved in without asking, saying she would have to stay with us until she could find her own place. She moved right into our room, her children were sleeping on our couch and Adi and I were left no choice but to sleep on a single mattress that we picked up in a garage sale.

I was so tired from working on my feet all day and I usually got home late, when it was really dark. I would open the door to the unit and find Rini there, hanging out with any number of strange guys smoking ganja, drinking alcohol, leaving empty bottles and cigarette butts all over my kitchen bench. Then shortly after my arrival home, Adi would turn up at the door. Instead of telling his sister to respect my wishes and stop the party, Adi simply joined in the party and together with their friends they turned our unit into a total mess.

I didn't care about Rini using our bedroom, so I went off to sleep on the bed with her kids and we closed the door behind us. I left early for work and when I came back at night all the mess was still there and Rini had been sleeping all day. Her poor kids were hungry and I took care of them by taking them out to McDonalds, which was the closest takeaway place to our unit. I got her kids Daniel and Noel an ice cream each and they were happy.

When we got back to the unit, Rini was up and it looked like she had just had a shower. She started telling me I should clean the unit before my husband got home, and trying to find fault with me.

"You should be a good wife," she said, and followed up with "How dare you take my kids out without asking permission?" and so on.

I didn't like Rini's treatment towards me at all. When my husband got home Rini started to pretend to help me clean and suddenly she was being so nice to me.

I told Adi about the way Rini had been treating me and he didn't believe a word I said. We ended up having an argument, and when I wouldn't give in and apologize to Rini, he gave me a huge punch just beneath my eye. So the next day I had to go to work with a nasty black eye. A gay guy who was the chef at the place I worked told me that being bashed, even by your husband, is not on, and my husband was breaking the law.

"You shouldn't go back home after work tonight," he said. He offered me a place to stay at his unit. I didn't want to involve him with my problem so I politely rejected his offer.

The next time the rent was due my husband asked me to pay all the rent from my wages. I asked him how he could be short of money for rent when he worked fifty hours per week and got Saturday loading on his paycheck as well.

"It's simple," he said. And he followed up with a glare. "Don't you dare question me. You have to pay it since you already got your wages."

He also asked me to reimburse him for the ticket money he had spent on bringing me over from Bali. I said "Ok" just to keep the peace. I couldn't work out what he was doing with all his money.

Eventually I found out what he was up to. It turned out that he was always spending time at the poker machines on his way back home after work. He had got into the habit of drinking in the pub and playing poker until all his money was gone. Eventually he wanted all my money too. When I refused him he hit me again. The beatings became more frequent and at one point he was so out of control with his anger that he dragged me by my hair until I fell on the public footpath. As if that wasn't enough, he made sure he kicked me a few times more while I was down. I felt that all my dignity was lost. My worst fears had been fulfilled. There I was in a foreign country where I knew nobody and my husband, the person who should be protecting me, was abusing me.

After that I quietly went about making plans, while trying to avoid further fights. I saved all my tips, and gathered as much money together that I could without arousing his suspicion. One morning, without Adi's knowledge I walked up the road to a travel agent.

"I have decided to cut my trip short," I said, and fortunately they enabled me to move the date on my return ticket to the following week. I said my goodbyes to my work friends and on the morning I had booked my flight I went to work as usual, just to pick up my last pay, and then headed to the airport.

At that stage I never wanted to come back to Australia. I had moved back to Bali with one purpose—to divorce Adi and not to have anything to do with him ever again. But I kept it a secret from my parents, as I no longer trusted my father to support me.

The divorce process was very lengthy and painful. I attracted a lot of attention. It wasn't every day they saw a 19-year old Balinese girl sitting alone in the Gianyar courthouse. Each person that passed me would ask what I was there for. I didn't know whether I should tell the truth, or make something up! Everyone was telling me that I should get a lawyer, or at least my parents should be there with me.

I started to feel so hopeless without a lawyer or support from my family. Eventually my name was called out; I looked around, and I could see I was being summoned to the Judge's office by a court official. I went in and sat down on the chair opposite a middle-aged woman, who scowled at me. I felt like she was looking at me with nasty suspicion in her eyes, and I didn't think I had a chance of convincing this woman of my plight.

I could tell by the way she wore her scarf tightly tied around her head, so that not a wisp of hair could escape, that she must be a very conservative Javanese woman. Without asking any questions she told me right away that I must reconcile with my husband.

"You must bring him to the courthouse for mediation," she ordered, "and you must bring a letter of permission from your parents."

"But I am over eighteen," I said, "so I don't need my parents' permission to divorce."

"Yes you do," she said, "as your husband has married into your family he has rights as a *sentana*. And you also need a letter from the chief of your village that clearly states you have reported your intention to divorce your husband, and have been granted permission from all the appropriate government officials," she continued. Before I could argue she dismissed me arrogantly with a nod and called the name of the next person in the line.

I knew that what she wanted me to do would be impossible, as I didn't want my parents to know anything about my divorce. I didn't trust my father to support me. I suspected he might even take his son-in-law's side against me, even though my husband had never fulfilled his duties as an adopted member of the family.

There remained only two options for me to take, either to bring my husband to court to prove that he agreed to our divorce proceedings, or to get a letter of permission from my parents along with all the other letters acknowledging this agreement, from government officials in my local community. Neither of these two choices were viable options for me under the circumstances.

Barely able to conceal my disappointment, I wrote down the lady judge's name and my file number for my next court mediation in my book, and then headed outside, where I found a place to sit under a tree in front of the courthouse. There I sat, overcome with misery, crying and sobbing, knowing there was nothing I could do to claim my freedom from this farce of a marriage with Adi.

It wasn't long before a stranger approached me, and introduced himself, offering me a cigarette.

"My name is Pak Komang," he said "from Denpasar." I gratefully accepted his offer, and we smoked and talked for a while as I told him my problems.

"I know a good lawyer," he said. "A really smart young lawyer." Smiling, he carried on. "He's good looking too! And wealthy! Don't worry," he said, "there is always one good one."

Then he gave me the address of his lawyer friend from Blahbatuh and suggested I go there and tell him about my case.

I couldn't believe my luck. In one day I had managed to find a good lawyer, and he was willing to help me. Not only that, he asked for nothing other than a small gift of money for his own ceremonial needs and a new jacket as payment. And he was able to take care of the case without me. I didn't even need to attend in court.

It was such a relief when I finally received my divorce papers in the mail. Unfortunately, my father had never changed his habit of intruding on my privacy and opened up my mail. He came after me waving the letter in the air, his face red and angry.

"You are a bad daughter, how dare you divorce your husband without consulting with your family."

This time I was not going to listen to my father. It was too late for that. I grabbed my papers right out of his hand, ran to my room and packed my things, leaving home just as fast as I could go. I did not expect my father to want to know or understand what I had been through, "for better or for worse," while being married to the Javanese stranger he had forced me to marry in the first place. I blamed him for that entirely. I didn't say goodbye, and I didn't think I would ever go back, although I felt sad to leave my mother and my sister behind again.

3

In sickness and in health

Tying the knot again

My second wedding—well actually I guess it was my third, as I was married twice to my first husband, first in Hindu style, and secondly as a Muslim—took place at a Registry office in a foreign country, far, far from home, without any of my family present. My partner and I were living in Australia by then. When I fell pregnant we decided to get married right away, and our wedding date coincided with Saint Patrick's Day. However, I don't think that brought us any luck, in spite of what my husband's Irish friend said. Perhaps I should have worn a green wedding dress. Instead I wore a very ordinary purple evening dress that matched the purple scarf I had bought at David Jones. Oh how I loved David Jones. *"There is no other store like David Jones"*—their advertising jingle still sticks in my head until today.

Our Registry-office marriage ceremony was brief and devoid of any ceremony, as far as I could tell. It seemed that all we were expected to do was to verbally agree with the marriage, then sign some papers. It was, however followed by a reception at a very atmospheric Japanese restaurant, with Japanese food. Both of the restaurant owners were friends of my husband—I had the impression that he was helping their family out in some way.

My new husband Bill was tall and thin, and he had wavy hair and a retreating hairline that showed his age. He was always doing kind things for some person or another, I could hardly keep track of the number of people who seemed to owe him favors, from any number of impoverished families with destitute children back in isolated central Bali, to various foreigners who had migrated to Australia and were still finding their feet down under.

Anyway, the wedding was supposed to be a festive occasion, but I was feeling very lonely on my Australian wedding day, as I didn't know anyone there yet. All the guests who attended were Bill's friends and even the band that played at our wedding was made up of his old mates. One of the owners of the restaurant also contributed a Japanese-style guitar performance and sang in Japanese.

Sadly, I was not feeling at all festive. I didn't even feel well on the day of my wedding. I was suffering from morning sickness, and in retrospect I think I was not really over the pain of my previous marriage. My decision to marry again was in a way a compromise. It was practical as I was pregnant, it would help me qualify for Permanent Residency in Australia and also to access Medicare so I would not have to pay hospital bills if I got ill during my pregnancy, and so on. Bill, who I had been living with for some time now, was so much older than me, nearly twenty years, but we had lots of things in common as I loved his music and we enjoyed going out together to hear live bands play. Plus he seemed to have really fallen in love with me; at least I thought he had. He did everything he could to cheer me up on the day of our wedding, trying to impress me with his friends and their kindness.

Everyone seemed to have a great time at the wedding, except me. Perhaps the feeling of foreboding was pressing upon me too heavily. It was more than just the nausea of my morning sickness making me feel ill. I knew in my heart something was going to go wrong. Sometimes I hated my witch-like ability to sense events in the future; I tried my best to reject the instinct of dread that was hanging over me.

As it turned out, I was right. I had only been pregnant for two months when things started to go wrong. In fact we had only been married for one month when Bill first got ill. It started with a horrible headache on our honeymoon in Queensland. With both of us feeling sick it wasn't the greatest honeymoon. We drove all the way from New South Wales to Gold Coast, taking turns to stop and be sick all the way. One minute it was my turn to vomit due to morning sickness, and then it was Bill's turn, due to his horrifying headache. We had to shorten our trip from two weeks to only one, so we managed to visit some of Bill's friends and we did get to stay in a nice hotel. But unfortunately I couldn't eat anything at any of the nice restaurant dinners my husband took me out to.

The whole time we were away all I could eat was instant chicken-noodle soup.

All I wanted at the time was just to go back to our home in New South Wales to lie down in my own bed, and vomit in my own toilet, instead of being so annoying to the people in the next room who had no choice but to listen to the sound of my being sick. It was so embarrassing.

A few days after we arrived back home, Bill decided to visit a doctor to get a scan to see what was causing his headaches. He returned home looking paler than ever, with news that he could have aneurisms in his brain.

"Not just one aneurism, but two," he said.

I didn't want to stress him out further by asking questions, so I tried to look 'aneurism' up in my English-Indonesian dictionary but I could find no such word, not even anything similar. Then I came across Bill's *Medical Encyclopaedia* on the desktop of his computer, the one that I used to do my English assignments. It described aneurism as "...a blood clot that could lead to brain damage..." Brain damage? I could understand those two words well, and they scared me.

Of course I had absolutely no clue what ramifications this could have upon my life and that of my child until Bill mentioned the doctor thought he might have to have a brain operation. Then I began to feel very scared about what could happen. My newly wedded husband could die. I would be left alone with an unborn child in my tummy, speaking very limited English, in a foreign country. How on earth was I to survive?

As soon as the doctor saw the results of Bill's scans he had to be hospitalized. Day after day I visited him in hospital and the time flew by. Finally, the day for his operation arrived. I was not allowed to enter the operation theatre. I had to sit outside for hours, sweat pouring down my forehead, and still there was no news. I was fully aware by now that the outcome of the operation could be fatal, as the hospital had insisted I join counselling groups and I had heard the grave tones in the voice of the counselors, although I could only understood some of their words here and there. The brain specialist had told me the operation would take three hours but five hours passed, without any news.

I was young, pregnant, knew just a few words of English, and there I was sitting alone in a strange hospital in a foreign country. My thoughts were floating, I felt so lost I could not even think of what I should do if he died that day. How could I go back to Bali? I had no money. Who was I going to ask for help? I knew nobody. My tears were my only comfort. There was no point looking at any pictures in magazines any longer. So I sat there for ages, staring at a white hospital wall and imagining my own tragedy.

Could this be more punishment for my ancestors' karma? Or was it my own? What bad things had been done for me to deserve these nightmares, one after another? Had I offended the two Dadongs and been cursed as a child? Or was it my own fault to get myself into such an impossible situation? A thousand questions went through my brain, and none of them seemed to have any ready answers.

Eventually, when I had given up to despair and my eyes were closing, my head nodding with tiredness, the specialist came out to inform me the news.

"Your husband is going to be alright," he said "he has pulled through the operation."

My heart lifted, and I sat back down, hugging my big belly. I gave in to my emotions and sobbed. But my days at the hospital were not yet over. Bill had to remain in intensive care for a while longer, and then they moved him into a hospital bed for a few more weeks of recuperation.

To make it easier for me to look after Bill without having to catch the bus to the hospital and back every day the doctor finally allowed me to take him home. But first I had to learn to change his colostomy bag and catheters each morning. During this time of nursing him I had to force myself all the time to forget about my own problems and loneliness, and tried to just focus on the future of my baby.

"What will happen to me and my baby if my husband dies?" I kept on asking myself.

I could still barely keep any food down. My condition

was very poor, my body had become very weak, and several times I had to admit myself to hospital just to get some fluid injected into my dehydrated body. I was taking anti-nausea tablets morning and night and still surviving on instant chicken-noodle soup. This was the only food I could eat that would stay in my stomach for more than a couple of hours.

There was no point buying anything else, I thought, while my husband was still in hospital,, so one morning I went to a supermarket and bought all the instant chicken noodle soup packets they had on the shelf. Then I went to two more supermarkets and bought all their stock as well. The noodles were easy to cook—all I needed was a bit of boiling water to pour over the dry noodles, then I would shake the spices and oil on top, stir, and leave the lid on for a few minutes. There was no way I could afford to go in and out of the hospital for meals while I was taking care of my husband, and I was also trying to fit in some Basic English lessons at Migrant Resource Centre.

There were times at this stage of my life that I did not want to go on living. My life seemed to be dominated by pregnancy and illness. And instead of being taken care of by someone I had to care for another. Endlessly. Bill was like a baby, incontinent and unable to control his bowels, always fouling the bed. Although he had a catheter attached, he often pulled it off by accident during the night because he was so deeply asleep on a high dosage of Valium. Life became unbearable, and I was still unsure of my visa, waiting for my residence application to be progressed by the Australian Embassy in Jakarta.

Finally a call came from Jakarta about my residency visa. It was good news, the visa had been granted. But I had to pick it up from outside Australia. So with my husband still sick, and not feeling too well myself, I booked a flight to Denpasar. I had to arrange for friends to look after Bill, so I could only stay away for a few days to visit my family in Bali, before flying back to Australia. At least with my residency visa sorted out I knew I would be able to work or at least study without paying a huge fees and I was also able to get a Medicare card that would entitle me to bulk-billing doctors and cheaper medication.

Despite my bad morning sickness and a very sick husband I was determined to learn English, so I enrolled myself at the Migrant English Centre. The course was designed for migrants in my shoes, who were trying to support their families but only spoke very limited English, and the teacher was also a foreign person. Louisa was German and she was the most caring lady I had ever met. She was very patient with us in the classroom, rewarding every effort we made as if we were little children, and she gave lots of praise to high-achieving students. It was in her class that I made my first real friends.

There were a couple of very smart and talented Bosnians attending the course who were very friendly, and they often visited my place with their two children, a boy and a girl. They felt sorry for me, as they could see I was trying so hard to do my English course while suffering badly with morning sickness.

I now realized it was very important for me to get out of the house, to meet and network with people of similar background. I needed so much support and on those occasions when I was able to support others it also made me feel good. There was another pregnant woman in the class, a girl from the Philippines, but she was very lucky as she didn't suffer from morning sickness.

I missed a month of my English class when my first child was born. It wasn't too bad having my baby all alone, without any family in Australia, because the hospital was excellent and the nurses and doctors were very caring. There were always voluntary workers around to talk to and they even offered support with home visits until I was ready to deal with a baby on my own.

Of course it was very lonely and sad being in a hospital bed and seeing other people with their mothers visiting and their sisters, brothers or close friends bringing flowers each day. Some of the new mothers didn't have enough space to place all their flowers, cards, balloons and new clothes for their baby. Their husbands were there all day long. "My Bill is ill," I would tell them.

I had a few Indonesian friends who visited me and some fellow students from my Migrant English class but it was the feeling of not having my immediate family at hand that really bothered me. So I asked the nurse if I could go home early. I thought it would be easier being at home, at least I would be able to see my husband all day as he had not gone back to work yet due to his illness. Luckily my baby was very healthy, and they let me take him home after only three days in hospital. I requested a home visit from a volunteer just in case I had problems.

I was very lucky to have a Malaysian lady come each day for more than four weeks. A nurse in Malaysia and now a voluntary worker for migrants like me, she was very kind, gentle and understanding and often brought me delicious Malaysian home cooking. She told me I mustn't tell the hospital, as a lot of the food she gave me contained chilies, which was against the rules. Of course I wouldn't have done any such thing. She shared with me her story of how she had ended up in Australia, and we talked a lot about similarities between our cultures—we even understood each other's language.

During the four weeks of regular visits from the Malaysian volunteer, we often went to playgroup together. She would drive me down to our local baby clinic, where they had a group of new mums and babies. It was great to be able to share our experiences of sleepless nights, keeping our breast milk flowing, and we were taught how to massage our babies after their bath. We would have fun competitions on the quickest way to fold nappies, as we were all encouraged to use cloth nappies instead of disposable. They were more economical and healthy, and reduced problems of dealing with the waste. I kept in contact with lots of mums I met during my pregnancy classes and from this playgroup.

By the time Indra was one month old I was feeling good about myself again, confident in my routine of breastfeeding, changing and bathing my baby and so on. I often took him along to my English class as it was only twice a week. He was a quiet baby and loved sleeping in his cot and no one minded me bringing him with me into our classroom. I managed to gain my English Beginners certificate and this paper was my ticket to enter the next level English class at TAFE College. I enrolled in a class called "English for Further Study."

Slowly my husband began to recover from his operation, even though he still needed to go to rehab for regular checkups and counselling was required for both of us. Bill was now able to mind the baby while I attended my English class. He felt so much better he said he was ready to go back to work. So, I enrolled my little boy in the only family day-care place that I could find. It was so far away I had take three buses from our house and then another two from there to attend English classes, but I didn't care. Of course, it took far too long and I was always exhausted. So after a while I had to quit my course while waiting for a child-care vacancy closer to our house or at the college

I was attending.

By then my husband was back at work doing his counselling job, although he was still getting tired easily and collapsed from exhaustion several times after work. Not only had he survived the operation, his recovery was also remarkably fast. But he had lost his confidence. One day he decided to put in an application for early retirement on medical grounds, as he didn't think he could handle his work any longer. He often got too upset with clients, felt sleepy all the time and even made mistakes in remembering his clients' names after having been told for the third and forth time.

By the time our baby was already two months old, I was still finding it very hard to find a childcare centre nearby our house, so I decided to take him back to visit my family in Bali while his father waited for his early retirement to be approved by his employer. Bill eventually came over and joined us for a few months, and then we all went back to Australia in December 1996.

My English was still very limited at that time, so I continued to study and I often took my young baby to classes. Luckily he was a very quiet and happy baby. I had also found a way to make some money for myself; after my English class I sold Avon cosmetics door to door, pushing my little baby in a pram up and down all the little streets nearby our house. Lots of old ladies bought Avon products from me, not because they needed them, but because they were so happy to have someone to talk to.

Elderly people get very lonely in Australia as their children grow up and leave home, following their careers to live in a different state or even abroad. So they love visitors and I enjoyed spending some time with them. I would entertain them with my stories of Bali in my broken English. Some of them had no idea where Bali is, although most of them had heard of the Philippines and Thailand, where most Asian people in the town we lived were from.

As well as my English lessons I also did part-time Secretarial and Accounting courses, until at last I got my first 'real' job as a receptionist in a child-care centre, which made it easier for me to get affordable child-care, as well as to keep an eye on my little boy. But my life was so busy that my little boy was growing up fast with a mother that had very little time for him.

Life back in Bali started to look more and more attractive. We often reminisced about the relaxed lifestyle, the benefits of our son getting to know the extended family. Bill especially missed having summer temperatures the year round, cheap beer and cigarettes. We seemed to be working all the time, and could barely keep ahead of the bills. It was still difficult for Bill to work, as he was not entirely recovered from his operation. He persisted in muddling up the names of his clients!

We decided to move back to Bali in early 1998 as I felt sure there would be lots of opportunities there to make money and I wanted to run my own seafood business.

When I first started, the business went well, but it meant getting up at three o'clock in the morning and driving to the southwest coast to meet the fishing boats as they landed on the beach at dawn, so I could get the freshest of the catch every morning. Once I had bought it then it all needed to be cleaned, transported, refrigerated and delivered while still fresh. I still had very little time for my husband or my son, but my boy was happy to be with his newfound extended family in the village.

It was rather awkward at first, coming back to live in Bali with my parents, especially as they didn't know Bill yet, and he was almost the same age as they were. But I was so excited to be with my family again and to be living back in the village, I ignored any awkwardness. The first couple of months went well, everyone was being sweet to us and we found life in the village relaxing. But it wasn't long until we all started getting bored.

I decided to go and study Balinese dancing with the elderly topeng dancer, Pekak Tutur, in Petulu village to occupy myself in my spare time. Bill was busy, and showed no interest in doing things with me. His passion for photography was growing. He spent his time nearly every day on the computer, retouching photographs of young girls that he had taken on his trips around the island to popular tourist attractions like Kintamani, Lovina, Tirtagangga and Tanah Lot. He would chain smoke the local 'Gudang Garam' clove cigarettes and drink 'Bintang' beer from early sunrise to sunset. Or sometimes he would make trips with a group of young children from a village at the bottom of Mount Batur, or a group of six young girls and a boy from Lovina who he loved to treat to outings. Once he got bored taking photos in Bali he then started to explore Java.

Bill's expeditions to Java soon became more frequent. Then one day he came home to my parents' house with a Javanese woman, who he said he had met in Sanur.

"She is going to show me a little bit of 'the real' Java," he said, "as she is going home to Solo to see her son." I asked her how old her son was, and she told me. He was only 2 years older than our baby at the time.

My parents asked me, "Is that a normal thing for a western man to do?" They couldn't believe that my husband would show up openly with another (married) woman at our home, and then tell us that he was going to Java with her.

"Don't worry about it, they are just friends," I told my mum.

In the meantime my seafood business was becoming more and more difficult to run because each time I needed the car for my second delivery in the afternoon Bill would have disappeared in it without letting me know when he would return. There were a number of times when he called me from Java, when I had no idea that he even planned to go to Java again. It became costly, having to rent a car each time I received a large order for seafood from restaurants. The smaller orders were no problem as I could deliver them in a styro-foam box filled with ice tied on the back of my motorbike. It looked as if I was running a very inefficient business; I was finding it impossible to make my deliveries and orders on time.

One rainy morning my sister and I were riding our motorbikes on our way to our seafood shop in Ubud when we spotted my Feroza on its side, stuck in a ditch near a Bale Banjar, at Jalan Dewi Sita. We stopped immediately as we thought Bill must be in the car. It turned out he had left my car there in the ditch because he was too drunk from the night before, then he had caught a shuttle bus to Gilimanuk port and that morning he was already in Banyuwangi, Java.

When I asked him what had happened he casually said he had met someone in Java and promised to be with her that day. I was furious, but I couldn't show it in front of my sister and all the people surrounding my upside-down car; I had to focus on calling a tow truck to pull my car out of the ditch and take it to the closest mechanic to be fixed.

A week later, Bill came back from his Java trip pretending as if nothing had ever happened. He showed no guilt and made no apology. He was being friendly to me as usual, and asked me for the car key.

"I don't think so!" I told him, "best you pack your bag

and leave me and my boy alone." But he refused to leave. So we continued fighting each day and he continued to take the car, do whatever his heart desired while I was trying to run my business without a car to make deliveries. I could feel my anger building up, it was so unfair.

Finally I had enough. I could no longer run my business properly under the circumstances, and I couldn't support my family without a well-paying job, so I asked Bill to do me a favour and take care of our four and a half year old boy in Bali while I went back to Australia to find myself a job.

It didn't take me long to find a job and set myself up with a place to live, then I called Bill and asked him to bring our son to Sydney. It was early 2000, the new millenium, and I was once more a single fighter. Bill did exactly as I had requested, no less and no more; he delivered Indra at the airport wearing a backpack.

"Here is your boy," he said, "he has got all his stuff with him." Then he left.

I arranged to divorce him a year later.

4

For richer, for poorer...

A simple, introverted man

I still remember the first time I met Jack. He seemed very conservative, and he was not exactly the best-dressed type. My impression of him was of a rather plain and simple, introverted man. In fact he barely spoke the first time we met, and when I got to know him better I realized that he was still rather innocent in a lot of ways, especially when it came to dealing with women. He had been a virgin until the age of twenty-four when he met his first wife, who had come up to him and asked him out. After a brief engagement they had married and they lived together for five years.

I met her at TAFE College in Australia when I was doing my accounting course back in 1998. We did a couple of subjects together in our course and ended up borrowing each other's books. When I visited her house she introduced me to Jack. I didn't take very much notice of him, as he wasn't the friendliest guy I had ever met and there seemed to be nothing particularly striking about him. In fact he seemed to be so ordinary that not for a moment did I see anything attractive or special about him.

Time went by so fast, it was as if it had wings. After I had completed my accounting course I left Australia and decided to live in Bali again for a while.

When my relationship with Bill didn't work out in Bali I went back in Australia without my child. I was all alone and missed him terribly, but I knew I had to find myself a place to live and find myself a job first, before I could ask Bill to bring him over. I was determined to get a good job and earn some money, as it was the only way I could see to keep my independence and support my family.

* * *

It was December 2000, one day after my arrival back to the Central Coast, when Jack rang me out of the blue, inviting me to join him at his client's Christmas party. I was surprised and touched that he had kept my mobile number all that time. He told me that he and his wife had been separated for a year, and were getting a divorce, and he wanted some company for the evening.

"Why not?" I thought, "I have no other invitations at hand." I didn't have any party clothes packed in the bag I had brought with me from Bali. All I had were a few T-shirts and jeans and sport shoes, as I had not planned to party, considering I had just arrived back in Australia and was more concerned about looking for work and how to survive as a single mother.

"What the hell," I mumbled to myself, "I'm not going to worry myself about what I wear. If worse comes to worst at least I'll get to meet people who might have some idea about jobs available."

I had a quick shower, put on a white T-Shirt, a pair of Levi's and my sport shoes, and went off to the Christmas party, doing my best to look happy. When I got there, I looked around for Jack, and I finally spotted him. He was with a young girl who was wearing a very alluring and sexy V-neck dress that exaggerated her breast size and showed off her firm young body. I forget her name but I do remember that at the time she was studying medicine. She seemed to me to be rather shallow and Jack later told me that he didn't like her because when he first attempted to talk to her, she snubbed him. She only started to show interest in him when she found out that he was a lawyer.

I was very nervous, as I didn't know anyone there and I felt so out of place. In comparison to the other guests I was dressed too ordinarily, more like a cleaner than a guest at the party.

"Well," I thought, "no chance to change now, so I may as well relax." Then I looked at Jack, and he didn't look that flash either and that made me feel more comfortable. The 'medicine girl' was hassling me to ask Jack to dance with her, so I did. "Ok," he said, and winked at me. So while they danced together I walked around to find the bar.

The party host was clearly trying to impress his clients, family and friends; there were so many good wines on display. I helped myself, pouring one glass after another, and felt myself slowly relax and start to go with the flow, just a little bit nervous and shy still. I felt as if all the eyes in the room were on me, questioning "Who is she?"

Finally Jack came to find me and asked me to sit with him. Apparently, 'medicine girl' had found someone better or richer—I forget exactly what he told me at the time. I was already getting tipsy by this stage. I continued to enjoy the good wine and food and I had met some other Asian girls at the party. Jack was a bit tipsy too, and he moved closer to me. He caressed my legs, my hands and played with my fingers and then we kissed. I suddenly felt a wave of dizziness, as if I was getting very drunk so I asked him to get me a taxi home. I didn't think I would be able to see the road clearly enough to drive, so I decided to leave my car parked on the street near the party and come back to get it the next day.

Jack suggested we share the taxi, as he also wanted to leave. Then he said it would probably be better if he stayed at my place because I wasn't well.

"That's not a good idea," I said. My next-door neighbor was an inquisitive Indonesian woman and I did not want to start off in the area with bad gossip about me being drunk and bringing a strange man home for a one-night stand. So Jack and I decided to go his place instead.

I still cannot remember much about that night so I have to tell you his version of our first night together, which he retold the following day, a version not very complimentary to me: "........ *we kissed at Paul's. First there was the touching of hands, and then I was stroking your hands with my fingers, then casual touching like rubbing knees etc, then we kissed. I took you back home soon after as you were close to passing out. However we also kissed even after you vomited (lol). Gotta love my work haha. I didn't kiss you in the taxi though—I was too busy watching you and telling the taxi driver you were ok because he wanted to stop and boot us out since you were somewhat indelicately telling him you were about to throw up. But being a good girl you held it in till you got to the driveway of my house..."*

I woke up the following morning with the worst headache and hangover I could ever remember. I needed to get my car back from where I left it the night before, near the party, and then go home to my own place. Before leaving Jack's house, I decided to ask him for a cup of coffee. I pulled my clothes on and wandered out to look for him. I was horrified by the state of the house. It looked like a neglected bachelor pad, and what a dysfunctional bachelor this one must be!

Jack was sitting on the sofa reading the paper with his two dogs—a rather big Rottweiler and a small pug—at his feet. By the state of the house it looked like the dogs must live inside most of the time. The sofa where we sat for our cup of coffee was covered with their hair, and the larger couch in his lounge room had a huge hole in the middle that looked as if it had been torn apart by the big dog.

The more my eyes wandered, the more disgusted

I became. I spotted some rats nesting inside an unused fireplace in the middle of the lounge, a bookshelf in the hallway covered in dust, spider webs and rat poops. The wooden floor of the house was scratched badly by dogs' claws, such a pity.

Jack had turned on the TV to watch the news.

"Can I have a shower before I go?" I asked Jack, as I finished my coffee. He waved in the direction of the bathroom.

"Help yourself" he said, and went back to watching TV.

It was very dark in the bathroom, and the damp wall was covered in mould; it looked as if the pipe must have sprung a leak inside the dividing wall. The bathtub was disgusting, with streaks of grime that looked like a mixture of old soap and dirt, thick and greasy. The toilet bowl looked as if no one had cleaned it for a decade or two. I had to try hard to hold back my nausea.

I realized I didn't have a towel, so I went back to Jack's bedroom to look for a cupboard but there was not even a wardrobe for his clothes, they were all piled up on the floor by the bed. Amongst the pile of shoes under the bed were some that looked as if they belonged to his ex-wife. Old sandals, even old condoms had been tossed into an open drawer under a dresser mirror. I spotted a towel on the floor that looked relatively clean, but when I picked it up, there was a pile of dried dog poop under it and I imagined there must be more amongst Jack's piles of clothes.

I changed my mind about having a shower at that stage, and, desperately in need of fresh air, headed towards the back yard. Through the window I could see a palm tree leaning over the pool, so I walked back through the house, past the kitchen where dishes were piled on the bench growing mould. I paused to open up the fridge, in search of something to whet my thirst, but it was also a disaster. All I could find was expired skim milk, five-year-old jam and sauces with black fungus growing in them—Oh dear!

I could barely see over the grass in the backyard and I am 167cm tall. It felt like a wasteland. I walked through the tall grass along a disappearing path, hoping I could get to a spot I had glimpsed from the house—out under the palm tree by the swimming pool—but I trod in a huge pile of wet dog poops.

I was becoming more and more disgusted by the condition of the house and garden of the guy I had just spent the night with. To make things worse, his swimming pool looked greener than any seaweed in the ocean.

"If only his garden was this green!" I thought, as I peered into water the bright green colour of chlorophyll.

But apart from a tangle of dried twigs the only things I could see that were healthy in that garden were some jasmine plants that dangled over the fence from the neighbor's side, and they too looked like they were struggling to survive.

I couldn't understand how anyone could be so dysfunctional as to live in such conditions. Even as a Balinese coming from an impoverished childhood, I was shocked. I began to wonder if he had been lying to me when he told me he was a lawyer.

It struck me that Jack was living like a homeless person in his own home. I went back into the house and asked him: "You could get sick living in this filth—why don't you clean up around here?"

"Can't be bothered," was the reply. He went on watching the TV, munching on a pack of chips.

The thing that surprised me was that he didn't seem at all embarrassed about his situation. He certainly wasn't trying to impress me. In a rather matter-of-fact way he told me the story of how he had gone to a chemist to ask the pharmacist for something to get rid of his body lice. At the counter he had lifted up his jersey to show his hairy chest, and—horrified by the sight—the pharmacist had screamed and chased him out of his store. I didn't know whether to believe him or not, but to prove his point he lifted his arms up and showed me an infected rash under both of his armpits.

"This is what the lice did to me," he said.

I recoiled in horror, and determined to get out of that place and go home and have a scalding hot bath in my shiny clean bathroom, as soon as I could.

I remember that morning Jack was wearing a very old

stripy jumper with vertical lines and a pair of striped shorts with horizontal lines. These odd clothes, much like a prison uniform, matched up with his thick glasses to make him look like a perfect dork.

"Oh my god... what a catch you are," I mumbled to him sarcastically, "I must have had a barrel of wine last night to end up with a guy like you." At least he had the grace to smile sheepishly, at my attempted humour.

There was something about that smile that made me decide not to judge the book by its cover; I had found our conversation very thought-provoking the previous evening, and beneath this morning's heavy hangover and seeming complacency I thought I could detect the odd spark that made me think he was not entirely lost in his own world. I already knew that underneath those stripy clothes was a body of well-toned muscles—so at least he loved his sports—boxing and karate, he told me. With a height of nearly 6 ft. it seemed Jack could actually be a good book just in need of a new cover—and yes, hopefully the hygiene problems could be fixed with time.

My decision to continue to see him was made like the kind of decision people make when buying a house. They make sure it has all the essential criteria, and compromise on other things they could live without, while they start planning their renovations. This particular 'investment' was looking a bit dilapidated, very messy, and certainly would need lots of repairs and TLC but I had all the patience and time in the world.

I sensed Jack's vulnerability, his submissiveness and neediness and I thought I might just be able to add my own personal touch in building him up into my ideal dream man. It was a wild card, but worth a try. No, it wasn't love at first sight; for me it was more about what I was prepared to do for him and what this relationship could offer me if the transformation actually worked. Most Balinese women don't marry their husbands out of love at first sight anyway, and my dad always told me love could grow over time.

My first criteria for accepting Jack was simple—to start with I simply needed to see if we could get along. The next important thing to me was that he must be able to be on good terms with my son who would soon be arriving in Australia. Jack was a single man of my age without a child; he was working full time, and he didn't mind that I was a single mum.

Fortunately he and Indra immediately liked each other; in fact they got on really well. If anything, I was the one who felt left out when they were playing their games together, mimicking various favorite funny TV characters I had never even heard of, as I had little time to waste on watching TV.

There were times when I was consciously aware I was making a compromise, as Jack did very little to help me in the house. But I didn't lose hope. I felt sure I would be able to slowly entice him into changing his ways, becoming someone more in line with my own ideals, as he was very easy going and seemed to want to leave things up to me. Compromising like this didn't seem to be such a huge challenge to me, as I really enjoyed having company and it was fun debating with him on all kinds of topics. Our conversations were always stimulating and Jack was full of good ideas for business—we shared a similar way of looking towards our future.

He seemed to like coming to my place to stay, and after a while Indra and I felt comfortable enough to stay with him at his house—although I spent a lot of time cleaning it first, as I couldn't stand the grubbiness. Step by step I uncluttered and vacuumed his house, scrubbed his bathtub back to its original white color, and watered his plants. I managed to get him to organize someone to cut the grass and tidy up the yard. When the swimming pool was finally cleaned and filled with fresh water the whole house looked like it had been transformed. Now it was my job to transform him.

One day he went off to play paintball with his work colleagues, and lost his glasses. Instead of letting him get a new pair of glasses I talked him into having laser surgery. It was a great success, and there was an added bonus— after the eye surgery he looked so different without his thick spectacles. He no longer looked like a dork—and was even quite handsome without his glasses. The next day we went shopping for some new clothes and he even had a new haircut. My beast was turning into a prince already!

Each time I managed to find time to drop in at a shopping centre I would buy him more shirts, pants and new ties. We even shopped for new suits. One by one I threw his old clothes in the bin, without his knowledge. Then one day he asked me "Where is the pink T-shirt that my grandmother gave me? And where are my striped shirt and pants, and my checked shorts. Whatever happened to my old clothes?"

"I don't know!" I told him. Then, chuckling, I winked at him "I think there must have been a robber, but isn't it lucky—he only stole your old clothes!"

After the first few weeks of transformation I felt more and more sexually attracted to Jack. He looked fine now, so fine. In fact he looked more than fine, and the temperature in our bedroom had heated up. My attraction to him seemed to grow stronger each day. Each morning there he was, dressed in one of the new shirts I had bought him and a new tie I had chosen, with matching pants and belt.

"Now you look like a smart lawyer Jack," I complimented him.

"Thank you Beautiful, I feel so much better about myself lately," he looked so happy and he kissed me goodbye as he left for work.

As we became closer, he told me why he had lived in

such a mess.

"I have been living like that since I was young," he told me. "I never knew anything different. My parents both drank too much and they were divorced when I was only fifteen. Mum moved to another state to live with her new boyfriend and took my younger brother with her. After that Dad lived in a one-bedroom flat, so I had to live with my paternal grandmother. All the clothes I wore were bought and chosen by my grandmother. Now I realize why no one wanted to go out with me at high school and during my years as a university student. My shabby clothes probably put them off—I looked so old-fashioned—and I had bad acne as well.

"What about your ex-wife, you've been living with her for almost five years. Wasn't she a nurse?"

He shrugged his shoulders and nodded his head.

"Right, surely you learned some hygiene from her? How come the house was so filthy then?"

"My ex-wife never cared about the house—let alone the garden. She had a bad back injury from her nursing days, and that made her depressed."

I remembered meeting his ex-wife in the days before Jack and I had gone out together. She had seemed to be dressed in a very sloppy way, but I didn't realize their life together had been that bad.

"We used to stay in hotels in Sydney on weekends, just to escape from our messy house," Jack told me.

"Well, I guess that was a good enough solution, at least you can afford an expensive hotel on your lawyer's salary, but wouldn't it have been cheaper to hire a cleaner? And how could you stand it living in it like that? It's hard for me to understand."

I chose not to dwell on it and moved on, continually changing things and making the house more livable. Jack seemed to be very happy and appreciative of my efforts.

My funniest memory of the early days of us going out was an incident at Botany Cemetery. We had gone to the airport to pick up Indra, who was four and a half years old at the time. I received a call from Bill to say the plane from Bali was delayed so to kill time we drove around in the neighbourhood. There we were in the industrial estate that is adjacent to the airport, ready for our adventure. Jack had a Land Rover and in those early days we were so close to each other and always horny. We drove into the empty Cemetery and parked. For a while we wrestled, enjoying a most delicious playful sexual arousal in the back of the car. It was very exciting and just as we finished a cemetery guard approached the car and knocked on our door. We were startled, as we had no idea how long he had been there. But he was very polite.

"Are you lost?" he said, ignoring the fact that we were lying, tangled together in the back seat. "Can I give you directions?"

In those early days, every day we spent together there

was always another sexual adventure. I remember the day we made love in Jack's swimming pool and there was a guy up in a neighbor's tree who saw us, ...we were more than a little embarrassed and then we dragged each other behind the fence, and continued having sex behind the grape vines until a big nest of ants started biting us in very painful places.

We used to make love in any space we could find: on the desk, on the floor, in the bathroom, in the garden, at any time of day or night, and anywhere convenient. Our love bloomed and we were finally able to tell each other that we were in love. One of our happiest early memories was of a song called '*Yellow*'. The last lines are "*...Look at the stars Look how they shine for you and all the things that you do.*"

My world seemed to be blossoming and I had never felt so happy before. My son immediately liked Jack. It was only a couple months before he started calling him Dad. Jack was so attentive to his needs; he was a kind, playful and truly loving father. He even used to take him to his business breakfast meetings before school, and then drop him to school after. At the time I was working as a bookkeeper for a mushroom farm and had to start work at 4a.m. Jack would shower and get him dressed for school, feed him breakfast and let him watch a cartoon before school. He was a caring stepfather; he even coached my boy with his homework and the three of us became very close. It seemed as if we were a perfect little family.

When Jack decided to buy a bigger family home it was the most exciting day for us. We moved into our new home, officially as a family of three. By then I was already working for a government office in vehicle licensing and registration. Due to my work, as I was only new in my job, I couldn't get time off when one of our friends had their wedding in Bali, so Jack took my son to Bali with him, just the two of them traveling together. It was while they were in Bali that I found out that I was late with my period. I rushed to a pharmacy and bought a pack of "clear blue" pregnancy test litmus papers.

I was very happy—thrilled with the results! I was positively pregnant and immediately rang the hotel where Jack was staying in Kuta. I could hear over the phone that he was overjoyed as well. He cried and I could hear him at that end, jumping and screaming and telling everyone "We are pregnant!" over and over again. That was a very happy moment for us both. I kept the test tube in the freezer and could barely wait to see Jack and celebrate together.

When they got back from Bali we had a special dinner to celebrate our happiness at being blessed with a child, our first child together. When I was two months pregnant with Dharma, Jack took me for a drive in his Land Rover to show me the town where he grew up into a teenager, where his mom and dad's house was. He took me to his childhood playground for a little late afternoon picnic of Thai food from a small takeaway shop around the corner. In that little playground he surprised me, with a proposal—in his shy voice and blushing, obviously afraid of being rejected, he asked if I would marry him and gave me a beautiful Belgian-cut diamond ring.

I cried tears of joy and happiness, and of course I said "Yes, yes, yes!"

Unfortunately, our trip home wasn't quite so romantic as I could have wished, as we had to stop each kilometer for me to vomit out the Thai food we had just eaten, due to morning sickness from my pregnancy. My pregnancy went well. We went to pregnancy classes together, and I was always on time for my pregnancy check at the doctor.

The birth of our child was for us both a time of true joy and happiness. I saw the tears in Jack's eyes; it was that special moment when two souls realized that together they had just created another soul on this planet. Jack was thanking me for being his partner, for giving him a child. Tears of joy were flooding that day. Then it was time for Jack to cut the cord, while I had to push one more time for the placenta to be out. Jack called his mum and dad, and spoke to them in such a happy voice, a voice I will never forget in this lifetime. I'm crying while writing this, remembering our happiness at that time, the joy we shared and the children we love so much.

That was 17th August 2002; a moment of truth

when love was so powerful, the hugs, the kisses—if only moments like that could remain, and be captured forever unchanged, the world would be such a happy place—a peaceful haven to exist in.

Going Belly-up... Facing Financial hurdles

It was only one month after the baby was born, however, that our life turned upside down. Not in terms of our togetherness as a family—we were still fine and happy together at that stage, but I had no idea of our financial situation.

One late afternoon Jack came home looking pale as a ghost. He had a few beers and then he began to share his bad news.

"I can't pay for the rent of the office, so the landlord is going to kick us out," he told me. "I haven't been able to pay the staff wages either."

He had six staff at the time.

"I am so behind on our mortgage—the bank will repossess our home if I don't do something soon," he said.

I was devastated by the news, but I had my baby and his seven-year old brother to think of. There was no way I would let my children suffer. Jack kept on drinking himself into a state, while I slowly came to terms with what he had told me.

When I woke up the next morning and saw him comatose beside me in the bed, I felt sad and confused. Could it be true? Would my children and Jack and I soon have no roof over our head? I had to make a quick decision. I gently woke Jack up, made him a cup of coffee, and started talking to him.

"Hey—what's the big deal? We can use my savings to get your business on track, pay for the rent and mortgage. You might have to lay off staff for a while, but at least we could pay them up to date."

I watched him, bleary-eyed, take a first sip of his coffee, and went on.

"I've got some training in the business world already. I can come in to the office and help you out with some of my typing and phone-answering skills and my accounting course is already completed so I can help with that too."

I was so overwhelmed with enthusiasm, imagining how I could work for him. I would put my baby in a sling just as my Balinese mother had done for her husband. No childcare had been booked or arranged as I planned to have six months off and wanted to do everything for my baby myself.

I had never worked in a law firm before. I had no idea of any jargon or terms used, I didn't really even know what went on there, but I was certain I could learn.

We sat in front of our house together, wondering if we could manage to keep a roof over our heads. I had some savings at the time, so I decided to give as much as I could to Jack to help him to survive his business crisis and prevent the bank from taking our house ownership. And that evening I went to Jack's office with him, while there were no staff there, to see if I could work out what was actually going on. It didn't make sense to me that his business could not afford the rent and wages for staff, let alone to pay other bills. There were massive creditors lists, but I could also see that there were a huge number of debtors. I figured that if I could chase them up we could easily cover all the debts. Even if 50% of our clients were to pay their bills I could see that would get us afloat in no time at all.

The more I looked the more amazed I became. It seemed that there was no system in place, not even any proper filing, archiving, or alphabetical files of work in progress, completed work, new clients and so on. There was no way of knowing what was going on in the office, no records of any staff actually doing timesheets, and most of their emails between one another seemed to involve planning what they were going to do at the weekends together.

Altogether there were six staff; we could not actually find much work that had been done, although boxes of files were everywhere. Jack was more often in court in Sydney, and whenever he came back to the office his staff were always giving him extra things to do. However, it seemed that no one was actually keeping on top of things. As far as I could see, whenever Jack was away in Sydney he would return home, go straight to his office and work there all night, catching up on the work that was supposed to have been done by his staff.

They seemed to be busy chasing just enough money to cover their weekly wages, and that was the extent of their effort. They were slacking along, none of them really working to their full potential, not really caring that if the firm performed better they might actually have a longer term job or even better pay.

In Australia employee loyalty is not great. Well I guess it's very rare that we find employee loyalty in any country for that matter. Even more so in a "lucky" country like Australia, where jobs are always available for those who want to work, as most people are not concerned about being unemployed and can rely upon social security support as fallback.

I got to know some of the people who lived in housing commission—houses provided by the government—just around the corner from our house. Many of them have never actually worked in their entire life. Some of the women used to take their kids to school still dressed in their pajamas, swearing along the way, cursing the government for making them wake up early to take their kids to school. They were always complaining: "How dare the government make us send our kids to school?" They couldn't see why any of their kids should go to school. Living on the dole, they could stay in a government housing all their life, paying a very low rent and still afford to eat and drink beer every day. They could see me working from early morning to late night every day, and yet my life was not much better than theirs, so there was not much incentive to change.

Working families like mine in Australia, especially those who run a small business, don't get support from the government. We felt hammered by tax left, right and centre, especially after the "Goods and Services Tax" (GST) came into place. Then there was also the Pay As You Go (PAYG) obligation, plus fines for not lodging on time, Superannuation to pay for employees—and business insurance.

Australia is indeed a lucky country for some but for those who are on the middle rung of the working class ladder it can be hell, plus a lot of hard work. If you are at the bottom, it means you will receive lots of help such as rent assistance, utility bills assistance, family assistance and a dole allowance. But if you are at the top level of the middle class with a high income it is possible to achieve a lot more. And then if you are right at the top, like the Australian mining tycoon, heiress of Hancock Prospecting, Georgina Hope "Gina Rinehart" who with her billions of dollars was touted as the richest woman in the world in May 2012 by BRW magazine, the money will not run out for at least seven generations.

In our situation I had no choice but to put my one-month-old baby in a sling and go to work. I got thrown in at the deep end, trying to help Jack to save his law firm.

He told the six staff that we could no longer afford them, which was true. They all knew that we were going to be kicked out by the landlord from our business premises and they knew the bank was about to repossess our house. There was some fuss about them needing to be paid on time, their superannuation and so on... but eventually we managed to get rid of all six employees.

I took a lot of work home with me, trying to sort out where all the accounts were up to and how I could assist Jack in doing work which was all new to me. I had no idea what the word 'conveyance' meant at that time; I had little idea even what 'filing' meant. I had to learn a whole new language full of jargon in a very short time

I remember on my first day of being in the office, I was alone there with my baby in the pram. Jack had to attend court and there were so many phone calls from clients wanting to speak to the staff. It was up to me to explain to them what had happened and that I would be the one dealing with their day to day phone calls and updating them on the progress of their work. In spite of their disappointment I had to advise them that our business was in trouble and ask them for their full support. Most of Jack's clients were very understanding and each time I looked at their files, I found they had work in progress for which no bills had been paid to date. Some cases had been underway for six months or more, but no bills had been issued for them.

Jack's law firm dealt in commercial litigation and also did some conveyance work. At the time I had no clue what the information I found in the files meant. On my first day on my own in the office I had to simply leave our phone unplugged as I had no idea what to say or who was who, which name related to what file, what type of work it involved or what progress had been made. I simply focused on organizing files, archiving the old files and putting them in boxes till we could find rental storage.

I put the files of finished work that seemed to be unpaid next to the phone, as I was planning to chase them up, to generate some cash flow for the firm. There was a huge amount of work in progress that had not yet been billed, so I put those files in alphabetical order in a separate filing cabinet. I also organized the new files alphabetically; the accounts were in a mess, so I was spending days and nights to organize receipts, receivables and payables while breastfeeding my baby every hour.

I sacrificed my mother-and-baby time to pick up the pieces, and be there for my husband as much as I could, but he was not always appreciative. That was the time when I begin to recognize his anger issues and his inability to control his temper. Each day working with him was like hell. He would yell at me in front of clients when things didn't work out in court, he would yell at me over anything and everything, he would even throw objects at me and slam doors. I learned to have quick reflexes and duck in case something as heavy as a printer suddenly went flying over my head. I had to continue working with him to save the firm, so I put up with all his abuse, determined to make it work for my family.

All my energy was devoted to getting his business back on track. It was slowly becoming our family business, with me and my baby hanging in there every day. I was almost at the end of my maternity leave holiday and yet my time was still needed so much. I knew it would fail again if I went back to my own full-time job. So I resigned from my government job.

The firm was slowly getting back on track and Jack and I could see the potential in it so we hired a receptionist to help out with my work burden. We also employed a business coach from *Professional Coaching*. Richard was very patient and so good at what he did. Even though at the beginning he was very unsure about our goals and he thought our expectations were unrealistic. We were planning to reach our goal of creating a half-a-million-dollar turnover for the following year.

When our firm started to go really well, we invited all our supportive clients for a Christmas party celebration, but as Jack and I were already engaged, we then decided to also invite our friends and families and to double up our party to make it our wedding day.

We invited almost one hundred people that day, it was a very happy moment of my life. Not only did our VIP clients who had supported us during hard times attend, but so did Jack's family from both his mother and father's sides. I was especially happy that lots of my Indonesian friends who had married Australians came too. We booked a wedding celebrant to conduct the formal part of our simple wedding ceremony; it was an elegant and rather atmospheric event.

Two weeks before the wedding Jack and I hired a personal dance tutor to teach us to Cha-cha and Salsa. We chose a theme song from one of Ricky Martin's albums called "No one wants to be lonely" and practiced for a couple of weeks. Jack, who had always been shy about dancing, totally impressed me on that day with the way he moved, twisted and turned and led me on the dance floor. Life was so wonderful and I knew for sure that he was my dream husband. We kissed at the end of the song and toasts were made with Moet & Chandon to our new beginning. I cherished that beautiful memory for many years.

We had our wedding photograph taken that day by a professional photographer, and I never thought life could be so beautiful, happy and as I dreamt it. That was simply the wedding that I had always wanted and dreamt of— my fairy tale moment—wearing a white dress, with my husband looking so handsome in his black tuxedo.

We went to the Blue Mountains for our honeymoon. Even though it wasn't exactly a honeymoon, since we took both of our children with us, nevertheless it was a nice calming trip. Jack took us for a long drive around the Blue Mountains all the way to Jenolan Caves. The scenery was so picturesque with its mountains, cliffs, windy roads and lots of trees along the way. We walked around the caves with a group of other people and a guide who explained the history of the caves. We spent almost half a day to explore the cave, all its nooks and crannies and the little rivers in between.

Richard would turn up once a week in our office to make sure we were on track and doing things as set out in his coaching manual. He set out tasks, monitored our progress and so on. I was always on track in collecting receivables and payables and the two tasks went hand in hand to create a nice cash flow. Our life began to look so much better, and we moved into a smaller office at the end of our lease so we could save a lot of money on the rent. Our new office was in a commercial building in town, closer to the business centre of town and the courthouse.

Things went remarkably well; Richard continued to coach us, encouraging us to reach our target. Then we hired one trainee lawyer, plus another part-time trainee lawyer and we were very lucky when our receptionist left us. Her exit was more like a punishment from me, as I sacked her for naughty conduct in flirting with my husband. I overheard her asking Jack to go shopping with her which I thought was rather cheeky considering I was only a meter away from her in the office. We found a really smart, efficient, good mannered and pretty young girl to replace her in reception.

I loved her dearly, she had a very entrepreneurial mother, and I could see that she was giving everything she could to the firm. Our trainee lawyers were also showing a lot of promise. One Christmas business had been so good that we were able to give bonuses of $5,000 to our trainee lawyer and $1,000 to our receptionist. We could now afford holidays and were able to take plenty of trips to Bali without needing to plan in advance, as money was no longer an issue.

All in all life seemed to sail along quite well, other than my husband being so naïve and doing work for some dodgy non-paying clients without taking any money in trust to cover our fees. And he was always forgetting to give priority to our family life.

My Angry Man

Even though business was achieving beyond our target, my husband was still an angry man and continued to be abusive towards me. I could sense that our relationship was breaking down, even though our business was doing so well. Sometimes I was overwhelmed by my feelings of not being appreciated and being neglected personally. His anger issues were not improving, so we sought help from a psychiatrist to prescribe him some medicine that would help him relax and slow down from his anxious life style.

I remember one particular night after a delicious session of lovemaking when he seemed to go mad. I was so satisfied with our long session of sex. He seemed to be deeply in love with me and I felt everything was perfect between us. After sex I fell asleep immediately. Then a loud banging and yelling from downstairs woke me. I rolled over and my husband was not next to me. I wondered why he was not enjoying the sensation of relaxation after lovemaking, that languorous after-sex feeling. I went naked, walking towards the stairs, and I spotted a light in our study room. A robber? But no—it was my husband in a foul mood, smashing the hanging light, kicking the bookshelf and knocking over our study table and chair.

"What happened?" I asked in a very weak voice.

"It's that f***ing stupid bitch of a local court judge! She made me lose my case today," he said. And he ordered me to go back to bed and told me to leave him alone. His mood swings were becoming more and more unbearable and violent, in spite of the medication.

Life was materially good. We owned our own 46-ft sail boat as well as a jet ski, and we drove nice cars. We had a new Saab Convertible as well as a Land Rover and our house was the best and biggest one on the block. We could now easily afford to travel overseas, and go on ski trips at the click of a finger.

But my husband's mood swings left me lonely and afraid, and it wasn't long before I started to seek comfort from another, more sympathetic man. He was just a good friend at the beginning, until I fell for his softness and kindness, and one day when my guard was down I slept with him. I ended up having an affair, something my husband tells me he has never forgiven me for until now, regardless of how many flings he has indulged in.

In my confusion, and trying to appease Jack, I even went as far as to have a threesome with him and my lover one late afternoon. I got drunk and I was still feeling so passionate about my new affair, I told Jack about him and how good he was in bed. I wanted my husband to learn about oral sex. It was a crazy thought, and even in my drunken mind I was still shy to suggest it, but my husband agreed. In retrospect I think that levelled the playing field, and he felt from then on that he no longer had to hide anything from me.

One night, just a week or two after that had happened, Jack got really drunk, and I realized he had gone to visit our neighbor Tracy. I went to find him there and asked him to come home.

"Let's go home to bed, it's already past midnight," I told him.

He followed me home but in a foul mood.

"Don't you ever do that again!" he shouted. "How dare you ask me to come home just when I was about to score with Tracy?" That was Tracy with the big boobs who the neighbors said was addicted to crystal meth—she was the focus of a lot of gossip in our neighborhood due to her grubby looking house and her druggy friends who hung out at her place day in and day out. Jack was on a mission to have his revenge for my recent affair.

That night Jack beat me up really badly. He managed to get me right down on the floor after knocking me over with one of his professional boxing punches, and then followed by kicking, choking and every torture imaginable.

I was in pain, and already black and blue with bruises, but as soon as he disappeared I still managed to drag myself up off the floor and take my children out of our house. I drove them to my mother-in-law's.

It was early in the morning by the time we got there. She calmed both of the children and sent them to bed in the spare room upstairs. Then she took all her frozen bags of vegetables out of the freezer and piled them up on the table in the lounge. She lay me down on a pile of towels and started to cover nearly all my body with her plastic packs of frozen peas and carrots to ease my physical pain and bruising. I shivered as she was tending to my aching, swelling limbs. She didn't stop talking in an incessant, nervous chatter.

"There, that should be better. I feel so sorry this has happened," she said. "What did you do to make him so angry?" I told her how the argument had started, and how cruel he had been, but she seemed to turn a deaf ear.

"He's a boxer, what do you expect?"

"Even boxers have rules about kicking a man when he's down" I told her.

"Yeah, but you're not a man, are you!"

I thought I detected a touch of compassion in her expression—maybe she did care for me a little bit after all. But then her thin lips hardened into their accustomed tight, straight line and she looked away. She started gathering up the bags of melting vegetables.

I was shivering, so she got some blankets to cover me and made me comfortable on the couch, but she made it obvious she didn't want me staying there long.

"In the morning, as soon as you feel better, you should ring your friends and go and stay with them," she said. "Give him a chance to cool down before you go back home."

"I'm going to report him to the police," I told her,

"I will take him to court—he could have killed me. He should go to jail!"

"Don't expect me to be your witness," she said. "I will defend him no matter what he has done. After all, Jack is my son."

"What about your grandson?" I asked her. "Do you think your son Jack has a right to bash the mother of his child in front of him? He will grow up traumatized. Or become a bully himself."

"I don't care what you say," she said, "if you ring the police you will be on your own."

Then she offered me a brandy to help me sleep.

As soon as the children awoke the following morning I dragged them to the car, leaving a note on the table to thank my mother-in-law for her help. That day we moved in to my Balinese friend Gede's apartment. Luckily he had a spare room, and was happy to have an instant family, although it was a bit cramped. He was very kind to the boys, treating them as if they were his own nephews.

I insisted upon having the boys with me and we left Jack living in our house on his own. Although I knew Gede was attracted to me, I strictly maintained our status as flat mates as I was still in love with Jack. Unfortunately I was always in love with Jack no matter how bad he hurt me physically. Perhaps I still am. But I was never worried about my pain as long as my children were not hurt. Pain was nothing new to me. It had been a part of my life since I could remember.

A new project

It was lots of fun flatting with Gede—we often cooked Balinese food together, and lamented about the fact that there was no good Indonesian food available in our seaside town. I thought it would be a profitable venture, as our home was a popular holiday resort, especially during the summer. But neither of us had any capital to invest.

Gede was originally from Denpasar and he was a warm, friendly Balinese man. Marriage to an Australian girl had brought him to Australia, but the relationship hadn't worked out. When they divorced he decided to stay on, as he already had a good job and he could not earn a similar wage back home in Bali. Luckily they had no children. By the time they broke up he had obtained a special Chef's accreditation at a College in Australia and had five years' work experience cooking Australian cuisine.

One day when I was early for my course and killing time by window-shopping downtown I discovered a rather decrepit looking Turkish café that had a "For Sale" sign in the window. I realized after trying unsuccessfully to order a beer there that it had no license to sell alcohol. It was in a good location, an old street-corner building—the bottom floor of a three-storey apartment block. The café had very dark walls, painted in a depressing combination of black and grey. I peeped into the kitchen which looked filthy. Most of the equipment appeared to be either not very clean or badly maintained.

The current owners were a middle-aged husband and wife team and they only served sandwiches, wraps, soft drinks and coffee. The place was often empty even during lunch hour and they didn't open at night, but it was right across the road from the Courthouse, and I thought that should be a great place for business, as obviously there would be a lot of hungry lawyers and barristers and judges working there who would not have time to go home for lunch.

I asked the tired-looking Turkish man what they wanted for it and how many years were left on the lease. Wiping his hands on his greasy apron, he named a very reasonable sounding amount of money. I tried not to look too excited and while paying my bill I told him I would be back—after I had talked to my accountant.

I took out a loan on the house to purchase the café. By that time Jack was being helpful again and starting to encourage me with my idea to set up a Balinese restaurant. We were on more friendly terms again by then, and occasionally I stayed over at our house again to keep him company. He didn't mind helping me borrow some money from a bank to fund my business with our house papers as collateral. Jack also helped me to organize licensing for the restaurant so I could start transforming it from a café selling sandwiches and snacks into a proper restaurant.

When I decided to take over the restaurant I made Gede an offer he couldn't refuse, and he agreed to work as my chef. He also knew a sous-chef who was looking for work, he said. He helped me re-organize the kitchen, clean the equipment and repaint the walls. We also changed some of the furniture and redecorated the space to make it feel more Balinese.

There was a huge amount of work to be done to bring the restaurant up to standard; it took us at least four weeks to clean the whole place and quite a lot of soaking and scrubbing before the actual colour of the cutlery could be seen. The kitchen bell, which looked black in the beginning, surprised us by turning a pretty golden colour after cleaning. Grey cups and plates glowed white after Gede and I spent at least a week soaking them with bleach in three large sized kitchen sinks.

Strangely enough, Gede had never actually cooked any Balinese meals, but he remembered the ingredients his mother had used to make certain traditional Balinese dishes and he was keen to experiment. I also did my best to remember the food my mum used to cook for me, as well as the Indonesian food I learned to make from the grandmother of my Javanese ex-husband when I lived in Surabaya.

Although at the beginning we opened with a menu of contemporary Australian cuisine, as that was Gede's expertise, we were determined to slowly build our menu up to be more Balinese.

In the beginning I wanted to just hang out at the restaurant occasionally, as a typical manager in Bali would do. After all, Gede was employed full time. I soon realized that the restaurant was going to be in huge trouble financially if I did that. It seemed to me that we were over-staffed up front as well as in the kitchen and there was no need for just one staff to stand behind our coffee machine as the demand wasn't there. As I had no working capital I maxed out my credit card debt but even then I started to get behind on rental. Letters arrived from the landlord of the unit where we were living, as well as the landlord of the restaurant, as we got behind with the rental of both.

I was in a very desperate situation and almost felt like giving up, when I suddenly realized that if I wanted to survive I should change the name and the concept of the restaurant to something more special. I knew we also had to learn to carry out our day-to-day operations more efficiently. I decided to work in the restaurant full time. Some days I worked at the front on my own and on others I had help from a part-time waitress (usually a university student). My twelve year-old enjoyed helping out during weekends.

It wasn't long before we developed our menu into a full list of Balinese specialties and we changed the name to *Bali Spices*, which proved to be very popular, as many of the locals had been to Bali and remembered the delicious spicy food of the island. I regularly worked from 8.30 in the morning until 1 a.m. the following day. As well as catering to the usual lunch and dinner trade we offered takeaways, which caught on very quickly, so I was flat out printing and promoting our takeaway menus, making lunch deliveries to nearby offices around the block. I even offered a coffee delivery; I was so afraid that I would not be able to meet all my debt obligations on time. I was terrified I would lose my business when it had only just begun, especially as the loan had been secured by committing our house to the bank as collateral.

Having a small business was quite complicated. First I had to pay for the local council to inspect my restaurant, and then there were council rates to be paid for my waste at business rates, not to mention the costs of maintaining Occupational Health and Safety (OH & S) in compliance with the law. I was busy learning about taxation, and was horrified when the council told me I would have to pay an "outdoors dining" fee on top of all the others.

I found it quite exhausting being a restaurateur and working so hard to make a living. Even though I paid high wages I found there was very little loyalty amongst my staff, so I ended up doing most things myself. I was working from 8.30 a.m. in the morning and stayed on the business premises until 1.00 a.m. the next morning on some busy nights. I would go home to have a few hours of sleep and then head back to work again. At the end of the week I would find myself with a pile of outstanding bills and not enough money to cover it all. It wasn't just the daily work that was exhausting. Whenever I took a day off I would have to catch up with bookwork, making sure all my receipts were in order and my bookkeeping and tax reports filed on time. If I let it slip there would be extra fines to pay on top of everything else and I would find myself dealing with auditors.

It wasn't until the second year that we finally started to meet our sales target. In the meantime our menu quality had improved tremendously. We continually made adjustments based upon feedback from our customers who tried our Bali specialties and compared it to their Balinese food experiences in Bali.

Once I made friends with our neighboring businesses and introduced them to our new menu at *Bali Spices* they showed their appreciation for our continual improvements and innovations to our menus by giving us lots of business. The addition of the ubiquitous Indonesian *Bintang* beer and a variety of good wines to our beverage list won us an even larger following.

There was a newspaper company just around the corner that employed around 200 office workers, and the courthouse across the road was always full of lawyers, barristers, judges—as well as their clients, of course. During a regular lunch hour we managed a table turnover of three or four times, starting with the early birds at noon, another lot at 12.30 p.m., then at 1.00 p.m. and the last of the stragglers at 1.30 p.m. seeking late lunches.

By our third year the restaurant was doing really well and I had built my reputation in our little town on the Central Coast. My name and the restaurant pictures kept appearing in lifestyle magazines and the food section of the newspapers. We had no need to advertise: word of mouth had spread the news far and wide that *Bali Spices* was one of the best places to go and be seen. In other words, our restaurant had become the talk of the town, even though another Balinese restaurant had already opened in a different area. We were renowned for our Balinese traditional menu and our specialty *Bintang* beer that everyone had tried in Bali once or twice. The other Balinese restaurant didn't have a license to sell alcohol, and our food was more typically traditional, so we still held the winning cards as far as the locals were concerned.

By popular demand we decided to expand our opening hours to several more nights during the week, including the weekends. I employed more girls to help out as waitresses. We played Balinese music softly in the background and a bamboo hut covered our cashier's corner to remind our guests of Bali; they would reminisce about their last Bali holiday and often came in for free advice on good places to explore for their next visit to the island. To build up my own personal branding I had a photo taken of myself in

Balinese costume by a good friend who was a professional photographer, and made it into a large poster that I hung in a prominent position on the wall. People admired my pretty picture—although perhaps it had been retouched a little too much, as some people were curious if it was me but others thought it must be a photo of my mother when she was young.

I often lit lots of candles in front of the poster in the evenings, to give it more romantic lighting, and that encouraged several guests to ask if perhaps it was my dead sister. I simply told them "That was me in my previous lifetime—look at me now—I've become an Australian, I even speak like one!" They would laugh and poke fun at me.

I knew that in some cultures candles are burned in front of a photograph in memory of a family member who has passed away, but I didn't mind, as the poster became quite a talking point and was a feature of which added to the mystique and attraction people felt for our restaurant.

We were doing so well, with hordes of loyal customers. During the day our regular clientele were the office workers, accountants, lawyers, barristers, judges, architects, and artists from the gallery across the road, local business owners, journalists, bankers, plus anyone who passed through our town for the day whether for their doctor's appointment or other purposes.

The thing I liked best about running my own Balinese

restaurant in Australia was the Bali connections that it brought to me. People came in to dine and to reminisce upon their experiences during their holidays spent in Bali—sometimes even their honeymoon—and this helped me to get over my sadness at feeling so far away from home.

The number of wonderful people I met during the time I was operating my restaurant was the brightest point in my life at the time. Such a lot of nice people became regular customers—one of them I even adopted as my family. She was my 'Australian Mum' who I called *Ibu*, in Indonesian style. She was extremely kind to me, offering me such a lot of support during my low times, and sharing my happiness in celebrating my achievements. She always told me that life could only get better. "You're going to be just fine," she would say, "and the restaurant will do well with your bright personality and yummy traditional Balinese cuisine."

She used to come to my restaurant almost twice a week, and talk about it to everyone, just to make sure that other people would follow. That gave us a great boost, especially during the early days of building up the restaurant when customers were still rather reluctant to try anything new.

Some of my customers became personal friends and we ended up swapping houses between Bali and Central Coast. We kept in touch on Facebook and via email, updating each other on our lives and they let me know what was going on in my old town. They still come to Bali on holidays and each time we catch up as old friends. Several of them still keep asking me come back to open another restaurant in the same town—almost 1.5 years after having left. "The new menu is not the same," they say, "we miss the chance to eat your Balinese food."

I am a people-oriented person. When I spend time with people I tend to forget my troubles, so the best medicine for me is being around lots of happy people. Over the years I developed a number of strong friendships with those who loved our food and the atmosphere at *Bali Spices*. We made a point to get to know each customer by their full name, where they worked and what their favorite recipes and wines were. In any business, knowing your clients is the most important part of the operation and it makes it easier to offer your latest products and ensure they stay loyal.

It wasn't long before we were getting requests for our recipes, so I decided to bottle the spice mixes that I used to prepare for the basic sauces in many of my Balinese dishes. Customers from out of town were thrilled to take a jar or two back home with them so they could cook their own Balinese meals. We earned extra cash from this and it was a great promotion when housewives shared stories about how easy it was to cook spicy Balinese food in their own kitchen.

The satisfaction I got from the achievement with my restaurant was great, but it wasn't what I wanted to do for the rest of my life. I decided to continue my education further by enrolling at the University to do a Masters Degree in Business. I also wanted to spend more time with Jack and my children, as we had resumed our relationship and were back living together in our home as a family of four.

Even then it was a hard decision to sell the restaurant due to customer loyalty, but the exhausting lifestyle I had taken on really didn't offer any other choice. I managed to sell the restaurant to an Indonesian businessman. I was happy to be able to focus on my studies and complete my degree within the required time.

Exciting ski trips and Happy Days in Australia

The first ski trip we did was when I was still working with Jack. At last the struggle at the office had paid off, and our law firm was beginning to do well. It was July and we were experiencing a very cold winter season.

"It's the best time now to go skiing," my husband told us one morning at breakfast. The snowfall is so thick—it's a really fantastic snow this season. We must go as soon as possible."

"It's too expensive and everyone says its over-rated," I said. But Jack went on and on about it.

"I want to share it with you—it will be the experience of your lifetime—you will either love it or hate it!" he said. He finally convinced me that I should give it a try.

"Life is too short not to have a new adventure at my age," I thought. We started gearing up for it, and went to the ski shop to find the warm clothes and equipment we would need to play out in the snow. My husband chose to rent his as he already had a pair of ski pants. We got quite excited with our planning and shopping. Jack was looking forward to showing us the snow. He promised us a fun-filled day on the snow and of course the TV was full of exciting skiing ads. He booked us accommodation at Jindabyne, which is near a lake and not too far from the ski slope. It was my first big trip in Australia. It was a very long trip for me—eight hours to drive from Central Coast to Jindabyne—but we were too excited to worry about the distance. We were so eager to see snow for the first time. My baby was still too little, but my elder son was young and brave.

Before we started our first day at the easy run on a snowfield called Smiggins, we sent our baby to a crèche and our older child to a ski class for beginners. My initiation was not exactly gentle. Jack took me up the slope on a ski lift and I had no idea how to get off it, so of course I fell, and when I looked back down I was scared.

"My God there is no way I will learn to 'plow' or use these ski boots and pole to get down that slope," I thought.

I just could not imagine how it would be possible to get all the way to the bottom of the frighteningly steep ski field, this being my first time ever on a snowy slope.

"Can I walk down?" I asked my husband.

"No way!" he replied, and he pushed me with his ski pole to make sure I followed him.

"We'll go down slowly," he told me. "Just look across to one side, don't look down, because wherever you look that is where your ski will take you," he said.

Of course it wasn't long before I looked down and, worried to death about how the hell I would get down there, lost my balance. My body tumbled down, rolling so fast, and it hurt like hell when I hit a huge rock and my skis came unhitched. I had not a clue where they had gone. Everyone passing me had a good giggle and laugh at my misery. Some of them asked if I was all right but they were skiing down really fast so they were out of earshot before I could even answer. I felt so dumb and so Balinese at that time!

By the time we went on our next ski trip, two years later, I had already started my restaurant, and we were trying to patch up our relationship. I told my husband in advance that I would only come if we didn't go so far, and I wanted to have an easy ski slope this time so I could get my confidence. He must have been feeling kinder towards me, as he agreed to go to the ski field nearest to where we were living. It was still a long journey for someone who grew up on a small island that can be crossed from coast to coast in less than a day. This time we stayed in a little town near the ski field called Tumut. It took us a few hours less to reach, and the slopes weren't as steep as the first place we went to. Our older son got so bored after one day because this particular snowfield didn't have as many lifts as the more popular ski destinations, Perisher Blue and Thredbo. It was only a small ski field by comparison.

However, I really enjoyed it this time, as I got to practice on the easy slopes, on relatively flat snow and I was able to get the feel of using my skis to plow. Our baby was just two and a half years old and we put him in a child-care place on the days we were in the snow.

Each day the little kids were allowed to play in the snow. I still remember watching him one afternoon, surrounded by other children who were playing in the snow. He was oblivious, deeply asleep, wrapped up in his cute snow gear.

I loved the drive back to our motel in Tumut. We saw lots of kangaroos, koala bears and snowbirds on the way. It was very dangerous if we had to brake all of a sudden because of kangaroos crossing, as the road was slippery with melting snow. We were very lucky to own a four-wheel drive vehicle; otherwise we would have had to install chains on the wheels before driving each morning.

The town was really small, and we hung out in a quiet local pub in the evenings, where they served freshly grilled kangaroo meat. They also had lots of cows in the area, and the steaks were fresh and tasty. On our way driving back home we spotted a nice looking local pub in one of the towns and there were plenty cows around.

It was the best steak I had ever eaten! So fresh, thick and juicy. You could choose a 1.5kg piece of steak or you can even get a 3kg piece on a one plate.

"Enough to feed a Balinese family for a week," I thought guiltily. I barely could move after eating as much as I could. It was a perfect stopover, our children had both slept through the first part of our journey and we still had a very long trip ahead of us, but we all had a great time.

It wasn't until the winter of 2011 that we decided to take our kids back on another snow trip. I had already moved back in with Jack, and things were going well between us. It seemed like our relationship had matured and we had forgiven each other for the past. I was working hard at the restaurant, so I felt I had really earned a break. We heard it was the best snow season ever and this time our younger boy was old enough for a beginner's class and he could start skiing. A long trip always made everyone agitated, it was a little bit hard on all of us when we finally arrived at Jindabyne when I realized that my younger boy didn't have the right size gloves. This was going to be his first time to ski properly and my husband was so excited he couldn't wait to get to the snow, so I gave him mine.

Jack had booked us to stay in a beautiful chalet right by the snowfield. Our big boy was rather disappointed, though. We weren't staying in town where all the bands and parties took place at night and he was stuck with us in family accommodation. The place was very nice, except it was really hard on our legs to climb up the four-storey chalet stairs after skiing all day. I found the best way to manage was to undo all my ski gear at the bottom and then head straight to the spa and sauna facilities, just to get my leg muscles relaxed so I could climb up to our room.

The view was magnificent when we opened our windows each morning. We could see the sun reflecting on the snowed-over lake. Jack told me it is a very dangerous lake, as often people forget it is there when they are walking on the snow and without realizing it go out onto the lake, and then end up drowning when the ice melted by the sun collapses under their weight. We had been warned to be careful and not to walk too close to the edge.

I'm such a scaredy cat, always scared of heights, whereas our little boy, after only just one day in the snow could already beat me at skiing. He would disappear and suddenly be miles away. The older we get, the stronger the fear factor becomes. We tend to get more and more worried about our safety, always concerned about what is at stake, whereas children are completely fearless and behave as if there is nothing in this world to worry about. I had little children skiing past me at great speed to my left and right, which made me even more scared and nervous in case I bumped into them. I felt sure I would roll down the mountain looking like a fat pig and give everyone something to laugh about. But skiing was always fun, very exhilarating, albeit tiring for me. Our children always had a wonderful time.

The part I liked best about our ski trip was the skiing lessons that I had each day; especially when I got to go on the chairlift with the young, very fit and good looking ski trainer from Austria. On my last trip my ski trainer was from Colorado, he was the most amazing gorgeous looking young fellow, so puffed up and handsome, and very friendly. I'm very sure good looking people are aware of their good looks, as they appear to be so confident and are so nice to everyone.

I have one regret though—I had the bad habit of losing my phone so I lost the numbers of those handsome young fellows. Their numbers could come in very handy now, especially since my husband has changed so much, and life has become very lonely.

Number one is a lonely number.

Beef Jerky in Shanghai

At the time Jack started consulting one of his client's offices in China I was in the middle of doing my Masters Degree in International Business. China was included in almost every subject I had to cover during my University studies, whether in relation to foreign investment or cross-cultural negotiation. It seemed China was the 'in' thing in Australian international business dealings. So it was very convenient that I could visit China and also take my 8-year old boy along while accompanying my husband on a business trip. It was the school holidays, and I left my restaurant in the hands of my staff who were very capable by then.

The Shanghai Airport was not very organized and it was certainly not well signposted. There were no signs in English, so we couldn't find where the taxi stands were... and I recall that we were too afraid to ask in Chinese. This was not my husband's first time in China, so he remembered some things from his last trip. We caught the fast train and I was in total shock to see on the screen that we were traveling at 400 kilometers per hour. Then we found a taxi stand close to the station, and got a taxi to our hotel.

A Dutch company managed the hotel we stayed

in, and it looked just like one of the hotels we normally stayed at in Sydney. The lobby was decorated with Christmas decorations and advertisements offering guests to celebrate Christmas together with all the members of their staff. We didn't book a banquet as my husband had to work on Christmas day.

When we woke up on Christmas morning it was still snowing outside, but the snowfall already looked grey and grubby. We got ourselves ready for the breakfast buffet. It displayed a huge range of different foods, from Japanese to Chinese *yum cha*, and Continental breakfast as well as a huge range of cereals and fruit. After breakfast my son and I went back to our hotel room and my husband off to work. He said he would only work until it was time for lunch. I went out for a walk, just close enough to a supermarket nearby, to a shopping centre like Carrefour where it was easy to catch a taxi. Jack didn't get back from work until very late that afternoon. He was very apologetic, and took us out for a Christmas dinner of Korean Barbeque.

I love Korean Barbeque as you get to choose your own ingredients, then cook them yourself at your table, so there's no rush to eat your food in case it gets cold. On our way back from dinner, heading back to our hotel, we passed a red light district. Sexy girls were hanging out in front of the doors of each establishment. Teasingly I asked my husband if he wanted to rent one. "I would never do that type of thing to you, beautiful," he said.

He told me he had learned his lesson from hiring a prostitute in the Philippines—at that time he had made the mistake of giving her his phone number. The prostitute rang his home and told him that she was pregnant so he went back to the Philippines and she wasn't. Also he caught gonorrhea from her which made his wife at the time very upset, and that had poisoned their relationship.

We flew to Hong Kong the day before New Years' Eve. The hotel was very busy as we arrived at night. I love Hong Kong… they have nice restaurants, and there is food, food, food as far as the eyes can see. The city seemed so alive and full of shopping and markets. We went to visit the Hong Kong islands by ferry and enjoyed seafood for dinner, looking at expensive shopping centres. In those days my husband was too tight to buy anything from an expensive place, and he was not interested in dressing up nicely so I had to be careful what shops I went into.

One morning we were out walking not far from our hotel when we bumped into a couple of Buddhist monks on the footpath. My husband always has a soft spot for Buddhism, or so he reckoned, and when the Buddhist monks asked for a donation for their new temple he gave them HK$200 and then he made me sign my name to give the same. I was reluctant to do it as I felt it was a lot of money just to give to a couple of monks on the street. How could we tell if they were genuine?

He got very upset at me and gave them HK$400

himself. Then we walked on further and we saw a sign saying: "Tourists please be careful of fake monks." My husband felt like such a fool, he got even more upset. He told me that it was not fair for me to be with such a stupid husband as him and we should get a divorce.

I left him in the park and went back to the hotel with my son. An hour later Jack turned up looking rather sheepish and apologized for having done the wrong thing in giving HK$400 to the fake monks and also for his bad behavior towards me. We stayed on another night in Hong Kong as we planned to return to Shanghai on New Year's Eve. When we arrived at the airport in Shanghai we found the fast train was not running due to New Year's Eve and New Year holidays. So we had to catch a taxi back to our hotel. The taxi stank of cigarette smoke and the trip was about as long as from Ngurah Rai Airport in Denpasar to Ubud, but the taxi driver was not half as friendly as a Balinese driver would be.

One night my husband took me out for an original Chinese *yum cha* dinner at a very big restaurant with his work mates. At that time I had a glimpse of how the business was going in his client's office. The staff seemed to be nice enough to me but I thought I perceived a deceptive look about them each time they spoke to each other in Chinese, followed by raucous laughing and then speaking in polite and stilted English to my husband.

I witnessed the cultural dimension as it came into

play that night and was pleased that I was aware of the need for cross-cultural understanding when dealing with a foreign language and the importance of body language. I felt as if I was seeing my University studies in practice that night. I felt rather uncomfortable as my Chinese was very much at beginner's level and all I could understand was the passing of food to each other; at least I knew how to say thank you.

I had to learn Shanghai Chinese quickly as people refused to speak English in Mainland China and they preferred to communicate in their local Shanghai dialect. They often assumed I was Chinese from the Mainland. During my short time in China I learned how to order food successfully in a restaurant and how to ask for extra chilies, etc.

One morning my husband and I went to a street market. I really liked the look of the beef jerky on a stall and I wanted to buy 100 grams of it. I felt confident that I would be able to do the bargaining, but my husband told me as this was my first time in China, while it was his third visit, I should allow him to do it. So I let him take over the conversation in Chinese. We ended up with one kilogram of beef jerky, packed in a huge plastic bag that we took to our hotel. And he paid far too many Yuan for it too. Luckily he had to stay another three months in China. Otherwise we would never have been able to eat all the beef jerky he bought that morning.

I think once again my husband felt like a fool… each time we talk about China since then we always laugh at our beef jerky story. For a long time when we went back to Australia I didn't feel like buying beef jerky anymore.

My husband organized an apartment on Nanjing Road so he could stay in China for another three months, and my son and I joined him for three or four days in the apartment before we left China. The apartment was awfully small. It only had one room with a double bed, a sofa bed, a combined bathroom-toilet and a tiny kitchen in one corner.

While my husband was at work my son would watch Chinese TV and sometimes I took him shopping or to a game centre. There wasn't a lot for us to do there, although it gave me lots of pleasure each time people understood my conversation in Chinese. It was satisfying learning another language and being able to practice it straight away. I was able to get my shoes fixed on Nanjing Road, buy my lunch and so on, but if I look back on my time there I don't think I would bother to go back to China for a holiday. I might go there for work if there was a lot of money offered, of course.

Overall I found China cold and unfriendly and people were not patient enough to stay in line—they would even push each other just to get in front of the queue to use the toilet and it was always a scramble to stay in line when checking in at the China Airlines counter, so many of them were lacking in courtesy and manners.

Maybe I'm being too harsh—at least they were consistent. Meanwhile my own emotional roller-coaster ride continued, as Jack's behavior to me changed like the weather, hot and cold and often unexpectedly blustering and unfriendly.

Our American Dream Holiday

The City of Angels was our destination and our tickets were booked from Denpasar to Los Angeles via Taiwan. In July 2012 Jack announced our trip out of the blue.

"Hey wifey, you always wanted to see America," he said. "Let's do it."

My jaw dropped so low it nearly hit the ground. I was thinking "Is he for real?" I stared at him in surprise.

"Yes," he said, "we're going to do it for real!" And he organized our tickets and accommodation so all I had to do was to get my Visa from the US Embassy in Jakarta. Jack and our youngest son only had to get their ETA online but because I have an Indonesian Passport I had to go home to my country and line up with other Indonesians to apply for my Visa, then make an appointment to attend an interview at the US Embassy, with a choice of either Surabaya or Jakarta. I picked Jakarta, as I hadn't been there.

I had dreamed of going to America for so long, our arrival at Los Angeles airport now seemed just like a dream come true. We caught a taxi to West Hollywood, passing Beverly Hills on the way and I felt like we were already in a movie. We arrived at Le Montrose, checked in to our 'spa-suite' accommodation with its huge bathroom, comfy queen-size bed, and tucked our little boy into his sofa bed. We even had a fireplace in our room plus two huge flat screen televisions, and we were close to the spa and swimming pool. I felt so grateful to have a husband who spoiled us like this.

On our first day we did a 'Walk of Fame' tour, looking at all famous names of movie stars and TV characters on the sidewalk. We had a fantastic time and it took me by surprise when Jack showed me Hollywood hill was just right there in front of us.

"Oh My God—I'm in Hollywood" I squealed.

In the late afternoon, we decided to walk out from our hotel and explore. On the way, we passed Mount Sinai Hospital. It was the biggest and most impressive looking hospital I've ever seen in my life and it was hard to believe that it had been there since 1852. All the houses around it were elegantly appointed and surrounded by trees. It was close to dinnertime, so we decided to look out for a place we liked. We found a small sushi place. Nothing special on the outside, it was simply called Café Sushi. We sat at the sushi bar next to an attractive couple, and in my gregarious Balinese manner I started a friendly chat.

"Hi—My name's Madé Angel—from Bali. You guys seem to know this place well! I didn't see you look at the menu when you ordered and the chefs seemed to know you."

"I'm Charlie," said the good looking guy, "and this is my girlfriend Morgana. Yeah, we come here a fair bit; this is one of our favorite restaurants."

"Are you from here?"

"I've been living here since I was sixteen," Charlie replied, "I'm originally from England."

"Are you some sort of movie star or something? You guys look too good to be just ordinary people living here in LA."

Charlie blushed red. Then he said "Aw, well, kind of. I have a TV series call *Sons of Anarchy*.'

"Is it on TV in Australia?" *Gosh now I realize what an idiot question that was!*

"Yes, apparently it is quite famous in Australia."

"Well, I never heard of it." Then I realized that wasn't very kind so I added "But I don't watch a lot of TV."

I kept on talking to them for a while and Morgana told me about her jewelry business and asked me about Bali. When we got back to the hotel, my husband searched on Google and came up with the name Charlie Hunnam and his TV series *Sons of Anarchy*. Wow, I was impressed! We looked up all the film and TV series Charlie had done. There was a famous series *Queer as Folk*, he was Guest Star in a film *Young American*, and many more.

"Oh Madé… you are such a dumb ass…" I thought to myself afterwards, "how could you not know that!"

I could have got his autograph right there and then since he was sitting next to me. I guess, as it was my first encounter with actors and actresses perhaps it was better this way, otherwise they probably would not have felt so comfortable talking to me.

That was my highlight of L.A.—meeting Charlie Hunnam and his girlfriend Morgana at Café Sushi, on day two. The next day we did a trip to Universal Studios with our ten-year-old son. This was the biggest highlight for him, witnessing full blown American film technology, movie creations, rides which blew his mind, stocking up memories for a lifetime. He was most impressed with the 3D technology and tricks, 4D and the amazing movie sets. Although it was very exciting, the rides were too scarey for a village girl like me, I felt my head was bursting.

On our last day in L.A. we hired a sedan and drove around Beverly Hills, stopping for lunch at the main shopping centre to get some affordable fashion items for me at the mall. Jack took us to see Santa Monica Beach and The Promenade. Then in the afternoon, he took us to his friend's place in Formosa Beach. We had a great catch-up night until he ruined it by almost killing us on the way back. He had been drinking way too much at his friend's place and drove recklessly so we ended up having an argument. Instead of saying sorry, he went out to get more alcohol from a bottle shop and got himself totally drunk. At midnight I got up, unable to sleep, and caught him sleepwalking. He was just about to pee over the balcony so I quickly stopped him and dragged him back in to the bathroom. That was the second time I caught him sleepwalking, the first was in our hotel in Kuta, on our last night in Bali before our L.A. trip.

We left the next day, flying from L.A. to Charlotte, which took 4.5 hours, and then took a short half-hour flight from Charlotte to New York. It was easy to catch a bus from New York airport to the nearest Subway station, and then from the Subway station we headed to Park Central Hotel on 7th Avenue, 56th Street—near Central Park. It was a really classy hotel, although it was much smaller than what we had in L.A. I was very grateful again and thanked Jack for sharing all his adventures in life—I felt very fortunate to have him, my loving husband, bringing all this luxury and excitement into my life.

The next morning Jack took us to catch the subway. We went to Liberty and Ellis Islands and to see the Statue of Liberty. Our visit there was interrupted by lots of NYPDs and water police trying to secure the area, as there had been a bomb threat. They ordered us to move away from the food area, which we weren't too happy about, as we had just got our lunch and really wanted to enjoy it, but we were out of luck as they were very pushy and they told us to catch the first ferry available to leave the island. "God Bless America" I thought—what is it with their crazy security preoccupation?

Wherever we went in the United States I always found it so scary that people carry guns and the police too. There always seemed to be bomb threats, and they take every little thing so seriously. If someone left a bag, then the area would have to be cleared until they thoroughly check if it contained a bomb. Before we even caught the ferry heading to the Statue of Liberty they made us pass through a checkup that was much more stringent than any of the checkpoints we had been through at the airports.

When we returned to the other side of the island we spotted a bunch of people watching black street dancers in the park. One of the things they shouted at the audience, which I will never forget, was "Hey, Obama wants change, we want dollars!" Of course I got sucked in and gave them US$10—I thought that was the least I could do, as it was a very good performance overall and they worked so hard to entertain the crowd.

Jack had always dreamt of having his aged steak at Gallagher's Steakhouse, open since 1927 and getting more famous every day. That night his dream came true, he was able to gorge himself on a 21-day dry-aged steak that weighed almost 1kg, grilled over hickory coals and insisted on enjoying the finest wine in the house. This gathering place has a history of entertaining New York's famous and notorious during prohibition days. Apparently it was one of the few 'secret' places where people with money could indulge themselves in pleasures of the palate and forbidden spirits. On their website it describes "a place where gamblers, sports figures, show people, novelists, playwrights and judges sat at tables across from gangsters, strippers, ballerinas and business titans." I didn't think of it at the time, but at least I was a budding novelist… although I was not sure where Jack fitted into that list, apart from his aspirations as a boxer.

Gallagher's is also famous as a sports bar and almost completely run by men. The only lady I spotted there was taking care of the ladies' toilet. My highlight of the night was a tall glass of Bloody Mary mixed with very spicy Tabasco sauce and garnished with huge olives. It was so delicious I had to have a second and then a third, even though Jack thought it was way too spicy. That was the best Bloody Mary I have ever tasted.

The next day Jack took us to Chinatown and we continued our walk to see the Supreme Court, Wall Street, Ground Zero—where the World Trade Center had been flattened on 9/11—and then on to the New York Stock Exchange and George Washington's original statue. There was the "original" Tiffany & Co. I looked longingly as we passed it, but unfortunately my hubby wasn't feeling so generous on that day. I was so excited to see the Donald Trump Building and then we continued our walk to Central Park.

We didn't do very much on our last day other than taking our son to New York Zoo at Central Park, and some sightseeing and window-shopping at the high-end fashion and jewelry outlets. I couldn't help but be amazed at how big the gap was between the rich and the poor in this country of the 'free and brave'. I loved the horse-drawn carts, something that I had always associated with Paris rather than New York, although the smell of the horse poop really stuck in my nose.

Central Park was very impressive, a huge area with lots of trees, playgrounds, full of people and food carts. We spotted a shop that specialized in cheesecake. I wished my elder son was with us, as his favorite cake is New York Cheesecake and I guessed the best one should be found here, in its home of origin. We couldn't help ourselves—how often does one get the opportunity to gobble a huge slice of New York cheesecake in New York! It was absolutely delicious, yummy and it melted on my tongue, its stickiness and sweetness seeming to devour my taste buds.

* * *

Now, back in Bali, the memory of that sweetness on my tongue had turned bitter. It was September, and it seemed like a lifetime ago that Jack had left me alone in Bali. I felt completely disoriented. I despised myself and yet marvelled at what I had achieved. I detested myself because I'd allowed Jack to cheat me so badly. I admired myself because here I was back on my own island wanting to create my long-term dream. I wanted to be here in Bali, reconnecting with old friends and introducing them to the new me, the person who had traveled extensively around the world and experienced life in their countries. I felt that I could be a new kind of Balinese woman, one who is accepted equally by high-achieving western women, a person on the frontline of change.

I had thoroughly enjoyed re-connecting with a number of long-term expat friends, some of whom I had met almost twenty years before. We were young then, and I had only just started going out with my north-American boyfriend in Ubud. Some of my original American friends had remained in Bali all this time while I was living in Australia, and others had married and settled down here.

I found them very interesting—many of them had achieved their dreams in Bali. They were now successful entrepreneurs, owners of cafés, yoga schools, founders of festivals. There was even one who had become a famous author of books on Balinese cuisine. I felt so privileged to be able to be involved in the Ubud Readers and Writers Festival, where I met so many writers from all corners of the world who had come to Ubud to share their work and spin their tales.

As a child I had dreamt an impossible dream, and now I wanted to show my old friends, my old teachers and the young children in my village that it is possible to realize our dreams. As long as we are willing to work hard, spend energy and time and make sacrifices in the pursuit of the knowledge we need.

It is not likely to be easy, as life doesn't offer a free ride to anyone and we are bound to make mistakes on the way. But if we are prepared to compromise, go without and persevere, I still felt sure we could get there in the end.

My old school teacher actually apologized to me for having laughed at my impossible childhood dream of flying in an airplane to see another continent. I was always telling them at school that I wanted to see kangaroos. I remembered my class teacher laughing so hard when I was in year five—she was also my class teacher in year six. She is so proud of me now and she is one of the few who has been prepared to take a leap of faith and understand me, a stranger who has lived in another country for the last twenty years of her life. I know I can rely on her to support my idea of helping other children in my village to dare to dream.

Being back in Bali is challenging to say the least. My approach to life after living abroad for so many years is more like a western woman, although of course I appear to everyone to be Balinese, so most people treat me as if I am a local who has never left the island. Nobody can tell by my appearance that most of my adult life has been spent in the west, so they expect me to understand their ways of thinking and talking.

I find myself harboring feelings of resentment each time I have to do business in local government offices where, as a Balinese woman, I am expected to keep smiling in the face of the rudeness of officials. More than half of the officials behave as if they are power hungry. It is as if they need to show their importance to make sure that I know where the lines are drawn—with a special set of rules because I am Balinese.

I remembered one afternoon at the Immigration office a lady in uniform came out of nowhere and from meters away asked me in a loud voice "Are you Balinese?"

"Yes," I answered.

"Then you should dress more respectfully when you come to Immigration," she said, pointing to my sleeveless top.

I was wearing a very nice top bought at a friend's shop called *Goddess On The Go* in Ubud.

There was a western woman right in front of me dressed in something that looked like unwashed rags, with uncombed hair and a pair of thongs on her feet. She did not receive any such reprimand.

It seemed little had changed in twenty years when it comes to double standards in government offices—one set of rules still existed for locals and another for foreigners. That I could be a victim to this kind of prejudice on my own island in 2012 was beyond my comprehension.

It works both ways. Back in my village I found some of my old school friends were still doing the same poorly paid work that we had used to do together when we were at Primary school. One day I spotted them cleaning a bucket full of chicken guts by the river and the next day I saw them spreading a basket of newly harvested rice to dry in the sun. One part of me wants to help them to find better work so they can improve their living standards but on the other hand I feel concerned they will think of me as interfering. Perhaps they will find me just too full of myself and think I am pretending to be better off than them, when it's obvious that I am not even able to maintain a stable family life for myself.

After all, I'm not wearing gold jewelry or driving a luxury car, neither have I built the best house for my parents in the village. Their measure of success is wealth that they can visually see. To them my knowledge or self-confidence is of little value—I'm afraid that nothing is likely to impress them other than a show of large amounts of money.

At one time a few years ago I had given free English tuition to some children in year six in my village. I received no support or encouragement from any of their parents. Not that it worried me to keep going without support, but I was disappointed when the number of students attending got lower and lower at each Sunday afternoon tutorial. There was nothing much I could do. By the end of my course, six months later, there were only six students left out of the twenty-two who had enrolled at the beginning.

To celebrate their completion of the course I took the six of them for an excursion to Bedugul to enjoy the botanical gardens and we went walking around the lake. I shouted them lunch and we had a great time—just the six kids plus our mini-bus driver who I had hired for the day.

I hope they went home with happy stories for their friends who had dropped out and hopefully their parents will be more supportive of their studies in the future.

My dilemma is that I want to help my people but it seems that they only measure success by money accumulated. I cannot tell them my stories of overseas trips or share the extra knowledge I have gathered over the years of living abroad. They won't understand my feelings of being a confident, independent person, the kind of person who doesn't have to put up with her man when his behavior is unbearable.

How could I tell them that I can confidently live anywhere on my own—whether it is all different parts of Australia, America, Bali or Singapore with my knowledge of business and experiences of traveling the world? The very thought of a woman being alone is suspect to them. I recalled Dadong Tinggal, the old lady from my childhood, and I begin to understand how she had preferred to act crazy, at least that was one way in which she knew they would allow her space and a kind of respect, even if it was based upon fear. I realized it must have been even harder for single women in her days.

After all these years of running away from home, here I was back again, digging in the soil of my parents' front yard. My sister and I had been planting papaya, herbs and flowers. I figured that this was a good place to start. Perhaps we could show them the benefits of planting our own vegie garden, transforming the bare earth of our own yard with fruit and flowers. Actions might work better than words.

I also set up a kitchen, had it licensed by the health department to produce food commercially and started experimenting with preserving my Balinese spice mixes in jars. If this experiment works well, perhaps I would be able to develop a market for it, increase the production. and eventually expand the business and employ some of the disadvantaged women in my village.

At a Women's Association luncheon at Sanur I saw a movie about mother earth and listened to a talk about Indonesia's Ibu Kartini, credited for starting the move for women's emancipation in Java. Kartini compromised by accepting a marriage arranged by her parents on the condition that her husband allow her to start a school for girls. Her tragic life inspires me to try to do more for our planet and make things better for mother earth and my fellow women.

We must do everything we can towards a sustainable future of the planet and this island we live in, both land and sea. My own struggle pales by comparison; helping others is so important to make the world a better place for human kind. I must continue my journey and accept my life's challenges, to be able to help other women achieve their dreams and share my concern for our environment.

Life is All About Taking Risks

We were still living on the Central Coast when Jack started making urgent unplanned trips to Sydney. One Saturday afternoon he got dressed up in a very smart and unusually tidy outfit and told me he had to go to Sydney for a Mardi Gras party.

"What?" I asked him, thinking I had misheard him. "What did you just say?"

"I've been invited to my friend's house to celebrate Mardi Gras. He will be in the parade."

I was confused, and didn't know what to make out of this. Sydney's Mardi Gras Parade is the highlight of the Sydney Gay and Lesbian Mardi Gras festival, and he had never shown any interest in it in the past, even though his brother was gay, and always spoke highly of it. It was a tiring one-hour drive to Sydney, or at least two hours in the train from the coastal town where we lived.

Jack came back the next day, very late in the afternoon, looking tired and strung out. I guessed that it was more than a hangover he was suffering from, he probably hadn't slept at all. Since that time, he began to disappear more often to Sydney and was sometimes away for a couple days at a time. The excuse was usually that he had appointments in Sydney on Monday morning.

It didn't make much sense to me that he had to leave on Saturday, but as he said, he always needed advance preparation for a court case, and I knew he hated driving early on a Monday morning to Sydney.

Not long after that he changed his hairstyle to a more trendy cut. In my opinion it was rather a 'gay' look, but I said "Wow, great hair cut, where did you get it done?"

"There's a really nice Thai hair dresser named Phoon on Market Street in downtown Sydney," he told me. Each time he came back from Sydney he would bring back some Thai food which his friend Phoon had cooked specially for him, and he always raved about how nice it was, although to me it tasted like a common green Thai curry, the kind that was made with a packet of curry paste, plus extra fish sauce and chopped green chilies, and maybe some fresh cilantro to top it up. He told me he liked to stay at Phoon's house and they spent lots of time walking around Sydney doing things together. It sounded as they had a very close friendship. I knew Phoon was gay and I doubted he had any idea that Jack was a high-risk partner.

When I told him that he still needed to wear condom with me, as I didn't want to take any risk, he told me "Look I don't need to have sex with you if you want me to wear that stupid plastic thing. Its that which made me lose interest in sex. I can find enough people to provide me sex without a condom—even better than that—I can enjoy anal sex these days."

Unbelievable! He was talking to me, his wife, without the slightest bit of remorse, guilt, or even any feeling of betrayal.

"Life is all about taking risks," he said, "or we will just never know."

We had fight after fight, arguing about morals and issues of integrity.

In the meantime it seemed that Jack was developing closer and closer ties to Phoon. From what I could find out by snooping through his diary and folders it looked like that Jack was even taking care of accounting, taxation and the legal side of setting up Phoon's company. Phoon's business visa ran out from time to time and I could see that Jack had filled in all his Immigration forms. I noticed that the Australian Government requirement was for a business to generate at least $95,000 per annum to be able to maintain a business visa in Australia. Jack lent him money time and time again, to support his hair salon, which looked to me like it was going broke. I couldn't imagine how any business could survive on Market Street, known to have the highest rents in the country, especially such a small salon, with very few staff. How could they possibly meet the Immigration requirement of income? He must have needed a very creative accountant to manipulate his figures.

Jack has always been a loner, and he never seemed to have any friends in the past. So now that Phoon was being so friendly I could imagine what a boost that must have been for his ego. It wasn't too long before Jack became a regular at the gay parties at Phoon's rental accommodation in Sydney. He told me that even when he told prostitutes he was HIV positive, they didn't care.

"Everything can be fixed with money," he claimed, "whether male, female, or other."

And then, as if to establish his sexual diversions as a right... "I was deprived of sex during my teenage years, so now I am going to make up for lost time."

It seemed to me that he was determined to enjoy every sexual encounter he could obtain with whoever was willing to do it with him, regardless of orientation. It was almost as if he was suffering from an addiction.

I struggled to find a way to separate him from all the bad influences in Sydney. Finally I managed to convince him that a move to Bali was very important if our marriage was to survive.

"Bali will free us both from our jobs, and all our mundane daily duties, and allow us to live again," I told him. Finally he agreed.

5

Till Death do us Part...

Betrayal from my family

We came back to Bali in early 2012, looking forward to finally doing something with the land that Jack and I bought almost nine years earlier when we sold our shares in the law firm. I had been dreaming of developing it and making some money out of it, as well as building a comfortable family home. Imagine my surprise when I went to my room in my parents' house, unlocked my cupboard and the original land certificate was nowhere to be seen. All I could find was a grubby looking photocopy. I immediately went to find my father, to whom I had trusted the keys to my room and my cupboard, and demanded that he tell me what had happened to the original certificate.

"It's a long story," he said. Suddenly he seemed older, tired and shaky. Looking rather sheepish, he launched into a long tale of what had happened to my sister and my brother-in-law in the past four years while I had been living abroad.

During all those years I hadn't been home in Bali at any one time for longer than a week, as I mostly came home on rather rushed trips, at irregular intervals, so there were a lot of gaps to fill in.

"Your brother-in-law got deeply into debt," my father told me. "We could have lost everything."

As I recalled, last I had heard my brother-in-law was still working at the Duty Free Shop. I remembered back four years ago he was getting very high monthly wages compared to local Balinese standards. He was in charge of merchandise stock for the big Duty Free Shops at Simpang Siur and at the Airport and earning wages of around eight million Rupiah per month.

At the time I helped my sister with a loan so that she could set up her own business on a prime location in the main street of Ubud, as I wanted her to have some independence. I lent her 75 million Rupiah to open up her business centre, to be known as the CBD business centre. We set up facsimile facilities, an international phone booth, and Internet connection with Wi-Fi for business people bringing their own laptops. I felt it would do well, as it also catered for locals by placing ads for their hotels, bike rentals, and so on.

I was so optimistic at the time, I also bought a Daihatsu Feroza on my sister's wedding day for my family to use in case they had to travel to Denpasar in an emergency due to sickness or needed to attend ceremonies far from our village.

"But things were going so well," I told my father. "How could he possibly get into debt? And why should that be my problem?"

"It was his sister," my father explained. "She had this fancy plan to get rich quick and she got him involved in it. He couldn't resist."

To cut a long story short, from what my father told me it appeared that my brother-in-law had become greedy—his own elder sister had convinced him to get involved in a scheme whereby she claimed he would easily get 200% interest for his money, so in a very short time he expected he would be a rich man.

"He began by investing 10 million Rupiah, and at first he was getting 20 million Rupiah back within a month. His Aunty was the leader of the mafia behind the entire scheme. Then he started recruiting more people, and getting more and more investors involved, including people in our village."

I remembered how my brother-in-law had tried to convince me to invest some money during one of my brief trips home. The way he had explained it to me the venture sounded like it belonged to a large company, more like a Duty Free business, in partnership with a Singapore co-operative. I was in Bali on holiday with Jack at the time and we were having lunch at Tiara Shopping Centre when he asked us to invest a large amount of money. He said we could easily double our money within a month.

"Wow, hang on here..." I said. "That's too good to be true! I need to see some bookkeeping, to believe that—shareholder's reports, etc."

But of course my brother-in-law could not produce any documents. All I could do at the time was warn him, and as I did not want to be seen as not supporting him, I offered him a trial investment of 10 million rupiah in his scheme.

"If I lose the money," I told him, "so be it." I just wanted to prove to him that I was 100% right.

"If you do lose my money," I repeated, "I will make you get out of that scheme! In my opinion it will only work maybe two or three months at the most!" I had heard no more from him on the subject.

As far as I knew, in quick moneymaking schemes people tend to get excited at the beginning, and that makes them vulnerable. It's not long before they start asking questions and new members—I prefer to call them new suckers—are hard to find. In a pyramid scheme they use the new members' money to pay the old members, pretending that this is the 'high' interest rate they had promised, in order to build their trust so they will work hard at bringing new members into the scheme. If they happen to recruit members who aren't able to bring any new members further down into the pyramid then that will usually be the end of the story.

Humans are so susceptible. Greed always gets the better of us. Anyone will be interested in getting rich quickly, it seems, and these were hard times for Bali's economy during the rather lackluster presidency of Megawati Soekarnoputri, Indonesia's 5th president. Apparently my brother-in-law had decided to go ahead with the scheme against my advice, and he had stayed involved until there was no money left to pay anyone.

"It wasn't long before the villagers who had invested started chasing him to demand fulfillment of his promise of doubling their money within a month. We were afraid to go out of the house," my father told me.

"What about his Aunty?" I asked, "Surely they should have chased her, not you?"

"His Aunty hired a local mafia group to guard her place and make sure no one was allowed to enter her house anymore. Why would she care about anyone? She had already collected her billions. She now owns lots of rice paddies in the Tabanan area, and a number of new luxury cars, and she can afford to pay corrupt lawyers and cops to protect her."

So my sister had sold her business in Ubud without notifying me. She knew I was against the pyramid scheme from the beginning, but she put all our money into it as she probably thought her husband was right—why work hard if she could get rich quick and pay my money back in no time at all?

Then they sold my car and put that money into the scheme too… that was when it all fell apart, my dad told me.

"He didn't dare to go back to his merchandising position at Duty Free as lots of people at his work place had already lost their money to his scheme, including his own boss!"

Each day more and more villagers came to our house to ask for their money back from the scheme, some of them threatening to kill my brother-in-law and my sister or my whole family if they didn't get their money back.

"We were desperate" my father said, "so we decided to mortgage your land certificate at BPD Bank Ubud." They got a loan of 150 million Rupiah, and due to my brother-in-law's stupidity he once more put all that money back into the scheme. His Aunty promised him this would be the last investment before she could give him 5 billion Rupiah in returns, which she guaranteed she would be able to do within just a few months.

So that was how my land certificate ended up at the BPD bank Ubud, guaranteed by my sister's fake signature! I knew that for them the situation was like the Indonesian proverb: *telur di ujung tanduk*—like an egg balancing on the tip of a bull's horn... a very dangerous situation, but it was more like *buah simalakama* to me—if you eat it your father dies, if you don't you will lose your mother... our Indonesian version of 'Catch 22'. It was such a very delicate situation. If I sued the bank then they could incriminate my family and all of them except my mother might end up in jail. My poor innocent nieces would no longer have their parents or grandfather to take care of them.

At that time I was absolutely overwhelmed with

anger; I wanted to kill them all for their betrayal. How could they have done all those dishonest things? Well, it turned out they could, and they had! I had to face reality.

I was dumbfounded as to how they had managed to do it. But I found out that the bank officials actually were equally responsible, as they had agreed to my sister signing all the loan documents, and even to her pretending to be me. She copied my signature and the bank's notary witnessed it. Perhaps he thought she was me. I don't know!

I had to research my Bank rights to see if I could still retain my certificate title in a case of forgery in Indonesia. I didn't want to pay out more money for a lawyer as it could cost a fortune and no doubt the BPD bank would be able to hire a much more powerful lawyer than I. So, I decided to set up a meeting with all the bank officials involved in approval of the loan. I took my whole family with me to the bank, as I wanted to find out just how they had been able to mortgage my land certificate with fake signatures and a fake ID from my sister, pretending to be me.

My negotiation with the BPD bank dragged on for two months. Eventually they decided to share the blame and cut the balance on the loan by 55 million Rupiah. I paid the rest just to get my certificate back. Two BPD bank officials met me at the BCA bank for my payment of 105 million Rupiah for the rest of the loan. I was feeling very hurt and at that time I really hated the stupidity of my family. Sure I forgive them now, but I can never forget.

New Place, Same Old Tricks

The deceit of my family hurt me badly, but it was Jack's behavior that made me wonder if life was really worth living. Several months had gone by since we had come back to Bali; it was already the end of March, and it looked like my good intentions of getting him back on the straight and narrow had gone astray. I was beginning to think I couldn't change him after all, no matter how hard I tried to be a loving wife. We had been living in Ubud for less than two months when he began taking regular time out.

"I want to explore Kuta," he told me. "I miss all the clubbing and fun I used to have in Sydney. There must be some clubs down there on the beach where people can enjoy drinking, drugs and sex."

I decided he must be a man with no shame, as not a twinge of guilt could be seen on the poker face he wore as he told me where he was going.

"Don't you believe in bad karma?" I asked him. "Or God?"

"Nah that's not for me," he said. " I don't have much respect for any figure of authority. Rules and regulations, laws and traditional culture are not my thing."

"Where have you been dad?" our ten-year old boy

asked him when he arrived back home at 10 a.m. on a Sunday morning wearing dark glasses and looking pale and twitchy.

"Oh I went to some night clubs to check out the pretty girls," he said with a wink, not even bothering to filter his news. "I started off at *Mint*, then we went on to *Pyramid* and we finished up at *La Vida Loca*."

"What are those night clubs like, dad?" was the next question.

"Well, *Mint* was nice and classy—for middle-aged types like me, then *Pyramid* was also similar but the music was not as techno. *La Vida Loca* was full of drunken Australians and prostitutes."

"So where did you stay last night, dad?"

"You wouldn't want to know, son, I don't remember much about it myself—some place up an alley in a back street of Kuta."

"Why do you like to go to places like that?"

"Oh well, it's fun to have a bit of recreation. The girls pay me lots of attention, and I pay them well in return. They make me feel good, and that's what I need when I'm stressed from working and feeling lonely."

Dharma didn't ask any more questions. The next day Jack was going on a business trip to Australia, so I bottled my anger away and tried to keep the peace by cooking breakfast, but by the time it was ready he was sound asleep upstairs on the bed, snoring, with his mouth wide open.

♔

Dirty Duck for Dinner

After Jack skyped me from the USA on Monday 12th November, I had told my son that his dad would be coming on Wednesday. As it turned out Jack actually arrived in Denpasar airport on Tuesday night, and his new 'flame'—girlfriend Ayu Ela—picked him up at the airport instead of us. He chose to stay at her boarding house room for the night and come to Ubud the next day. The first I heard of this was when I received an sms from Jack's Bali number on the day before I was expecting him, letting me know that he was already in Bali but he didn't know what time he would be able to come to see us because he had to look for a car he wanted to buy.

I was shocked to receive this message, as in all of our emailed correspondence since he had been in Los Angeles we had agreed we were going to share our Honda CRV, he was going to stay in the villa, and so on... Now he had changed plans without consulting me.

"But then, after all who am I?" I thought. After all, he had been referring me sarcastically as his 'ex-wife' for some time now, even though we hadn't decided to separate. As far as I was concerned we had a great holiday in the United States, and everything was still fine between us right up to August 3rd—the day my ten-year old boy and I left Sydney after our brief stopover on the way back from America to Bali. But it turned out Jack and Ayu had been seeing each other since June. Or, I was starting to wonder, could it have even been longer? I didn't know what to think or to believe anymore.

Finally, on that strange day, Jack turned up at our villa around 4.30pm. American Annie, my best friend in the local expat community, had kept me company while waiting. Jack took out a bottle of wine, my favorite Pinot Noir that was supposed to be just for me. He hugged our little boy tightly and cried. Annie left discreetly, to give us some space. I went and put my arms around Jack; he was emotional and in tears, just telling me how much he missed me. He missed all of us, he said, including our dog Kenzo. I opened up a beer for us to share because I was feeling pretty emotional as well. I hadn't seen my husband for more than two months, since he had been in L.A.

At this stage I had no clue what had been going on in L.A., and did not even suspect that Ayu had actually been there with him. I only knew of her as his 'new friend'.

We went to have a beer by the pool. In the midst of our conversation, I showed Jack one of Ayu's ads that I had found on my smartphone at *indonesiancupid.com*.

"Look what I found," I said, and clicked my way to the image of a pouting Indonesian woman, gazing out from the screen. She listed her name as Ayu, and put her age as 30, a young woman without a husband, living in Kuta,

Bali, Indonesia, looking for a man between 32 and 45, for the purpose of: Pen-pal, Friendship, Romance/Dating, or Marriage.

"*Willing to relocate to another country*" it said. She was wearing huge earrings, had pouting Botox lips and a plunging cleavage that separated two pendulous breasts.

"I'm looking for a nice husband and a good life," the caption continued.

"What date was that ad?" Jack asked me.

"28th September," I replied.

Jack exploded in rage.

"Why the f..k didn't you show this to me earlier?" he said in a harsh voice.

"What's the difference if I show you now or a month ago?"

He exploded again, even worse this time, slamming the beer bottle on the cement by the pool and at the same time smashing both our beer glasses. I leapt onto the path to get away from the broken glass and the anger, but he came after me, chased me to the gazebo and grabbed me by the neck. While he was shaking and choking me he kept on yelling at the top of his lungs.

"Of course I blame you!" he said. "If you had shown me that ad much earlier, I would not have committed to a relationship with Ayu."

He went on yelling at me. "On 28th September I was in the process of getting her visa to join me in Los Angeles!"

This is the first time I had heard any of this. He had never mentioned in any emails that he had taken anyone with him to the United States. Wow! Already two brutal shocks earlier today and now another, right under the solar plexus, just for good measure. But right now all I wanted to do was to escape his cruel grip on me, which was tightening by the second. I leant backwards to put him off balance and then ducked to the side, escaping through the garden.

He continued his rampage, shouting and smashing things, so I decided to grab our son and take him to Annie's house. I dragged my boy with one hand, clasping my laptop in the other. Even then Jack continued yelling at me abusively from afar. I could see in the distance he had started bashing my Xeon motorbike, kicking and punching it. My poor motorbike, only a few months old, was fast becoming the latest victim of his anger.

"Well," I thought out loud, "it's better than my head or my child getting hurt."

I ignored the show and continued on walking up the path as fast as I could, resisting the urge to go back and try to stop him smashing my Xeon.

It had been a bad enough shock to find out that my husband had not only arrived at the airport a day early, on Tuesday night and spent the night with some strange woman. Then he told me he's going to live in Kuta, and now he is going to buy a car? I was reeling.

As soon as my son and I arrived at Annie's place I asked her to look after him, and told her I would probably be out for a while. Before I left I made a quick phone call to my friend in the Ubud police, told him where I was going, and asked him to give me some support, in case I had trouble. Then I looked around in Annie's kitchen and found a solid oblong block of limestone that she used as a knife sharpener, and slipped it into my bag. I didn't know at that stage if I would need it for attack or for self-defense, but I was sure I could swing the bag with gusto. I felt like a volcano about to explode.

In a calm voice that belied the fire in my belly I asked Wayan, the gardener, to take me to the restaurant called *Bebek Bengil* (Dirty Duck), as Jack had let slip during his yelling bout that his new girlfriend was having dinner there, and he had promised to meet her.

Wayan took me there on the motorbike and dropped me without a fuss or asking too many questions. I gave him my helmet to hold, and told him I would be a short while, because I needed to see a friend. I asked him to wait for me at the front of the restaurant.

I had never met Jack's new friend Ayu before, but I had studied the images on Facebook many times, so I went inside the restaurant to look around for a tall woman with long straight hair and a nose that looked like it may have undergone plastic surgery. There weren't many customers there as it was still early—probably around 5pm. I passed a "*lesehan*" style table with pillows to sit on, and I saw two transvestites there, one wearing makeup and one not. The eyes and the pouty Botox lips of the one wearing makeup looked familiar, so I went closer, and asked her "Are you Ayu?"

"What?" they both asked, speaking in unison.

I looked again at the nervous looking transvestite with the makeup on, studying her closely.

"Sorry. I think I made a mistake," I said. "I was actually looking for a woman."

I was convinced that my husband must have cheated on me with another girl. I kept on moving and looked at all the other tables at Bebek Bengil restaurant but no girl there had the slightest resemblance to the image I had seen on Facebook under the name of 'Ayu Ela & Jack Sullivan'. I headed back to the place where the two pretty boys had been sitting, and saw their pavilion had been vacated; only two untouched milkshakes remained where they had been sitting.

Something about those two untouched drinks suddenly made my mind clear. I shuddered with a mixture of anger and horror at the thought of those two transvestites guiltily leaving their table with two full glasses of milkshake untouched, because one of them must have been 'her'. It made me tremble even more thinking that it was a very real possibility that my husband was seeing a man. I blindly turned back along the garden path and found the two strange men in women's clothes waiting in front of the restaurant: one with makeup and one without, both of them with artificially large breasts. I approached them again.

"So do either of you ever use the name Ayu?" I said.

One of them raised his hand, a nervous, but decidedly cheeky grin on his face. My jaw dropped—not believing what I saw with my own two eyes.

"OH MY GOD…."

I felt as if I was sinking into the ground, and I desperately needed someone to slap me to wake me up so I could tell the world that this was the worst nightmare I had ever had!

As I was swinging my hand back, ready to hit the guy who admitted to being Ayu with Annie's limestone knife sharpener, Jack suddenly arrived at the scene and hastily got in between us. He turned on me and slapped me on the face, then moved closer to the two lady-boys. As they walked back together to pass me; I leant forward and grabbed Jack's crotch and pulled as hard as I could. He screamed with agony, and the boy-girls squealed and nearly tripped over each other in their haste to get away. A crowd had gathered, but I didn't care. I yelled at the top of my lungs at Jack.

"What the f..k is wrong with you? What the f..k are you thinking?"

The cops that I had alerted earlier on arrived just in

time, hurrying through the crowd, to see Jack approaching me. They moved forward to protect me by grabbing Jack's arms. In that moment I took the stone out of my bag again, and whacked the back of his head, shouting at him "This will fix your f..ked up head!"

I didn't realize I had made such a big dent. Blood started to drip down over Jack's clothes, but he couldn't budge, as the police still had him by the arms.

As I turned away I saw them release him so he could take his singlet off and use it to cover the cut on the back of his head.

"I hate you!" he was yelling. "F..k off, will you, I never want to see you ever again."

I was beside myself with fury, and if the police weren't there I swear I would have attacked him again… I was fueled with so much anger and frustration and now my fourth shock of the day, the realization that my husband must be in love with a man, had come so suddenly. I had only seen Jack for less than an hour and my world had already fallen apart.

The police were calling more of their colleagues to come to the scene and all four of us ended up being rounded up and escorted to the Ubud Police Station.

It was really weird entering the police station to see my own husband, who had arrived there first, busy trying to lay charges against me. Not to mention both his *waria* 'girlfriend' and the other transvestite standing beside him, as his witnesses… I found it so ironic that they were posing as witnesses against me, on my husband's side.

Now, viewing them for a second time, I found them both very masculine, especially the one in makeup, who called himself Ayu. I could not stop thinking—"Could this creature be the person my husband calls 'beautiful' and 'gorgeous' on skype?"

Jack had even used the endearment *'Sayangku'*—My *Darling*—when speaking to him, a love-name that used to be reserved for me!

Was this some sort of joke God was playing on me? I imagined them sleeping together and it really bothered me. I had a mental image of my husband kissing this man's face with a hard lump looming down below, and it made me shudder.

I walked towards the two female impersonators, holding my head and my shoulders high, my body straight. I was determined to walk with dignity and not let them take me for granted. I looked Ayu in the eye and then spoke slowly and scathingly.

"Huh! I wonder how my husband can do it to you, unless he takes drugs—you're the ugliest thing I have ever seen, an absolute insult to womanhood!"

"Wow," she defended herself by saying, "Just listen to you talking…" and her friend chipped in "Your husband left you for people like us because he got bored!" They kept on alternating: "We created a new fantasy for him!"

"We gave him the fairytale he wanted."

"Wow," I said. "Some weird fairytale that must be!"

I was taken into a private room by one of the police detectives to be interviewed about the incident. I asked him what the 'witnesses' had said. The police were happy to fill me in. I don't imagine that in western countries the police would tell you what the other side had to say, but here in Ubud they were happy to tell me exactly how Jack and his companions had portrayed the incident. I was able to defend myself.

The interview went on and on and to make it quicker, I helped out the police by typing the report, as I felt sorry for the officer who could hardly type at all—he was using two fingers! I knew I could probably type much faster than anyone in the police station.

In the meantime, Jack had started to put on a big performance of protesting to the police that the interview was taking so long. At first he complained loudly, then, when they didn't respond, he started to throw things around and worked himself up into a temper tantrum. The police didn't do anything; they chose to ignore him. Jack was swigging at a bottle of red wine right there in the police station. He went out the back and started angrily punching their boxing bag.

To make matters worse, the electricity at the police station suddenly went off. This is a very common thing to happen in Bali. The room was stinking hot with all of the fans off. The police were still smoking in that tiny closed room, and we had to wait for their computer to come back on so they could complete their report. I went out to the darkened waiting room to get some fresh air, and sat on the wooden bench near the door.

That was when the lady-boy hooker, who I now knew as Elvanda—I had seen the real name on his ID card and typed it into the police report along with the other information (*sex: male, place of origin: Palembang, Sumatera*)—all of a sudden dropped to his knees at my feet. It looked as if he wanted to kiss my feet! I was sitting on a chair, and I edged backward as far as I could go, tucking my feet underneath me.

"Please forgive me," Elvanda said. "Don't be angry! We can be friends—on Facebook, skype, even in real-time! Please let me reintroduce myself: my friends call me Carla. I swear on my mother's grave that I never wanted to hurt you or your children."

"I love Jack," he went on, "if you don't want to be with him, I would love to continue my relationship with him with your blessing." I looked down at him, and in spite of my anger I felt a pang of compassion. Did he realize just how dangerous it was to swear on his mother's grave? Especially to someone like me! How desperate he looked.

Then one of the policemen butted in. "What a liar and a drama queen you are," he said, looking aggressively at Elvanda. Ignoring him, Elvanda went on.

"If you don't agree, I promise not to have anything to do with Jack again," he said.

The other transvestite, whose name I had typed into the police report as Serai, from Sulawesi, approached me too and squatted in front of me, his hand on my knee.

"I want to be your friend too," he said. "Now that we're going to be friends, please call me Franceska."

I pushed them both away from my feet and stood up.

"Don't touch me!" I said.

"How can someone like you, working in a beauty salon and doing cheap tricks, afford to buy a brand new car?" said the policeman.

"Don't you imagine I have a new car because of Jack," Elvanda said. I thought I detected a flash of pride in those mascara-smudged eyes. "When I worked in Australia I earned $300 an hour. I will never ask Jack for money, my love won't cost a thing!"

Then Elvanda continued, in a husky voice that betrayed his sexuality, unwittingly incriminating himself even further.

"I bought land in Palembang," he said, "from my own hard work."

"Yeah," I said, "I heard about that. You were working on my husband."

Of course as it turned out Jack had paid for the land, Elvanda had asked Jack to pay the whole amount for the new car and Jack had also paid every expense incurred in Australia—even for ads on the call-girl websites to promote Elvanda's services. Not to mention all the travel and shopping expenses while in the United States.

Thank God finally the electricity came back on and I was able to see Elvanda's face clearly again. This time it seemed to me to be a fake face filled with lies, but still doing its job quite well in convincing my husband. Elvanda had got his teeth into Jack and I could see from the expression on Jack's face that he had willingly turned into a zombie. He could no longer tell right from wrong.

I found Elvanda's deep voice really annoying. He kept on telling Jack "Don't be angry, honey!"—angry pronounced *un-gry*. A hard and vicious anger was welling up inside me. I really felt like bashing up Elvanda's ugly face. I couldn't stand hearing my husband calling this travesty of a person '*Beautiful, Gorgeous*'—all the names that he had used to call me.

I begged the police to finish the report as quickly as possible, making up any excuse I could think of.

"My ten year old son needs to be fed dinner. And my friend Annie is ill and most likely having a panic attack!" I used every excuse I could come up with that was based on truth. I had had enough drama for one day. In fact it had only been a few hours, but since 4.40 p.m. that afternoon, only 10 minutes after Jack's arrival in our villa, my entire life had been turned upside down.

In the end there were no charges laid, and we all

went home and on our merry way, none the wiser for the experience.

As we were walking out the door of the police station Elvanda asked me if I wanted Jack to come with me to my villa.

"Is this some kind of joke?" I replied. "Jack is in love with you. You take Jack with you because I don't want him, especially after he slept with you."

Jack went back to Kuta with his travesty and her friend, and I went back to our villa in Ubud.

*   *   *

I didn't expect to see Jack for a while after he disappeared with the two ugly ducklings, so I was shocked when he burst through my door the very next morning at 4 a.m. looking upset. I was still in bed, snuggled up with Dharma.

"What are you doing here?" I asked him, rubbing my eyes as if I had seen a ghost.

"I had to jump over the wall," he said. "Those f...ing transvestites left me alone in their room in Kuta and flew back to Jakarta."

He slammed the door and went on upstairs to bed. We didn't see him for the rest of the day, until late that evening, when he appeared again, looking angry.

He started shouting "It's all your f...ing fault" he said. "My girlfriend went back to Jakarta because of you."

Left out in the Cold

More often than not, when we realize we need someone to be there for us, there is no-one available. In fact it is not even likely that anyone is even aware how bad our situation is, or how desperate we are in that particular moment for a hug or a few nice words of comfort.

All of my sadness, my sorrow and my pain seem to have blended into one dreadful ache inside, especially if I think back over the events of the past few weeks. My ten-year-old son and I had returned to Bali on the 3rd of August. My husband and my older son Indra remained in Australia and were to follow in ten days time when Indra's visa was ready. I remembered how excited we had been when we went to the airport to meet their arrival flight, but when they came through the doors at the arrival area there was not even a hug to reciprocate. Jack was clearly preoccupied and he looked at me with weird eyes and a cold expression. Indra was equally distant. Jack made excuses that he had been working too hard in Australia, and hadn't had much sleep.

As soon as we arrived at the villa Jack immediately unpacked, set up his computer and started checking his email and Facebook accounts. We could hear him chatting on Skype upstairs. It was as if he hadn't noticed how excited my little boy and I were to be with him again. Our last time together had been our 'dream holiday' in USA and we had missed him ever since.

Over the days that followed it seemed that he was putting a huge gap between us. He was glued to his laptop on most days, and I often caught him out of the corner of my eye, staring at naked images on the Internet. He started making regular trips to Kuta, and coming back at odd times. When he got back he would stay up staring at porn sites, or pretending to be busy with workload. Then he would sneak off to sleep in the tiny room at the back of the house.

On those occasions that he did come to bed, he would sleep at the furthest edge, on his side, with excuses of having a sore back, being too hot, etc. There was no more cuddling like a pair of spoons—not even a goodnight kiss. Sometimes he would disappear into the toilet with his laptop or his Samsung tablet, and he had begun to lock the bathroom door. Every time I came home from going out on my own he seemed to have a guilty look on his face.

One day when I had just got home from the Gym I spotted that furtive look on his face again, and couldn't help myself asking "Have you been playing with yourself or something? You look so smug, just as if you had been masturbating," and he blushed and nodded his head.

I became more and more upset about this strange behaviour, and I started to imagine that he must have met somebody new in Sydney or Kuta, so I approached him about it.

"So what's going on? Have you found somebody new then?" I asked him one morning after another lonely night on my side of the bed. He looked pained, but did not bother to answer me, grabbing a towel and heading for the bathroom. "It's better just to be honest to me," I said to his retreating back.

I couldn't bear being ignored, so I kept on at him "Come on, tell me who it is," I would hassle him, whenever I got the chance. But he would go red in the face and shout at me at the top of his lungs "Just leave me alone!" The last time I had bailed him up was late the previous night, after he had had a few too many drinks, and he had finally grabbed me and shaken me, and shouted at me: "Can't you see? I am in love with somebody else. She is beautiful and kind, and I want to be with her." I went limp, all the fight and anger draining out of me, when I heard these words.

He went on. "I still care about you and our sons, but I am IN LOVE with her, and I want to share my life with her. I want to share my life... I want to live half the time in Ubud and the rest in Kuta. I'm going to Jakarta tomorrow to be with her."

And then, before I could reply, he had pushed me out the door, locking it behind me. I was only in my shorts and a skimpy top; I didn't have the motorbike or car keys, and it was late at night, so I had no choice but to stretch out on the lounge chair by the pool and hope he would relent and open the door. But I must have cried myself to sleep. Now here I was, awake again, and locked out in the cold.

I couldn't believe my situation.

At the mature age of forty years, here I was crying like a baby for my mother, wailing in desperation, longing for her warm hands to stroke my hair, her wise words to warm my heart. I had never felt so alone in my entire life.

I had finally realized that I had lost my soul mate to a world that I had never known or even imagined. Jack, who had been so kind, gentle, my best friend, my lover and a wonderful father to our children in our early years, was now in love with somebody else. Somebody who I now realized was a lady-boy who worked as a hooker. A man who wished to be a woman despite his physical maleness— so much that he had surgically-added breasts.

Jack had chosen to be with this lady-boy, rather than at home with our children and me.

And then I remembered that our seventeen-year old boy was planning to come home this evening with a girlfriend who wanted to meet his parents.

"Luckily Jack is off to Jakarta to see his lady-boy," I mumbled to myself. I was determined I would make up for his absence by being the best mother possible. My poor son didn't have much choice. It was unfortunate that one parent had gone astray, and I was the dismal other.

I dozed off, my racing thoughts turning into wild horses that carried me off and dumped me in a graveyard where old ladies with fangs and long dangling breasts jumped up and down on the graves and pointed at me, laughing. Rather than be left out, I joined them, and enjoyed the wild freedom of their disrespect, as the night callously retreated, bowing, and then continued its limping dance towards morning.

I heard the click as my son came down and unlocked the door when he went for his morning swim. I pretended to have just finished meditating, shouted him a cheery "Morning Darling!" and then dashed inside and put the kettle on. I tidied up the kitchen and made myself a coffee, then checked for messages on my cellphone in between scalding sips of hot, sweet Balinese coffee.

Thank goodness Jack had locked me out, I thought. Things looked different in the soft morning light. If my anger had got out of control and our fight escalated further our children might have been orphans by the time the weekend arrived.

I decided to pull myself together and promised not to ever be so stupid ever again. The children had suffered enough from all our fights, temper and rampage. They were sad, upset and confused by the changes they had witnessed in their parents. I was confused enough myself, and had no idea how things had escalated to this level, but I had a feeling it was not over yet.

Jack is trying to be two people

The months went by so quickly in Bali, and suddenly I realized we were already half way through November. The humidity and heat of the build-up to the rainy season were taking its toll on me, as I tried to be there for both my children, and make up for Jack's increasing absences, and his erratic and violent behaviour whenever he came home to us. For the first time in years I didn't look forward to Christmas or school holidays the way things were going.

On one hand it seemed that Jack wanted his family, his wife and two children, but on the other hand he desired something else.

Jack had always dressed simply, and anyone could pick him for an Ozzie bloke—especially when he was relaxing with the family. Usually in Bali he would discard his professional ties and jackets and hang out in a plain Bintang singlet and a pair of shorts. He used to show lots of love for both of our children, especially our ten-year old who loves him back with the same intensity. Dharma used to laugh all the time when his dad was around— they would play out the roles of their favorite comedies together.

Jack the family man used to be so focused on the corporate world and his business adventures; he had many creative business ideas to discuss with me and was always happy to take us on family holidays.

Now since having a taste of the underworld it seems like he has shucked off that role as easily as changing his costume. These days all he can talk about is how much he enjoys getting high. He even takes liquid G when he is doing exercise—he showed me the bottle, and told me he had found that it gave him more stamina.

He started off telling me that his life was very boring in Bali, and how happy he was that had changed since he joined the crowd in Kuta partying and taking drugs.

"I bet you are footing the bill," I told him.

"Yeah, they think I am a big rich man, I feel so flattered and accepted."

It was really strange to hear this from someone who I had always thought of as being so intelligent. At the age of forty-one he now seemed to have the emotions of an adolescent. The new Jack was so immature that he was crying in front of me when the radio played a song that reminded him of the first kiss with Elvanda at Dee Jay's nightclub in Kuta. He had absolutely no shame, often phoning her while our boys are around. We could hear him upstairs, saying things like "I love you beautiful" and "You're so sexy!"

The boys couldn't believe what was happening, especially when Jack explained to them "What difference does it make if your dad dates a female, male or she-male?"

"The Indonesian term is *waria*: '*wa*' for *wanita* or woman, and '*ria*' for *Pria* or man," he told them earnestly. By this time both kids were staring blankly at their father, aghast.

"But Dad, what about Mum and us, and the family?" they asked him.

"I still love you," he replied, "but I need more in my life than the same old boring stuff.'

The boys are so hurt and ashamed that their dad is dating a hooker who is a she-male *waria*; they cringe with embarrassment and go and lock themselves in their room.

Jack seems to me to be lost in his own world—immune to our feelings, and it is as if he can't tell right from wrong anymore. All he wants is to have a high life, to live his 'fairytale' and be completely selfish.

What next?

In spite of everything that has happened, tonight I'm hoping to have some plain boring family life. Tonight we're planning to go to dinner with the boys in a nearby restaurant. Last time we managed to have an ordinary family dinner it ended up in disaster on the same night just because of a small issue: the Internet wasn't working and Jack couldn't skype his 'darling'. Tonight seemed to be pretty average, we got through dinner without any major drama, and Jack and Dharma had fun joking together as usual, but when I got home I still felt sad and confused.

I felt like I was sleeping with the enemy, and he was trying to confuse me. From now on I had decided to look for the real concrete evidence and to believe nothing less.

But Jack's behavior was causing me to become more and more distracted. When your hopes and dreams are drowning in a sea of regrets and sorrows you can no longer be fooled by moments of peace. Even my son's smile seemed stiff and forced. It was like the quiet time before a storm; I felt a kind of pregnant pause of anticipation as if something bad was about to happen. All I could relate to was heavy rain and thunder. Even when it stopped raining, I felt sure my skin would not even notice the warmth of the morning sunshine.

As each grey day transformed itself into an even darker night I was feeling so alone and confused. I dragged myself through the days with little hope, trying to fight down the tears that seemed never far away.

When a light appears in the midst of chaos, we want desperately to convince ourselves that everything is back to normal, regardless of how bad the last screaming match has been.

How could I understand my addiction to this man, and the crazy things he expected of me, when all he could offer was brief moments of lucidity amidst a turmoil of lies and chaos?

Could it simply be that I love him more than any other man I've ever met in my entire life? I must admit that he is good in bed, and we had some wonderful high points in our marriage, that's for sure. But that was in the past.

Perhaps I am too insecure to be on my own? As for seeking another partner—my low self-esteem makes the possibility of finding a new husband seem a formidable task, even in this yoga and new-age hippy-frequented part of Bali.

Perhaps most important thing for me is maintaining my self-respect as a Balinese woman. Deep down I'm terribly afraid of my father's rejection. He will never understand my failures in relationships and the whole family will be affected by what others would say about me in the village—gossip is a terrible thing.

I guess I just don't want to be seen as another *janda*—the word for divorcee has negative connotations in Bali. Divorced women are well known to be easy victims of men's sexual desires in my village neighborhood, so it's not easy to survive on your own. I guess I don't really want to continue living in Bali as a single mum again—that was probably why I decided I had to go back to Australia to live when my marriage with Bill failed.

Balinese culture encourages us to keep 'face' no matter how bad things are, no matter how much we suffer. But I have noted it is generally the women paying the penance for this—there seems to be another set of rules for the men. Having lots of women in your life and marrying a number of them is seen as a rather admirable feat of accomplishment for the opposite sex.

My father's visit

For the first time ever my father actually rang me twice yesterday, expressing his worries for my life—he said he wanted me back home, so he could take care of me and perhaps give me some support.

Today he actually came to visit me at our villa.

"He must be really concerned over my wellbeing" I thought. "Perhaps my sister and brother-in-law have described how brutal Jack can be."

I was surprised to actually see him coming down the path later on in the morning, wearing his best trousers and a batik shirt, and carrying some fresh green coconuts from the village.

"He probably has my best interest at heart," I conceded, "even though all he ever talks about are the other troubles we have in our family, how his son-in-law Agung is such a failure, cannot produce a male grandchild, and so on."

He stopped by the garden *Balé* at the front of the house where I was taking a break, reading a book.

"Your mom is concerned about you," he said. Now I knew who was behind the visit.

"Hopefully, with you coming to visit me Dad, Mom will feel more at peace about my situation." I gave him my biggest smile, but I couldn't make it really convincing.

"Madé, you must remember that the man comes first in the family and when women interrupt the flow of the man being in control, the family will fall apart," he said. I knew my father wanted me to have a stable family life. In any traditional Balinese family the women are not supposed to disturb the peace.

"Whatever you do this marriage cannot fail," he said. I knew he was thinking of his grandsons, the only male grandchildren, my boys. Boys are important for the continuity of the family. I could not explain to my father the weird reality of my situation—it was just too hard to describe. No matter if my heart had been broken to pieces, my father didn't know the truth and he wouldn't want to know.

"If you didn't disturb the man," he said, "your family life would still be peaceful. You have to stop nagging, nibbling at him and being smart. You should be more like your mum, accepting and content."

I smiled, bitterly. My mother is just like a mushroom, left in the dark about everything. She can't read, she can't write, and she is so powerless that for years she tried to keep it quiet that her husband was out having affairs, until I found her in tears one day. Imagine how useless she felt. She had no place to go, no way to earn any money. She was totally dependent upon my father.

I tried to keep quiet, but my resentment was growing. I thought he had come because he was concerned about me.

But it turned out he had just come to give me a piece of his mind, advice that I really didn't appreciate. He wanted me to repair the damage between my husband and me.

"I just want to see you together, I love you all," he said. My husband had produced him a grandson, therefore he could not be anything else but a perfect son-in-law in my father's eyes. Even my brother-in-law could only produce girls, and he was the one living there in the family compound, much to my father's disgust. He referred to him as 'the painter without a job'.

"Sure Jack has a bit of a temper," my father said, "but he is working and he seems to care about his children."

I knew my father could only see the surface, as I'd never confided in him about any of the problems in our marriage.

"There's no point in telling someone who will never understand," I thought to myself.

My father asked me if I wanted him to come to our villa and check every three days, to make sure my husband is happy and content!

"Probably not necessary," I said, and tried to keep the sarcastic tone out of my voice.

He went into the house where Jack was sitting by the window having a cup of coffee and they had a friendly chat.

"*Apa Khabar?*" he said. "*Kenapa tidak datang ke rumah?* Why didn't you come home to visit us?"

Then he pointed to the broken tiles and chair and asked him "*Kenapa rusak?* What happened?"

"*Banyak hujan!* The rain did it" Jack said.

"Right," I thought to myself, "the rain, as in the song '*Rain all over me*'….. the tingles like rain-drops on your body caused by ecstasy and a family of similar drugs."

On his way out my father stopped by the *Balé* again, and suggested that Jack should come to our village more often.

"I will let him know, but no promises as he is meeting his girlfriend this Friday in Jakarta" I said.

I had downloaded the hotel reservation the night before from his laptop. Jack had booked himself into a brand new Prada Suite at the Merlynn Park Hotel, where even the shower had a panoramic city view.

All this is to impress his lady-boy in Jakarta, after already having impressed her by staying together at Beverly Hills Wilshire and taking her shopping for Prada at Beverly Hills' Rodeo Drive in L.A. Just lucky for me that they had argued, and she left early to go home to Jakarta, otherwise a lot more money would have been spent as Jack was planning to take her on another spending extravaganza in New York.

That wasn't the only spending he had done on her behalf. I had found in his notebook a list of supporting documentation required for an Australian visa, and amongst that were papers for 'car ownership' and 'land ownership' in a man's name, not one I recognized.

"Does Ayu have land?" I asked him. "Who bought her land?"

"I did," he said, without even blinking.

The figures were mounting up. At the police station I had asked her how much my husband had spent on land for her in Palembang.

"Not much, only Rp.15 million," she had said.

She had also asked Jack to pay the balance of her new Black Honda CRV, which cost Rp.350 million. I checked the notes in Jack's diary—the total money spent in 15 days so far added up to AUD $31,000. A good portion of our family savings had already been thrown away on his new passion.

I thought back to my childhood in those days when my father was seeing other women, and any money he had earned had disappeared without trace. He had always protected himself by anger, so that we would avoid him and not dare to question his ways. I wondered how my mother had managed to keep calm and work from dawn to dusk to put food on our plates. I had never heard her complain or raise her voice against him.

Perhaps I am my father's daughter, I thought. I seem to be lacking in all the qualities of Balinese womanhood. Suffering silently is not for me!

My mother the inspiration

When I think back to my childhood of violence I remember that my mother was always there to patch me up and comfort me, no matter how naughty or badly punished I had been. In those days her life was not easy either, dealing with a husband who was prone to bursts of unreasonable anger and frustration, who often blamed her for his own difficulties in life. My mother did not only have to deal with my angry father and his tantrums, she also had my grandfather to take care of and he was even more egotistical and sarcastic than his offspring. How she managed to keep her temper, work hard from dawn till dusk and continue keeping the home fires burning and the family fed in those difficult times I will never know.

These days my mother is less tired, with my sister having taken a huge weight off her shoulders in dealing with village and temple duties. She has now grown into an aging, rather chubby old lady who always walks across the yard dragging her sandals loudly as she goes, instead of just lifting her feet to take another step. She never used to wear sandals in the old days and it is as if she has taken to wearing them reluctantly, and is tempted to leave them behind at every step.

No matter how hard we try to dress her up, she remains

unconcerned about what she wears, preferring to tie her sarong loosely with a knot at the top end where she likes to twist some cash notes from her daily sales into the worn batik fabric, just enough for the day's frugal spending. She refuses to wear a skirt unless she has to go to town and would rather wear a ragged t-shirt than a clean one.

"I don't want to get my good shirts dirty," she would say, as she twisted her hair into a lop-sided bun at the back, poking some fragrant flowers into it from her prayers.

I think of my mother as a living Buddha, as she is one of the simplest and gentlest human beings I know. She has survived until now without learning how to read or write, keeping herself busy and happy with all the ceremonial duties she is entrusted. It seems she harbours no resentment towards life; she prays each day that her children and her grandchildren will be given enough good karma by our ancestors. She wants all of us to be happy and get along well together. I know Mum is right when it comes to money. "Money is not the key to happiness," she always tells me.

She is an entrepreneur in her own right. She collects frangipani flowers all day long, drying them and then selling them when she has filled a big bag. She loves to take young coconuts, veggies from our yard, banana plants, banana leaves, chilies, papaya, jackfruit, and mangosteen to the market—she can sell or trade anything and everything superfluous to our family's daily needs.

My mother loves being busy, and on those days that there is nothing to be sold from the garden she sits down all day on a mat on the verandah making palm-leaf offerings to sell in our local market. She also helps my father grow banana trees and rice on a small piece of land nearby that belongs to a generous Indonesian man of Chinese descent who lives in Denpasar. As the land is in our village fields, too far away for this man to send his employees to care for it, instead of letting it turn into a wilderness he prefers to let my father grow whatever he likes and harvest it too. My mother enjoys helping him on the land as she gets to spend time with him. She also knows exactly where he is, and whatever he can grow provides her with a welcome new source of produce to sell in our local market.

I would imagine I've inherited some of my mother's high spirits when it comes to selling. She can sell anything to people—even if she just takes a couple of papayas to the market which look rather small and not at all of good quality, someone will still want to buy them from her. Her infectious laugh reminds me of my own.

My mother forgets her trouble when she has company, and she is happy when she can sell things, even for a little money in return. She never asks me for money. Each time I give her some—even though it is not much at current value, for example $10, around Rp.100.000—my mother would say "Oh this is too much, are you sure you can afford it?" She is such a humble person and so appreciative towards any of my gifts, the direct opposite to most of my Balinese neighbors and cousins, who never seem satisfied with what I give them. Whatever I give her, my Mom says a simple "thank you" and offers me a big smile, while the others would look unsatisfied and ask for more.

I love my mother dearly and each time I think of the way she lives her life it gives me a more positive perspective, encouraging me to see things from a better point of view. Life has not been easy for her. She is a person who accepts things the way they are and thanks God for everything she has been given each day. I would love to be able to appreciate this life the way she does, one day.

Women like my mother and others of her generation selflessly devote their lives to our Hindu and ancestral family temples. They are the keepers of the knowledge and wisdom of our clan.

But if I think about our Balinese Hindu religion and our traditional adat lore and all the work that goes into the lavish ceremonies we devote to our Gods and ancestors, I feel the weight it imposes upon on Balinese women who are expected to devote so much of their lives to making and dedicating offerings. I figure that my mother's generation of dutiful women, many of whom were never lucky enough to go to school or have a career of their own, may be the last of their kind.

My mother and most Balinese women of her age grew up at a time when schooling was out of reach and home and village was their entire universe. They had no more pressing duties in their daily life other than taking care of the children, making offerings and doing bits and pieces of daily selling in the market to supplement family income.

Life was tough, so the women of her generation made offerings to their Gods in the simplest way possible, using fruit and palm leaves grown from their own backyards or bartering other fruit with their neighbors and sisters in the area. The making of offerings was not such a financial pressure as it has become for the young married women of today, especially those who live in an urban environment and have to buy all the materials.

Life has become more expensive and complicated for the women of my generation, with so many more choices and opportunities due to our education. Those who left school early to help their families, or because they could not afford books and uniforms, have a very low earning capability so it is hard for them to survive.

Emancipation has many challenges, and I wonder if Ibu Kartini, the renowned Javanese woman who fought so hard for Indonesian women's rights to education during colonial times, could have every imagined that literacy was not going to solve all the problems women have to face in society once they become a part of the work force.

Indeed, Kartini had to deal with being "married off" to an older man who she had never met and did not love— a man who already had three wives. In those days arranged marriage was common and no doubt she was expected to please her father by marrying a man in a high position— her husband was the Mayor of Rembang, in central Java.

But Kartini was smart enough to make a deal with him before she agreed to marry. She insisted that he respect her education and allow her to open a school for women, where she could teach others how to read and write, as well as other important skills.

Sadly she died still a young woman, just a few days after giving birth to her first son, but her letters were published, and her words went on to inspire many. That was 1904, and she was only 25 years old. I wonder what she would have done in my situation? Women had little choice in those days, so I guess she would still be with husband number one, no matter how difficult it was. In those days divorce was not possible.

Being able to stand on my own two feet, travel, and get an education had enabled me to be independent. Now I must pay the price of my freedom and make my own decisions for the sake of my family. To compromise on my strange situation with Jack did not seem an option. But like Kartini, I too am driven to write, in the hope that my stories might help me find a way, and also light the way for others.

A magical night

Perhaps my father's invitation was already bearing fruit. Or maybe Jack was feeling guilty about his impending trip to Jakarta the following day... whatever the reason it was good to see him in such a happy mood after the past weeks of ups and downs, rages and confusion. I decided just to go along with him to keep the peace.

"Lets go and visit your family in the village," Jack proposed at breakfast time.

We set off for the drive up into the hills. My son was so excited at the prospect of seeing his two beautiful cousins. They are perfect playmates for him at the ages of nine and six years old. The two girls are always very excited to see him too.

After having heard about the past few weeks of anger and fighting between Jack and I, my family was shocked to see us coming up the path together, chatting with our son Dharma—and most pleasantly surprised to see that my husband looked happy.

They looked even more confused when I whispered behind my hand that I was only putting on an act and humouring Jack; I tried not to mirror their confusion, realizing that I didn't know who Jack really was anymore. But as always they all made him welcome and everyone seemed happy to show him around.

Jack was very impressed with our gardens, which my sister and I had created over the past few months since his last visit. He loved our sunflowers, he admired our unusually large round papayas and he seemed to genuinely enjoy looking around.

My brother-in-law Agung took him to see his beautifully coloured "Koi" fish. Then when he came back and sat down his attention was drawn to some bright and colourful paintings that were hanging on our walls, walls that had always been so plain in the past. So I took him to see the piles of Agung's abstract paintings stacked up in the back room. Jack seemed astonished and delighted by the professional quality of my brother-in-law's art works. We had a pleasant day with the family.

As we took our leave in the afternoon he hugged and kissed me in front of them and told me that he loved us all. For one brief moment I almost believed him! Perhaps, I thought, we had the real Jack back; he seemed to enjoy so much just being with us. Then we set off to have a Japanese dinner together at a restaurant called *Ryoshi*, one of our favorite places to eat in Ubud that serves fresh sushi, salads, soups and a delicious Bento box dinner.

I wanted nothing more but to enjoy that moment, I was determined to live in the 'here and now'… so happy to see smiles on my little boy's face. Jack and Dharma were laughing and joking all through dinner. We ate so much we could eat no more and then we decided to go home and have an early night.

That evening everything seemed to have returned to normal between Jack and me. I was feeling very comfortable, and we both slept naked. We cuddled up just like we used to every night before we split up; he became aroused and we made love. It was just like the lovemaking when our marriage had been normal—nothing semed to be out of place. He told me that he loved me, he always has and always will. Just at that moment I heard a gecko clucking, a sign that confirmed in my superstitious mind that Jack was actually telling me the truth, except this time the gecko tricked me.

I set my alarm at 6 a.m. and was up early morning, to make sure I would have enough time to make Jack's coffee and prepare him some breakfast before his flight to Jakarta. While I was making bacon, eggs and toast for breakfast Jack got ready to go, showering and getting dressed. I was very impressed by how good he looked in his new suit and jacket, just like a professional business man—I really wished he would be able to focus and reconsider the importance of our family life once more. I had pushed the knowledge of why he was going to Jakarta into some dark and deep recess of my mind and I was able to 'play the game' of the dutiful wife right up until he left. I even walked up the road with him to find the driver I had arranged to take him to Ngurah Rai airport at 6.45 a.m.

Love being Tested

How far should we be prepared to go in sacrificing or risking our own life or sanity for our partner or husband when we have children who need us more?

Jack was back home and in tears tonight, telling me that he hasn't changed as a person. He is filled with remorse, he says. He feels so guilty that he has been with prostitutes during our marriage and also had unprotected sex with me since that encounter.

Could I believe what he said? Was this a sign that he really want to change? I didn't think so. After all he was about to leave first thing in the morning again. This time he was planning to stay with Elvanda for at least five days—including Saturday night—giving him ample time to party with the lady-boy he now called his 'girlfriend'. They would be staying at the luxury Thamrin Residence apartment that he had rented her in the most expensive part of Jakarta, with its extensive gym facilities, jacuzzi, sauna and Olympic-sized swimming pool.

I had no doubt in my mind that it would just be the same old story. No doubt he would have another five wild days of glamorous clubbing and drugs and then come home and dump on us all of his anger and negative emotions as he slipped back into his other personality, the one that was disconnected from our family, especially me.

I remember how—when he caught HIV after his calamitous trip to China—he took me on a holiday to Bali before he broke the news, and I really thought he loved me. When he tried to tell me at breakfast the day after we got back that I needed to have a blood test I must have blocked it out completely as I was totally unprepared to receive any bad news from him.

That night I came home from work at the restaurant around 1a.m., totally exhausted after my first day back at work. After a glass of wine to wind down I took a hot shower and got into bed with Jack. My hand stroked his shoulder, and there was a gauze bandage taped to his upper arm. He rolled over and I noticed he had one on the other arm, and another on each thigh.

"What's this?" I asked him. "You've got bandages all over you! Did you have a blood test?"

"Don't worry Beautiful, just go to sleep." He peered at me, bleary-eyed. "You must be tired out. I'll tell you about it in the morning," he whispered.

It was his doctor who notified me the next day by phone that I had to come in to the clinic for a blood test.

"Who are you?" I asked, bewildered.

"This is Dr. Robins," he said, " from the HIV Clinic."

"Oh My God!" I said, and then I realized I was shouting at him, "In this age of HIV Jack has been putting my life at risk?"

It's impossible to describe the shock and fear going through in my head at that time. I felt like I had been stabbed, and my whole body trembled. I went back to bed and cried for hours until I really thought that I had slept and it was just a nightmare. It wasn't a nightmare.

I was wide-awake for my usual morning coffee before getting ready to take my kids to go to school the next morning and then off to work before I realized that Jack had tried to break the news to me the day before. I realized my entire body must have shut down and told my brain to suppress the incident and deny it. I had lied to myself, told myself that he would never do such a thing. After all, when I was in China with him recently, didn't he tell me he would never hire a prostitute because he loves me so much?

Well, in retrospect I guess he didn't lie. He didn't hire one prostitute—he hired two on that occasion—and at least one of them, or maybe both, had been HIV positive.

Fortunately, after having all my tests the doctor told me that my results were negative. But it was enough to frighten me badly, especially as Jack kept on insisting that he still didn't need to wear a condom during sex. I went for a discussion with the specialist where my husband and I were tested and the doctor told me that as Jack was HIV positive I must always use protection during sex to be one hundred percent certain. Jack hated that—he even tried to tell me the specialist was wrong!

"Even if you can prove them wrong, who are you to make that decision?" I told him. "You are not a doctor you're just a patient who selfishly wants to be told it's safe to have sex without a condom. What happens if there is a tear inside, or even just a tiny scratch? I would easily catch it from you."

Jack hates condoms because he says they take the pleasure out of sex. I have to admit having sex with a condom doesn't give me the same pleasure either, but I would rather be safe than sorry. And I wasn't feeling very attracted to this man I had married and had a child with right now. Just the way he had contracted the virus, while he was in a relationship with me was enough evidence of his lack of integrity. It was obvious enough that he had no respect or love for me as his wife at all.

I didn't understand how he dared to take me straight away on a holiday, right after his dangerous adventure in China and tell me that he loved me? It was beyond belief and I felt betrayed and depressed. I felt as if I had lost the last vestiges of my self-esteem.

That was when things began to get even more complicated. Whether it was out of his frustration at being unsatisfied by having sex with a condom, or through the influence of people he met at counselling, I don't know. At that time the counselling sessions were full of gay people, so he started to find out more about the gay community. He started taking drugs and hanging out with his new friends, all along pushing me to believe that it was safe to have unprotected sex with him. I was desperate to save my marriage and I didn't want my family or anyone else to know what had happened in Australia. I was determined to forgive my husband so we could start a new life in Bali. I felt sure we could rebuild everything! I wanted to prove to my father that I could make a success of the relationship with the man of my choice—not his!

I knew it was crazy but I gave in and sacrificed my life for Jack because I loved him. Sometimes I would wake up in the night in a cold sweat, my mind churning. There I was having sex with a high-risk person—who just happened to be my husband—hoping against hope that I wouldn't catch anything, and praying he would love me with all his heart for all the things I do for him, including risking unprotected sex.

I prayed to God each night that my husband would recognize this sacrifice, that he would love me tenderly and stop being angry and violent. I accepted him back without stigma and treated him like a normal healthy person. I tried to pretend that the entire nightmare had never happened and would not come back to haunt us again if only we could live happily ever after.

Forgiveness can be misunderstood as acceptance. Perhaps if I had reacted in a different way I wouldn't be where I was today, wondering what my husband was up to in Jakarta.

Alone again

I have often heard it said that if you live in Bali you will never be alone. Indeed, now I am back living in the land of my birth, after living abroad so long, I realize this is very true. It is very unusual to be alone here, because Balinese people think it is impolite to leave you alone. My people are so curious and caring, they want to know what you are doing day and night. But since I have come back to Bali to live, after twenty or more years of living abroad, I have tried to keep a gap, clinging to my western lifestyle, and carefully guarding my own space as I find I need solitude to focus.

Perhaps that is why I feel so alone in this overcrowded island, full of curious Balinese, and fly-by-night tourists, full of yoginis and hippies busy doing their detox and working hard at being beautiful people. There are so many foreigners in Ubud, and most of them seem to come for health retreats. It must be a fantastic business for locals and resident expats, but I wonder why all these Australians, Americans, English and Europeans decide to come to Ubud specifically?

When I look at my old village now, after having lived overseas so long, I feel sad. The place has become so built up, and is getting polluted. It has always been the central market for the region, but now the drains are becoming blocked with rubbish and plastic bags, the lanes dusty and cluttered with building construction projects that seem to be out of control and the rice paddies are disappearing at a rapid rate.

Another thing that bothers me is that there are now too many cars on the road for its size, so we have traffic jams all the time. After having lived in a city that has plenty of public transport and well-organized roads, I find it really hard to drive in this madness, with motorbikes zooming in all directions like angry bees. I know they are not going as fast as they drive in Australia, so perhaps accidents will not be quite so bad, but it seems that nobody knows the rules, or perhaps they just make up their own as they go along. The main rule that I can discern is "Give way to anything bigger than yourself"—unless, of course, you are driving a motorbike, in which case you can change the last four words to "anything you cannot dodge."

Perhaps I have developed a critical western eye. I am pleased to hear that some of Bali's farmers are planning to go organic—not an easy thing to do when the government has been pushing all kinds of artificial fertilizers and pesticides and fungicides on the farmers for years. All our land is connected with our neighbors and irrigated from the same source, so I can't imagine how farmers can achieve this goal in the next ten years unless everyone changes at once. In western countries to be certified as organic you need to either use virgin land or make your gardens in a place free of artificial fertilizers, weed killers or pesticides for at least 15 years. If your neighbors use any of these things you will be disqualified immediately.

I feel sure, however, whatever my parents and I grow in our backyard in our isolated village north of Ubud must be pretty much organic as we have never been able to afford to put fertilizers on our land. All we use is our own leaf compost, which rots in a hole in the ground at each corner of our house compound.

So why is it I no longer feel I belong in this bustling, traffic-choked place called Ubud? It is, after all, named after the Balinese word *Ubad* meaning 'medicine' or 'healing'. I may not be one of the beautiful people seeking bliss, but I certainly do need healing.

After my high profile life as a restaurateur in Australia I feel so alone in this paradise—no one seems to be aware of my existence here. It is as if I have suddenly become invisible. I no longer have any feeling in my bones that I'm true-blue Balinese, nor do I belong to the expatriate cliques or the intoxicating detoxing souls.

Who am I then? Again and again I tell myself I cannot reverse my life; what's been done cannot be undone. But I would like to think that there is still some room in my life to find the answer to my questions.

I decided to go and visit a famous Balinese spiritual healer, and see if he could guide me. In need of a personal cleansing ceremony—perhaps it would help me find the right direction—I went to visit a famous *Balian Usada*. Tjokorda Rai is a Balinese spiritual healer, with a reputation of being able to purge negative energy and enhance recovery from illness and trauma. I decided to ask him if he could help me reclaim my soul, as I was feeling so lost and unable to come to terms with my past.

Tjokorda Rai is one of the descendants of the last King of Ubud. He is a renowned Balinese healer who began to use his gift of communing with deities and spirits over forty years ago, after discovering an ancient *lontar* book passed on by his ancestors in his family temple. In my eyes he is the most humble person of such distinguished origin that I've ever met in Bali. He was very polite and gentle and made me feel comfortable and vulnerable at the same time.

He shared a very special story with me of how as a teenager he had run away to Jakarta, although he didn't know anybody there. He had been destitute and lived on the street, traded from one person to another, struggling to survive in Jakarta's underworld of thuggery and desperation. He almost died, and when he finally came back to Bali he was very ill—so ill he could find no healer who could cure him.

"It must have been my destiny," he told me, "otherwise why would someone like me who had everything I could ever have wanted at home in Bali, run away to Jakarta?"

"Sometimes our life's journey does not work out the way we want it," he told me. Upon his return to Bali, plagued by insomnia, he started reading the holy *Lontar* palm-leaf scripts stored in his family temple. He came across a special book of *mantra* and found that when holding it he was able to fall asleep at last. Slowly he was able to heal himself and he realized he could help others to heal and cure their illness.

Perhaps, I thought, sharing his story with me was his way of empathizing with my sorrow and pain. He appears tall for a Balinese man, draped in sarong and cotton shirt. Undeniably charismatic, he radiates warmth and a brilliant smile. He carries the knowledge of his spiritual and healing powers with a rare sense of humility. There's a sparkle in his eyes—even when he speaks with utter seriousness.

Tjokorda Rai sat on a chair and he asked me to sit on the floor with my back towards him and my legs stretched out in front of me. He placed the palms of his hands on my scalp, then moved them down to either side of my head, his fingers prodding various parts around my face and right into my ears. He pushed and prodded, commenting on those parts of my body related to that point of my visage.

"This is fine, this also fine, you are very healthy and strong" he said.

I was then asked to lie down on the bamboo matting on my back. He sat next to me, lightly drawing all over my body with his healing tool, a small bamboo branch, while reciting *mantra*.

"I am opening up your triangle and getting rid of bad energy," he said. And then he sat on the ground near my feet and once more picked up the small piece of bamboo. I tensed up at the mere thought of what was coming next. He poked the pointed end into various meridian points under each toe of my left foot.

"Your liver, ok. Your pancreas, ok. Your spleen, ok. Your lungs, ok. You have very strong hormones," he said—maybe he sensed that I was nearing my period. Then he poked his stick in between my big toe and its neighbour. I screamed in pain as it hurt like hell and I twisted from side to side on the floor to find some release.

"That is your heart," he said. "Your heart is in huge pain, it is being torn apart by your love for someone and your boundaries have been knocked down—you have lost all your strength in your heart."

Suddenly, I saw him stand at the edge of the matting. He closed his eyes and placed the soles of his feet against mine. Without any introduction, he began whispering a mantra or goodness-knows-what, twirling his hands around in front of him, as if he were drawing a mandala in the air. He waved his arms over my body in a circular motion, and in moments he was done.

Sitting down by my lower left leg once again, he pressed the same points as before between my toes with the piece of wood. Something had evidently shifted in my mind or body because, where earlier I had nearly leapt from the floor out of agony, now there was no pain, although the point of original pain remained tender and sensitive to his touch.

He asked me to sit up and held my head in his hands, touching two spots in the middle at the top. "In this spot," he said, "you have a trauma from a recent blow, and this one—a bit smaller—is a trauma from your childhood." Whispering more *mantra*, he moved his hands around my head. Then he held the right side of my head for a moment, exerting a gentle pressure, and once more I felt a dull pain. "This is caused by stress," he said, "too much stress and the right side of the brain gets exhausted."

I remained seated on the floor and he put my left palm on my chest, my right palm on my forehead, then gently moved my hands around in the air. "This will clear your heart and your head."

As my friend and I changed out of our sarongs and drove away together I felt a lightheadedness that I hadn't known for ages, a release borne partly by the touch of Tjokorda Rai's kindly spirit and ministrations, and partly from freeing myself, letting go of the dead-weight I'd been carrying around for so many years.

Not long after I dropped my friend off at her place I began to cry, and although I was driving the tears didn't stop till I reached home, feeling sensitive and tired. I went straight to bed and slept for a couple of hours.

Later I realized what it was that I had particularly appreciated about Tjokorda Rai. He's not just a healer—although some call him a shaman—neither is he simply a man with ability to connect with the divine and the spiritual world; he is also a good mentor for life in general. His treatment and his words were painful and yet sweet, good for the body and soul. Just what I needed, right when I was hungriest for it.

"You need to be patient," he told me before I left. "Your triangle will open up now you have got rid of your bad luck—return it all to *Ibu Pertiwi*, mother earth. Miracles will follow. You will discover a lot of new creative energy and your pain will slowly be replaced by happiness and many achievements to come."

I waited for him to continue, soaking up his words like a sponge.

"You will have to work hard," he said, "but you have the ability to rebuild your life. You will succeed despite your karma, or that of your ancestors."

Wrong! Wrong on so many levels

This week has been the hardest week for all of us. If I am to believe what I read in the brochures for the spiritual retreats around Ubud, it would seem that our five elements are so out of place that our cosmos is imbalanced and—I looked up the definition of the word 'normal' in the Australian Oxford dictionary—life is far from 'normal'. I'm still trying to be patient and just keep on wondering if we can only find a way to take a step back through the sliding doors to those days when we were happy as a family, when our life was more or less balanced and what I considered to be 'normal'.

Then I looked up the word 'wrong'. According to the definition, if I stay with my husband it will be wrong at every level.

The definition of the word **wrong** as an adjective would mean:

1. (of conduct or actions) contrary to justice or to what is right;
2. incorrect, not true;
3. not what is required or suitable; (like backing the wrong horse, I decided)
4. (in Aboriginal English) not according to law, esp. marriage laws;

5. not in a normal condition, not functioning normally;
   (Yeah, there is something wrong with the gearbox, I
   told myself.)

Regardless of my lack of gambling skills, or mechanical knowledge, I still decided after looking at the above definition that my staying with Jack was clearly wrong.

I added up all the things I had to consider. Jack wanted me to stay with him now, when he already told his new love that we have been separated since June 2012, although we went together as a family to America for a holiday since then, and had a great time. Well I certainly did, I'm not sure about Jack in retrospect, as he was already dividing his heart between me and someone else at that time. He obviously has been hiding lots of secrets from me all along.

It didn't make sense to me. I thought back to August, when our marriage still seemed to be quite good in my opinion. We made love each night while staying at my friend's house. I sensed nothing wrong at that time; Jack was passionate and seemed to reach a climax just as a normal man would.

But it was still wrong, I decided. Wrong for Jack even if he has opened up and confided in me that he is so much in love with a man, who he prefers me to refer to as 'her'— regardless of her made-in-Thailand silicon implants. Wrong for him to openly call this man on the phone in front of me, calling him 'Beautiful' and 'Gorgeous' over the phone, telling him he loves him so much. Wrong even that he missed him so much, or at least that he insisted on telling me that he 'missed touching his sexy butt'. Everything seemed wrong to me now on so many levels. Especially wrong for Jack to tell me how Elvanda is aroused when Jack kisses him and his penis is poking Jack.

What do I do now? If I leave, Jack has threatened to cut all support for our children. If I stay how much more of this abnormality will I have to swallow and struggle with, trying to work it out logically in my own head?

I'm feeling as if I'm being controlled and manipulated, and I don't like it. One minute I'm being his emotional pillow, doing my best to rescue him after one of his hour-long crying spells, although he is driving me absolutely mental. The next minute he is laughing and seems to be back to normal. But then suddenly he erupts and goes on a rampage, trying to destroy all of our belongings.

Tiny things set him off. Even such a little thing as the Internet connection being down sparks his anger and he starts abusing me, yelling at the top of his lungs. He seems to have lost any feelings of shame or sensitivity; even in front of our villa staff, he treats me like his slave. Yesterday he snatched the modem out of my hand and glared at me in anger then stomped off to his room, slamming the door behind him like a spoilt child.

I have suggested he see a psychotherapist but he has not done that yet. For the kids' sake and overall welfare it is clear they need their dad back in a normal and balanced state, but we can no longer predict when that might happen, if it happens at all.

My children have become withdrawn and tearful, and I feel it is becoming more and more dangerous for our safety. We have no way of knowing when the mood swings will next happen, so we tip-toe around him and keep our distance. I felt I was putting my children in a very difficult situation by staying with Jack. But when he was about to leave our little ten-year old boy started crying.

"I love you daddy." And then, "Please don't go daddy!" I couldn't bring myself to do the same, I felt so relieved he was going.

The boys and I had a proper discussion yesterday. I was surprised and relieved when they both agreed with me. As much as we love Jack, we must learn to let him go. The boys are really hurt that he should treat me so badly and they are feeling totally neglected by him.

I feel sure that he must be having some kind of breakdown; some kind of imbalanced chemical reaction must be taking place in his brain, making him confused as his moods change by the minute. It is as if he is fighting a huge conflict in his head—he loves the stability of having a family but he is also in love with a strange exotic creature.

"Any sane or normal person would choose to fix up their family and support their children," I told him when he calmed down enough to have a conversation. "Instead you are creating so much pain for us all."

It's obvious to me that Jack is living in a fantasy world right now. I have no idea how or when he will eventually return to the real world—in the meantime, the reality of family life and responsibilities for the children have totally reverted to me.

"She is so pretty," he tells me, tears in his eyes. I peer at the photo on the screen, but all my eyes see is the surreal face of a feminine man with a strange but exotic composition of features that have undergone numerous operations—a long nose, pouting lips, a jaw that looks reduced in size.

"She is such an eye-turner, all the guys couldn't keep their eyes off her when we went to pubs and clubs in Australia," he spoke in almost reverent tones. He is such a child, I almost feel sorry for him. He doesn't even realize that other people can see through the façade—but I guess by 'other people' I mainly mean women.

"Of course men would be able to sense that this ladyboy is a hooker," I tell him. "They stare at her as they would gaze at something alluring they see in a shop window—a thing they can rent at an hourly rate to play out all of their obscene fantasies."

But that excites him more.

I notice on Facebook that she calls Jack her 'King' and he calls her 'My Queen'. Sure, I had to agree, the drag queen does have a particular tragic beauty; I could see it now. Tragic because she has to be dishonest to make him love her.

I still could not understand how a common street prostitute lady-boy could find it so easy to be sponsored for a three-month visa to Australia. My friend, who is a manager of a large non-profit organization in Australia, owns her own house and is of good character, has been trying to sponsor her Balinese friend to come for one week's holiday to Darwin. But no, her application has been rejected twice. The guy she is trying to sponsor has a respectable job, his own business in tourism here in Bali, and so on...

I tried to apply for a visa for my father to visit me for a little holiday in Australia some years ago. I wanted him to meet my husband's family and his relatives, friends and so on. At the time I applied for my father's visa I had a house in my name, I owned my own restaurant, had plenty of money in the bank and credit facilities available. All of that was not security enough for the Australian Immigration to grant my father a visa to come and see how his grandchildren live in a different country. It was a huge disappointment for me. Even our local politician who knew me personally wrote references for me to the Department of Immigration to let them know that I was someone well known in the area, of good character, and so on. In my case it was just not good enough.

And then I compared it to another Indonesian friend of mine who simply wanted to sponsor her friend to babysit her child for two to three months. This Indonesian person had never held a job in Australia, spoke very limited English, and was living there in rental accommodation. But that was no problem! They granted her a visa right away.

I know the inconsistency of bureaucracy drives most people crazy everywhere in the world, and I certainly don't understand how red tape becomes so tangled and illogical in any country. I have a Master's degree in International Business from a university in Australia and of all countries in the world I thought my adopted home would be more genuine and fair towards someone like me who has worked so hard to make a success of their life in Australia.

One day I had time on my hands, so I decided to do a little research on the lifestyle of my husband's new flame. I went to the hair salon my friend had told me about in a back-street of Kuta. She had told me she thought it appeared to be a base for a number of young transvestites from other islands of Indonesia living in Bali.

A pretty girl attended to me right away, and I had to look twice to ascertain her gender. It was her deep voice that gave her away, but she was beautifully made up, and proceeded to charm me with a flick of her comb and a bright smile as she set about colouring my hair in a most professional manner.

While we were chatting—she asked me all the usual polite questions like "Where are you from Miss?" and "Are you married?"—a number of other brightly dressed 'girls' clattered in and out on dangerously high heels, calling to each other, teasing and joking in loud voices as they went up and down the stairs.

"Wow you have a lot of people working here!" I commented. The hairdresser shook her head.

"No," she said, "those girls hardly ever help out in the salon—they work the night shift, playing 'escort' to lonely foreigners in Kuta."

"Goodness, that must be dangerous! Are they well paid?" I asked her.

"They can earn about $50 a night," she replied, but nearly half of that disappears in pay-offs to the security guys and the police. Sometimes they get lucky. All they need is a gullible Ozzie guy to sponsor them, and they can go to Australia. It's easy to get work as escorts in Sydney and they earn at least $300 an hour there. I've got one friend who was only three months in Australia and managed to come back to Bali and buy a new car."

"Wow she must be doing well," I said, wondering if her friend could be my husband's paramour.

"Yeah, but she's really cute, she has the men eating out of her hand," she answered. "Her 'sponsor' followed her back to Bali and set her up in a fancy apartment in Jakarta." The plot was sounding alarmingly familiar.

"It must be dangerous in the Clubs," I said. "My friend tells me you have to watch your drink or they slip drugs in it."

"Well I haven't heard of any overdoses lately," she said, "but it's easy to get hooked on getting high. The 'girls' are pretty much aware of the dangers of alcoholism and addiction, although some can't resist."

"I guess they earn lots of tips too?" I ventured.

"Well, my friends all pick up extra money from the bar sales—whether its alcohol or drugs there's a big commission to be earned if you encourage your pickup to indulge—and most of them make a deal with the barman. He pours them weak drinks, and bills the 'sponsor' for expensive cocktails. The 'girls' just pretend to participate and later on they split the tab with the barman and take their share of the money. It's a pretty good lurk."

By the time I left the salon I had the lowdown on how the transvestites were able to get rich quick, picking on lonely white Anglo-Saxon males that were desperate for attention and not averse to trying 'sex with a difference'. "No doubt they are easy prey," I thought, "and the business is probably the same all over the world."

I also had a beautiful new colour in my hair and sparking elongated pink fingernails encrusted with tiny bejewelled flowers.

Between a Dream and a Nightmare

I woke up on the morning of 20th November 2012, and realized I was not in my own bed. I was lying on a double bed at my friend Annie's house. My son Dharma was sleeping soundly in the middle and cuddling Annie for his dear life. My head was thumping and when I got up and peered in the bathroom mirror I realized I had a black eye.

My husband's mood swings had gone from bad to worse, and it had taken its toll on us both. It was a tiny problem that set him off around 9 p.m. on the previous night—the Internet could not be connected and I had asked him to email me a copy of his passport for our villa contract. He started yelling at me, letting off a stream of endless abuse. Then when I got up to leave he punched me. I ducked, but his fist caught me on the side of my head, just above the eye. He went on threatening me as I tried to beat a hasty retreat.

"If you dare to leave the house I will never come to see you or our son again and I will stop all financial support for both of the boys!"

I did not want his threat to become reality, so I sat in a chair not too far from the door, just in case I had to make a dash for it. I forced myself to stay calm as he got more and more abusive. It wasn't long before he started throwing chairs around. One chair flew over my head and crashed into something. Then he started slamming the doors and went to the bathroom. I took the chance to try to get my son out of the house, but unfortunately he was already in bed asleep and had locked his door from inside.

I went into panic mode, grabbed my bag that I had prepared in case of an emergency from under the stairs and hid myself under a coconut tree in the dark in the middle of the adjoining rice paddies. Luckily there was a security guard from the villa next door who I knew, named Doblet. He was not far away and he had a huge torch so I wasn't too scared and I ran directly to him.

I told him my situation, then I rang my landlord to ask him to help me to call the police but he refused to do anything, as he didn't want to get involved in my domestic affairs. I called the police myself, and then while waiting for them to come I kept on listening in case my husband got worse or tried to do anything stupid to our son... but twenty minutes later there was no more noise coming from the house The gate had been locked and the lights were off. The police still hadn't arrived.

It eventually took half an hour for the police to find our villa, although the station is only ten minutes away. I realized now I couldn't depend upon them in an emergency, even when I was so afraid for my son's safety and my own. By the time they finally got there and we got back into the villa Jack was already asleep.

Six cops had shown up, and all they could do was take photos of broken chairs and tiles. Finally they asked Jack to come out from the room. He came out entirely naked—his penis hanging uncovered—and started yelling at me again as soon as he saw me. He looked deranged. The police were so embarrassed they didn't ask him anything at all; they just told him to put some clothes on. He ignored them and went back to bed. They suggested I take my son to a safe place, and then they wanted me to go with them to the station.

Feeling more secure with six policemen in my villa, I did my best to wake Dharma up, opening the doors and putting a shirt on him so we could leave for a safer place. I took him to Annie's place next door. Poor Annie had been supporting me through my reality series of 'bad movie' scenes for the past five days, day and night, with ongoing surprises and shocks from each continuing day of Jack's rampage. My son was already used to using Annie's house as his safe haven and it was starting to feel like a second family home to us both.

Once Dharma was safely tucked in Annie's bed, I then went on down to the police station to file a report of damages. My landlord, who had finally showed up to give me some support, accompanied me with his driver. After we had spent half an hour at the police station with me airing my grievances, and asking for protection, the police finally told me there was nothing they could actually do to protect my safety.

"Jack is still married to you," they said, "it is your joint property he is destroying and as yet he hasn't caused you any bodily harm." At that stage my eyes still looked red and swollen, but no bruises had appeared yet.

I was so amazed to hear the four cops debating amongst each other.

"What law does this come under? What can we charge him with?" Their conclusion was that there was nothing they could do—there were no specific charges they could lay against Jack. Never had I felt so helpless in my life. I came out in a cold sweat, asked the policeman for a glass of water and went and sat in a corner, as far away from the men in uniforms as I could.

Taking pity on me, one of them approached me with a suggestion.

"Perhaps we can take some film of Jack and his girlfriend while having sex, to prove he ejaculated," he suggested. "We can use a hidden camera. Then he can be charged for infidelity."

When I told him "But it's not a girl, check out his KTP! It's a man with breasts!" he looked dumbfounded. To my amazement, I was then told by one of the more senior policemen "If the sexual act was not between a man and a woman—therefore, by definition there is no ejaculation into the vagina—it isn't considered infidelity according to our National Marriage Law Number 1, 1974."

The other policemen all stood around nodding their heads and agreeing.

"Do you have any bruises?" they asked, "any cuts?" In the end all the police could tell me was that I had no recourse to the law to protect myself or charge Jack unless I had cuts or bruises or bodily harm as proof of his aggression.

"Just be careful," they said, "and if he does it again, let us know in time so we can get someone to take photos, or a video, someone who is willing to be your witness in court."

I thought about potential witnesses, and shook my head, knowing perfectly well that none of my neighbours would want to get involved with the law. The legal institutions had such a bad reputation on my home island, nobody who got involved with them ever came away unscathed. It was very hard to get witness protection, and any interaction with the police or the courts would cost money as well as time.

The driver dropped me home. I felt completely lost and let down. What was the law worth in this country of mine if it could not protect women? Very little, obviously. Here, men write the laws, women have very little involvement, so of course laws aren't designed to protect women. It is a patriarchal society and the men are in charge!

In Australia Jack could have been charged for property

destruction or for endangering a child, at least, and the police would take him away. They would have asked me if I needed an 'AVO'—an Apprehended Violence Order. I had asked the cops here if they could do that too, but they had no idea what I was talking about.

It seemed to me that in my country the law was still stuck in the past—just a useless pile of stupid words written on paper, created by men, designed to protect men, and only men.

* * *

At the end of my tether

Waking up this morning at Annie's I felt a total loss of self. I was feeling weak; it seemed that I had completely run out of steam. I didn't even have any willpower left. I didn't know where all my strength had gone, so I asked Dharma if he wanted to go back to our house. We said a reluctant goodbye to Annie and headed home.

But when we got to our house, as soon as Jack saw us, he started yelling straight away, abusing me again in front of our son.

Dharma started crying. He stood there staring at his father abusing me, listening to him yelling louder and louder by the minute. No matter what I said was wrong, no matter what I did was wrong. I felt like giving up on everything. I headed for the kitchen and made myself a cup of coffee. There, on a shelf, I saw my husband's liquid 'G' medicine. I decided to pour some into my coffee. I put at least one large tablespoon of it into my drink—enough, I hoped, to end the pain forever.

I have never been a smoker and I have always left drug-taking to others. But at that moment, on that dreadful day, I felt my world was over. I simply wanted to end the pain. Perhaps everyone would be happier without me. Of course deep down I knew there were lots of people who cared about me and were willing to help me. I just wanted to stop feeling anything, to reach that dream-state between conscious and unconscious. I really didn't want to die but if I died at least Jack was right there to take care of our son. Perhaps it would teach him a lesson.

Less than twenty minutes later my legs started to shake, my entire body felt hot and my sweat started pouring like rain after a sudden huge thunderstorm. Suddenly my respiratory system began to fail on me. I felt breathless and began to cry, knowing that I was actually going to die. My legs became very weak and then I could no longer see. My world had gone dark. I felt Jack's arms grabbing me. He dragged me to the bathroom and put me under a cold shower. I heard his voice in the distance. He was shouting in my ear. "Stay with me! Listen to me!"

Each time I drifted away into the white mist that was enveloping me he tried to make me do something. I heard him calling our son but I could only feel the cold water and could still not see anything. I heard Jack giving instructions to Dharma to go to a little *warung*, the local roadside shop where they sold cigarettes and drinks, to find a few bottles of Red Bull. I remembered calling out to him "Get Annie!"

After that I could not remember much. It felt as if I was losing momentum. One minute I thought I was in a dream and then a few minutes later it had become a nightmare again. Then I remember vaguely asking my husband to take me to the toilet. I felt his arms lifting and dragging me and placing me, dripping, on the seat. I could hear his agitation as he complained about the smell and then he had to hold a bowl for me to vomit into while I was sitting on the toilet. I felt like my insides were purging themselves from both directions.

In the meantime Annie had arrived and was staring at me in horror. No doubt this was not the best side of me she had ever seen but I was too far-gone to feel embarrassed.

Annie then decided to take my son upstairs to comfort him and apparently she helped herself to my fridge and open a bottle of large Bintang beer to calm her own nerves.

Poor Annie suffered from panic attacks time and time again due to being bipolar. No doubt she had been going through hell with me. She must be suffering so much extra depression and anxiety with us running to her every night, seeking a safe place to hide. She had been keeping her phone by her bedside and making sure she always had her security guard on standby, in case anything happened.

Annie is the best sister anyone could dream of having. She is so gentle, has a very kind heart and she means every word she says.

All these thoughts were going through my head as I slowly regained consciousness, and I realized I could see again, but just dimly. Now I was starting to feel a bit better, I looked at the luminous dials on the clock beside my bed. It was already 9 p.m. and even though I was just waking up, I felt so tired I could hardly move. But at least I could hear clearly again.

Upstairs I could hear Jack's voice. He was making a phone call to someone.

"Hi Honey," he said, "Do you want me to come to Jakarta to be with you?"

I realized he must have been calling his 'girlfriend' again to ask if she wanted to see him. If I remembered rightly, this must be the fifth or sixth time he had called her since yesterday. He sounded anxious.

"He wants to test her to see if she really loves him, if she wants him to be with her in Jakarta or anywhere else for that matter," I thought, and I could hear myself mumbling out loud.

It was all such a familiar scenario to me. He sounded just the same as he had been when he was wooing me in the past, a younger Jack, in love with me in a former lifetime, at a time when his ex-wife wanted him back.

My heart sank down to my boots. Even after my near-death experience, it was 'business as usual' and he was still thinking of somebody else. It seemed so ironic that I had stood by this man for so many years.

I felt like a leaf, after having been tossed and torn by the storm, now weightless, falling into some dark and distant corner to rot.

* * *

Around four hours after my attempt to kill myself with the 'G' substance my body temperature had dropped back to normal and I could see again, but my mind was still in a misty dreamland. In my semi-conscious state I realized that my husband was there in bed with me, stimulating my G-spot. It felt amazing—as if the sun had suddenly come out and was warming me from the inside out. I was so turned on that I completely forgot my situation or even where I was. He continued to make me feel so good—then the next thing I knew we were kissing, we had amazing sex—and he came inside me. I tapped my arm to see if I was dreaming, or still in my nightmare. I still didn't really know where I was or how I had got there.

Even now I remembered bits and pieces and it had felt so extremely good—like the first time I fell in love with someone. But then another hour later as my mind cleared a little more I remembered vaguely that we must have had unprotected sex. I forgot how it had happened but now as my consciousness started to come back I began to panic.

The horror in my mind grew steadily as I moved my tired body from the mattress. My God this must be classified as some form of rape, especially as I had no idea at the time what I was doing. I had heard that the substance which I took in my stupid attempt for suicide was often used as a rape drug to snare innocent victims. Was this what my husband had done to me? But then it was I who had taken the drug in my state of desperation, wishing to put an end to it all. I was still half unconscious during sex and he had completely disregarded his promise to always use a condom and taken advantage of me without using any protection.

The conflict began to get worse in my head. Oh my God—did I just have sex with the enemy? This man who I used to love now seemed so revolting. A man so deeply in love with another man. Perhaps he was trying to kill me. How could I live with myself now?

I felt as if a part of me inside had died, and the numbness was spreading like a disease to the rest of my body.

Wake-up call

Today it seems that Jack has decided to stay with me to watch over me and make sure that I am OK. He refused Annie's suggestion to call the doctor to come to our place, so he must have been nervous, perhaps apprehensive of the consequences of what had happened yesterday. I dozed uneasily. But whenever I woke up he was still there. He kept on telling me how much he wanted to be with me, and how much he needed to be a part of the family. I did not respond.

What a fool I had been. I had thought that after all his cheating in the past at least this time he would really feel sorry about it. But he obviously did not feel any remorse at all about his sexual liaison with this other person, whether male, female, or a mixture of the two. Jack was more concerned that I should understand his own personal dilemma. He was confused, he told me. He needed me to be supportive and expected me to be willing to wait till he sorted himself out.

I decided to reserve judgment for a while, but I could hear so many conflicting voices—a forest of wild animals in my head. I stopped trying to listen to them and let my mind wander. I needed respite and I wanted to forget about the voices in my head and focus upon healing my pain. I tried thinking about all those things I had noticed on my early morning walks in the ricefields—the delicate green shoots of the newly planted rice plants and the busy gurgling of the water in the irrigation canal, the clarity of the water as the mud settled, bringing an upside-down universe into reflected view in the morning light. I sought to recognize at least one clear voice, but they all blurrd together; none of them made any sense at all.

Once more I back-tracked to the beginning of our relationship... trying to remember the details from when we were first dating. Could I have been so blind as to miss something? I recalled my personal memories of those regular fun outings that built our identity as a couple.

We had known each other for twelve years, but in one moment of vague, semiconscious limbo the power of sex and ego was a force like no other. He had abused my trust in him and everything I held sacred. My right to live a healthy life and take care of my children was at stake and he was the one threatening to take it away.

Today I am still alive and regretting every bit of yesterday. Regretting my own stupidity and attempt to kill myself, and my gullibility in letting Jack take advantage of me while I lay in bed under the influence of the drug. Most of all, I regretted having let him put my life in danger again.

"I am a mother. I must think of my children first," I told myself. "Yesterday is gone and the main thing for today is that I'm here and still alive for my ten year old boy—to see him each day after school, and my older son—to be there for him on weekends. I'm thankful for being alive even though I might have been better off dead. I have no wish to ruin my children's life."

* * *

The end of November was already approaching. I had been trying to focus on Dharma, as his teacher had warned me he was no longer responsive in class. I had been getting calls from her every second day telling me that he had been upset and crying in class. She told me he was oversensitive with the other children and the tiniest incident would upset him.

I waited till he came home from school one afternoon, and after I had given him his favorite dinner, sat down with him and asked him what was wrong.

"It's you and dad, mum," he told me. "You're not the same any more. Dad is always angry when he comes home, and you're always sad. I don't know what to do. Where is he now, anyway?"

I couldn't answer his question and I felt like he was blaming me for his father's absence. I searched back over our past to see if I could find any clues as to where I had gone wrong. I remembered Jack complaining about one of my emails back in June.

"It struck me in the gut," he said. "You told me I needed to be a more successful person."

We were here in Bali at the time, and we had been fighting. That was five months ago, but I could remember challenging him on that day.

"Why do you bother going to Kuta clubbing all the time?" I had asked him, and followed up with: "It's a place for cheap young drunks, prostitution and drugs, not for people who live in the real world. You'll never have any success in life if you hang out in the underbelly with the dregs of civilization!"

He told me that my words had spurred a change in his way of thinking and made him determined to achieve success in whatever way he could.

"That was one of the reasons why we went to America back in July," he said, "to look for opportunities, as well as to have a holiday!"

"So what kind of success did you think you would find in Kuta, after we got back?" I countered.

I didn't realize at the time that he had become deeply involved in a relationship with his 'she-male' escort. He was already exploring a different plane of existence, a world to which he was relentlessly drawn. This new involvement no doubt included the use of drugs of some sort and the embracing of a life without any certainties or even likelihood of success. More certainly, if I was to believe what I had read in the newspapers, it could end up with some sort of deal from hell—perhaps a jail term or even a death sentence in Indonesia.

What confounded me was that he now seemed to have turned into someone completely different—a complete and total stranger. This man next to me now was someone I felt I had never known in my entire life, a very fragile and confused human being. I felt sure that the person I knew—the one I had married—was in jeopardy. My feelings vacillated between anger and concern.

"How could you do it?" was my most consistent question.

"My mind has been playing up. I don't understand it myself," he tells me in one of his more lucid moments.

It seemed even he did not quite understand how he had so suddenly become very comfortable kissing a lady-boy who he described as having "large balls and a penis larger than my own." But from his point of view the pretty face and a pair of large breasts rendered these distractions irrelevant.

"I am questioning my own sexuality," he told me, "and that has caused a huge conflict in my head. I don't know—perhaps I have always been bisexual or gay. I'm always attracted to people who are strong and aggressive characters."

To make matters worse, last night he was back in my bed after two and a half months of separation. I lay there looking at this man, imagining him passionately kissing his strange lover—was this really my husband or could he be an imposter? I am still consumed by doubts that all of this is actually happening and not just a bad dream.

* * *

In my culture, especially for women, sex and sacredness are intimately joined. In Jack's head sex is just an act for a savage man to enjoy his selfish and narcissistic release of sexual tension. He regards sex as a means to a physical end, rather than as a transformative energy that connects us with larger cosmic energies. To me sex is a way of creating and sharing a special kind of energy, a practice that helps me bind together with my husband more deeply and intimately, enhancing the love I want to share.

How could men and women have such different fantasies? Men want to conquer, do battle and celebrate their victory, then move on to the next conquest, while women desire to have and hold and nurture forever.

Midlife crisis – living a fairy tale

My latest theory has me giggling. It seems that Jack thinks he is some sort of Richard Gere character out of the *Pretty Woman* movie. He always wanted to be a hero, the kind of rich man who could make a hooker's dream come true. Why else would he take his lady-boy girlfriend to Los Angeles, stay at the most luxurious hotel in Beverly Hills, and shop with her at the most expensive Rodeo Drive shopping centers?

I found the pictures on the Facebook page that she had put up under his name, and they supported the entire *Pretty Woman* cliché. I read their messages to each other— he called her "his queen" and she reciprocated in kind. I could see he was spoiling her, trying so hard to impress her. He seemed to have genuinely fallen in love.

I recalled my surprise when he returned from Los Angeles with a suitcase full of expensive branded clothing, original Dolce & Gabbana labels, a Cashmere T-shirt with a price tag of almost US$2000 and a suit of similar value. It was all for him—nothing for me!

I remembered when we stayed in West Hollywood, Los Angeles, he had told me to avoid Rodeo Drive, as it was not within our budget. We were staying at a very expensive apartment but it wasn't as luxurious or as expensive as

Beverly Wilshire in Beverly Hills, a Four Seasons Hotel. If anyone ever wonders how much does it cost to stay in a hotel at Beverly Hills per night, Wikipedia will tell you it ranges from US$2500 at the lowest price up to US$15,000 and some places cost as much as US$25,000 per night— The Atlantis Bridge suite penthouse, for example.

After all our scrimping and saving to get ahead it was heart-breaking for me to know he had spent around US$31,000 from his business accounts, which were supposed to be dedicated towards the purchase of a property in Santa Rosa Beach for us. All this to spoil a drag queen, while our family had been budgeting so tightly on our day-to-day expenditure to save up for our American dream.

I waited for an opportunity to flip through the pages of his diary while he was upstairs with our son. On nearly every second page I found a reference to large amounts of money transferred to Elvanda. First $2,000 then $1,600, then $3,000 for visa, then $10,000 to pay apartment rental, another amount with a note "to pay Thomas's baby-sitter" (I knew Thomas to be Elvanda's two-year-old adopted son), a room in Kuta, electricity. Then there was Elvanda's budget for shoes and bags, and a note regarding the price of a house ($80,000 in Cibubur). By this time I was too angry and upset to continue looking and I heard Jack coming down the stairs, so I stuffed his diary back under his pillow and pretended to be sweeping the room.

* * *

On Thursday morning, the day after he got back from visiting 'her' in Jakarta, he didn't look happy.

"My lady-boy hooker is so stupid she would rather run away back to her job as a prostitute, back on the street than stay with me" he said.

"In *Pretty Woman* the hooker stayed and it looked like they would live happily ever after," I replied to him, making a joke of it— I was unsure whether my joke would cost me a huge fight but I made it anyway. He scowled.

"The difference between the hooker in *Pretty Woman* and yours," I told him, "is that your hooker actually has the balls to run away."

I wrote in my diary that day.

Some fairytale now is causing my husband a huge conflict in his head because he is feeling guilty of having spoiled a lady-boy street hooker instead of spoiling his own wife. He is now regretting that he could even care for someone of the same sex. He is trying to tell me that he needs to break away from me so I can learn to totally let go of him and then we can begin dating again. I really don't understand any logic behind these confusing ideas he has…

I wondered if I could contemplate going back down that path. Now our relationship had even deeper scars to cope with than after our previous separation, and that was hard enough. It would take such a long time to get any one of those scars to start healing, and we would have to try healing them one by one. Now, the conflict in my own head could not stop, thinking of my husband kissing and sleeping with a man, believing that he had actually genuinely fallen in love with that person.

I wrote in my diary later that day:

My 'normal' husband is no longer the man I loved in our early days together. He is already in a different category altogether. Now he is officially bisexual.

Knowing this, I found it so difficult for me to find any common sense or logic in his suggestion that we get back together, as I was not interested in exploring or sharing his strange new direction. My tastes were beginning to look decidedly conservative in comparison to his.

How on earth could we roll back time so that we could return to the way things were, or at least the way they had seemed to be, before June 2012?

I was deep in thought about this when my friend Putu, who I met not so long ago, arrived unannounced one afternoon at my villa. It just happened to be a day that Jack and I had been having a screaming match. Our argument had been very loud and Jack had ended it by announcing his intention to go to Jakarta and never come back to us again. He had then gone into his room, slamming the door.

I was totally deflated, but relieved to see my friend's

cheery face.

"What's up *Mbok*?" she asked me. She always called me 'elder sister.'

"Nothing I can't handle," I told her, defensively, and then followed up with "Shhhh!" and pointed my finger to the newly slammed door. "He's on the rampage."

Putu had heard about my being used as a punching bag in the past. She looked very concerned.

I started to make some coffee for my guest, and was just about to put it down on the table when Jack reappeared. He burst out of the room, laden down with all his bags, screaming at the top of his lungs.

My friend Putu took one look at him and stepped nimbly out the back door, taking her daughter with her, leaving her coffee behind.

"I haven't even left and you're moving someone else in!" my husband accused. I looked around for my friend, but she had driven off swiftly in her car.

Without my knowledge she went directly to the police station and sent a few policemen back to my house, just to make sure I would be safe, but Jack was already on his way by the time they got there.

Since that incident, Putu continues to remind me that Jack is not a nice man to be around, and especially not good for me and my son. We have become close friends; we often share our stories of the highs and lows of marriage. We regularly message each other to make sure both of us are keeping on top of our daily struggles. She is also putting up with a man who is not very nice to her. By comparing our ups and downs we have come to the conclusion that both of our marriages can only be fixed if we change our own expectations and demands towards our husbands and the way we react to things. It seems we are both learning how we can enjoy more highs and avoid the lows, but it takes an awful lot of dodging and disconnecting to be able to do this.

Funnily enough, we both seem to have come to the conclusion that maybe our marriages aren't that bad, even though the experience of being married has severely shaken every conviction and belief we ever had. It is amazing how the human brain adapts under stress—it seems we have both discovered a new basic goal in life since getting married—simply to endeavor to remain undisturbed in spite of whatever might happen. We have both discovered that pain can be buried, hidden away.

In spite of the disruption and disorder that has become a part of both our daily lives ever since marriage, we had separately come to the same decision that we'd rather not live without our husbands for the sake of our children. Out of this decision has arisen some of our biggest challenges, not that we would trade them for anything in the world. However I don't think our children have benefited from it, in fact I fear it could have done them a lot of damage.

My friend Putu and I decided to make a conscious

effort to apply more insight into marriage to help us navigate. I started by observing my sister's marriage and some of my Balinese friends' marriages to local men in my village. I also asked the girl who works at my villa lots of questions about her marriage—luckily most Balinese don't mind being asked personal questions. No matter how disappointed they were in their men they seemed to all think it was their fate and their responsibility to carry the burden.

Slowly I am becoming more aware of what other people's marriages are really about in Bali—the demands and expectations they place upon each other and how they compromise to hold it together. I'm especially interested in their highs and lows and how they deal with the worst moments without becoming violent.

In Australia, statistics say that more than seventy percent of people who say "I do" will not be sleeping in the same bed eight years on from the date of their marriage. And though religious scriptures allude to the fact that adultery and abuse are acceptable reasons to end a marriage, I'd be willing to bet that the major challenge to any marriage is ignorance.

Playing with Fire

Jack has always had a tendency to be interested in a variety of darker worlds other than just our boring world of day to day living and married life. He has always been curious how people from a very unfortunate and disadvantaged background actually manage to live their life and survive. I used to think that his curiosity could have been the reason that he had so often ended up getting involved with prostitutes, out of interest to closely observe their way of life, but perhaps that was too simple a theory. No doubt it was just his cover-up for looking for something different in sex.

I remembered his weird fascination with bike gangs and back-street prostitution from comments he had made about his travels in the Philippines, Thailand, China and Hong Kong.

"They are not afraid of anything or any one," he would tell me.

But now this was a different story. How could I be expected to watch him, even support him, as he got himself deeply entangled with his lady-boy prostitute in Kuta and the night-clubbing drug scene, right in the back yard of my own island home?

I remembered the stories he had told me about visiting

black ghettos in the States and talking to the homeless hobos and girls on the street.

"Some of those unfortunate people were living on the footpath, with blankets and no roof over their heads," he told me. "No doubt many of them had been in and out of jail because of drugs, murder, rape and so on…and yet they were still able to laugh and joke with me. When they knew I was Australian they asked me if I was Crocodile Dundee!"

In my experience, normal people usually wanted to avoid visiting areas like these, or talking in close conversation with such desperate characters, but my husband was extremely curious.

"Curiosity killed the cat," I thought. "Why does he always have to play with fire?"

Putu gave me a book to read that promoted the idea that marriage is the *'fire of life', somehow designed to refine all our dysfunctions and spur us into progressive wholeness.* In this light, contrary to what most people think, the goal of marriage is not happiness. And although happiness is often a very real byproduct of a healthy relationship, this book claimed *'marriage has a far more significant purpose in sight: it is designed to pull dysfunction to the surface of our lives, set it on fire and help us grow.'*

I could see that if we're willing to see it this way, the points of friction in our marriage could quickly become appreciated as 'gifts' that consistently invite us into a more whole and fulfilling experience of life.

This fits in pretty well to Balinese philosophy, which takes much from the ancient Ramayana and Mahabharata chronicles, although women never seem to get a second chance. When Sita, having been carried off by the evil monster Rahwana, is finally rescued, her husband Rama no longer believes she has been faithful to him. She undergoes a test by fire, to prove she has been honest, but he is still consumed by jealousy and never really redeems her love, in spite of the ordeal she has been through willingly to prove it.

Living in the 'here and now'

I found a positive inspirational post online today: "*Live in the here and now!*" and I thought it would be something great for me to focus on doing, so that I could put my past behind me, and face the future as it comes.

On the way back to the villa, my heart sank once more, thinking of how my life had been unfolding into such a tangled up web of misery—worse than an American TV soapbox drama, I told myself.

Then, remembering the long list of things I had to do; I chose to let go what I could not control. I took a little early morning walk, and looked at the dew on top of the rice stems, so clear and so beautiful, reflecting rays of morning sun, and I was determined to watch each drop as it fell to the earth.

The green colors of the young rice plants and the coconut trees, and the sounds of nature and the sight of the hard working Balinese farmers in the fields made me realize how beautiful this place really is and how lucky am I to be here in Bali, especially Ubud. I felt lucky I could call this place of my ancestors home for now. My footsteps slowed down until I came to a stop. Standing still, I tried to listen to the voice in my head telling me to enjoy this very precious moment, appreciate everything I could see, everything I could smell in the air, every sound in the atmosphere.

After a while, the humidity of the air began to distract me from my enjoyment of the morning sunshine and my feet started to itch where insects were biting me. I started to feel very hot even though it was only 7 a.m. I walked back to our villa to settle myself into a chair and enjoy the rest of my coffee.

Luh, the girl who takes care of my villa, hovered nearby. I could hear her bustling around and making kindly noises, offering me nice words of comfort. She seemed to feel the depth of my sorrow. After having witnessed the fights between Jack and I she had a good idea of what I was going through in my broken marriage.

Pushing a bowl of fresh sliced mango towards me, she suggested I should eat something.

"You must look after yourself," she urged.

I tasted the mango and enjoyed every bite of it, so sweet and juicy. I listened carefully to every word Luh said. She was expressing her concern for my little boy, being hammered with all of life's stresses, with an uncaring father who didn't bother to hide his violent temper or his noisy professions of love on Skype, when calling this strange person she had heard me refer to as "his lady-boy."

"Who is this person?" she asked me.

She hadn't heard of a *waria* so I described Jack's lover as a 'boy with boobs'. She was nonplussed.

"You mean a boy who dresses in girls clothes, like a *bondres* mask dancer, or a *gandrung* boy legong?"

"No, this boy actually has taken hormones so he can grow breasts, and had an operation to put silicone implants in them to make them even bigger."

She shuddered and looked horrified.

"You mean a doctor's operation? In a hospital?"

The idea was obviously too fantastic for her to believe, so I went on to tell her about gay marriages overseas; in parts of the world where it is accepted as normal for a man to have another relationship with a man, or a woman with a woman. "It happens here too," I told her.

Luh had never been out of her village. She could not believe it was true. So I told her about how many gay relationships are happening in Ubud, right near us, as we speak, but I could see it was too much for her to comprehend.

"It's normal for boys to hold hands, and play around with each other" she said. "Then when they grow up they get married."

"Yes, its normal for girls to do that too," I told her, but in the west both men and women do it after marriage when they get bored. Some even change their sex. Sometimes they marry each other, too."

This was too much for her to believe—she blushed, and looked at me disapprovingly.

"We should accept what God gave us," she said,

pouting, and then she ran off to clean the bathroom, as if scrubbing the tiles white with bleach would keep these dreadful new ideas at a safe distance.

I kept on telling myself that there are so many secret paths of life hidden from us. In comparison to Luh my eyes were wide open. I had seen and experienced a lot of life. Perhaps too much, I thought. But even then, with all my worldly experiences, there were some things I still found hard to accept. Especially a bisexual husband who preferred the same sex.

We never know when we will have to cross a certain path, or turn in a new direction, and there is no guarantee whether we will be ready or not at that stage. But why did it have to be me?

My mother always told me "Life is all about accepting our path." Learning our role and acting in this movie we find ourselves in, without any script to follow is not easy. Our ability to play our part well will determine how successful we will be in this lifetime.

Someone like me who had already given up on life and attempted to kill myself certainly wouldn't win any Oscars acting... but then what? I wondered what the next role I had been set up to play would be, and if I would be ready to accept it and truly live through it in the 'here and now'.

Blame it on the Weather

It was so hard to drive. I was stuck in a very heavy rainstorm all the way from Ubud to Tegal Pisang, and the road was like a river. I still couldn't get used to driving a car in Bali. I had always driven a motorbike, and in the old days of my fish business I had hired a cousin to drive me around.

My brother in-law had called me for help. His scooter had let him down, stopped in the middle of nowhere, dead. The only mechanic he knew of had a *bengkel* at least 4 km away and no phone. It wasn't only the difficulty of driving in the rain that bothered me, I found it even harder to drive at that time as I was so down, so many tears falling down my face had made my eyes swell, I could barely see the road.

I drove carefully over the flooding road, dodging floating debris that made it hard to see the roadside. An upsurge of plastic rubbish was no doubt blocking all the drains along the way. Many shops were filling up with water. Probably all those drains had never been designed properly in the first place.

Balinese are not very renowned for their planning or engineering skills, unless we talk about our terraced rice fields and *subak* irrigation. They know how to deal with nature, building channels connecting their rice fields using the simplest materials of mud and grass in the most artistic manner. Unfortunately when it comes to asphalt roads and ditches that do not contribute to producing a harvest, there is a lot to be answered for in regards to caring for our public roads in Bali, and this is in the hands of the government.

The floodwaters got deeper as I went further north and plastic was everywhere; the roads looked more and more like rivers. I felt lucky I wasn't riding my scooter. As I drove through these unfamiliar scenes of flooding and destruction I began to wonder if this was how the world would end.

"Will God be so angry with my Balinese friends and families that no ceremony will be good enough to prevent a disaster and everything will be destroyed?" I wondered.

In my mind's eye I could picture the destruction happening all around me in Tegal Pisang—flooding, landslides, problems with health due to the dirty floodwaters entering shops, markets and villages.

People had been dying in my village recently, and it seemed to me that they were dying younger. There are hardly any of my dad's friends left and not so many of my mom's friends either—they had all died due to illnesses their families blamed upon the curse of black magic. With my western eyes I could see how flies were partying on their food, right after partying on pig stools. Anyone could see how the pig waste was left in the open, you could smell the stink of it. In many homes the kids were eating their meals near the pigsty—only a small wall divided it from the kitchen.

On rainy days like this I could imagine the excrement of the pigs mixing into the river along with the rubbish and I knew the children were being washed in the same water. Even their clothes were washed in it. Mind you, I used to swim in the very same rivers. Now, just even the thought of it made me feel sick.

What ceremony can we do to fix this problem? I'm sure the *dukun* next door—a shaman, who had barely managed to finish his primary school education—will have all the answers for my village.

Our village *dukun* continues to treat people with diseases in a very imaginative way; he crushes the hair of a black dog and a black pig together, mixes with coconut oil, and gives it to the sick person to drink. How could anyone do this and who is going to stop it happening when more than half of the villagers believe in this *dukun*'s power to heal?

I was amazed when I heard that the God from Pura Dalem had taken up residence in his family temple.

"Why?" I asked. "Is our Pura Dalem no longer good enough? Why would the God of the Pura Dalem want to move to this guy's family temple?"

"What is happening in my village?" I thought. "Perhaps

I'm not the only one crazy here!"

I finally found my brother-in-law. Poor thing, he was squatting, soaking wet and cold, near a cemetery. I told him to leave the bike there until the rain stopped and took him home. As soon as we got there I told him to get dry and change into warm clothing right away, to avoid getting ill. My mum burst into hysterical laughter when she saw him, "You look like a wet rat," she said. No sympathy at all.

I realized that is one of our Balinese habits; instead of giving sympathy we often laugh when we see people fall over. We laugh when we see something wrong with others, even if they are mentally ill or physically disabled. Perhaps we do it because we suspect they have earned their bad karma, and in the case of my brother-in-law this certainly fitted. But what about my difficulties, would everybody laugh at me and think I deserved them too? I decided to be more caring and sympathetic from now on, even towards Jack.

My Sister's burden

My sister was born seven years after me—yet another disappointment for my mother, another girl. However, my mum managed to justify her new daughter's existence by earmarking her to take over responsibilities in the village. She knew this little girl would be able to take a load off her shoulders when she grew up—all those time-consuming mornings, afternoons and evenings of making offerings for the temple, attending ceremonies for the dead, life-cycle ceremonies and helping out at religious festivals within the community required a lot of energy.

I have always taken care of my little sister. While I was robust and strong, she was small and skinny, although she did inherit a big rear end from my mother just like me. When she was a little toddler I used to watch over her to make sure that the other village children didn't bully her. I carried her around on my hip, balancing her weight with a strip of grubby batik wrapped around her bottom and tied over my shoulder.

Now we are both grown up and have families I am sad to see that she already looks so much older than me. She always appears to be carrying a heavy burden on her shoulders and is generally stressed about her duties in our village. When I called her the other day she was so ill she couldn't get out of bed. She had been getting up very early each day to juggle her duties as a wife, mother, small-scale village entrepreneur and member of the village *Banjar*. Her obligation in the village to help prepare for a large temple ceremony has been wearing her out, as the preparation for the *karya ngusaba desa* at our temple, a ceremony to give thanks to Dewi Sri, patron goddess of fertility, for our bountiful harvest in the rice fields. It has been going on for months now, requiring her presence for hours on end, day after day, at the temple.

When I spoke to her she sounded so sick of being overloaded with life's never ending tasks.

"I wish I could be you," she said. She wanted to be someone who she saw as having escaped from the boring details of life to travel the world—someone who was able to simply stop over and join the family to pray at our temple at her leisure. She wished that she could be the one with a permanent resident status in Australia on her Indonesian passport and a business visa to enter the United States.

"If only I studied as hard as you did and appreciated education as much as you!" she told me.

Even though I have offered her financial help again and again, she still feels guilty for not being able to pay me back her already large interest-free loan. She reckons it will take her a lifetime to pay me back what she has already borrowed.

"I don't want any more loans." She was adamant. I

often just give her money and tell her she doesn't need to return it, but I empathize with her feelings of pain at having no other choices in life, being torn between her wishes to be more like me and doing her duties as a traditional Balinese woman in a village like ours.

Now she is trying her best to cope with it all. Each morning she gets her two children ready for school—they are still small, just nine and six years old. She also has to help her husband in the day-to-day running of their small business, selling ornamental fish. Then she helps me out in my little kitchen, preparing the spices that we mix to sell as sauces. After that she still has to attend community working bees and her devotion to temple ceremonies takes priority over everything else.

Her recent absences from the temple due to business commitments and trying to make a living have been a subject of discussion among her friends. They have been talking about her being too lazy to attend *banjar* events, although she has valid excuses with a mountain of debts to be paid plus other daily expenditures. She also needs to earn enough money to pay her family's share of each temple ceremony.

Change is in the air, it seems. Instead of talking badly about her, now her friends are starting to follow in her footsteps. If they find themselves standing around waiting at the temple they head home or go back to work. They don't think it is any longer appropriate, when the work at the temple could be completed by only twenty people, that women from all one hundred and fifty families in the village should be expected to show up at every working bee. They want to implement a roster system.

My sister and her friends have started to make their voices heard within the *banjar* community meetings. They are complaining that their burdens are overwhelming; it is no longer possible for them to juggle. The costs of supporting ceremonies are becoming so high in both time and money; they cannot see how their Hindu religion can be sustained at the same level of participation for another generation. I wonder too—will my sister's daughters and their friends be able to follow the example of their mothers in the future?

The community head of the *banjar* organization has started to listen to them and recently he announced some changes. One of their first steps to make it easier was to decree that expensive imported fruit should be replaced by local fruit in making offerings for the temple, a wise decision that will save our families a lot of money, considering there are so many temple ceremonies being held at any one time. It has for some time been a matter of prestige to have brightly polished red apples from New Zealand, Sunkist oranges from Australia and green grapes from California gracing the tiered fruit offerings we make for temple festivals, so I felt encouraged to see these expensive items replaced by yellow *sotong* guavas and red *jambu* rose-apples at our most recent temple gathering.

Since I have been back in Bali I have met a number of Western women married to local Balinese men who have become a part of their local communities after marrying into local families and joining our religion. It takes time to learn to make the intricate woven decorations used in ceremonial offerings, but is not so difficult for those who are good with their hands, and there are many simple items that can be easily made. Balinese women are always very welcoming to those who show an interest in joining in and contributing in festival preparations. In my experience, judging by those I have personally become acquainted with, only a very few foreign women are willing or able to adapt to local customs, joining the regular offering-making working-bees and carrying family offerings to the temple on their heads. Like me, many of them have families to support.

Most foreign women I have met who now live in Bali shake their heads in admiration and marvel at the seemingly endless energy of their Balinese counterparts once they realize what an immense amount of devotion and personal sacrifice needs to be made to fulfill the expected role of a woman in Bali. Preparing the family offerings for temple anniversaries and family life-cycle ceremonies, plus daily propition of evil spirits and monthly full moon ceremonies is exhausting. Even the most simple of offerings to keep the balance between the good and evil spirits in the family compound, which become more complicated at full and dark moon, and on special days of the calendar, involve hours of work in preparation and distribution to all of the house shrines and other points of the spiritual compass that mark the most important locations within the yard.

As many of these women are, like me, breadwinners in their families, they are able to resort to buying offerings or pay their staff to make them and dedicate them 'on behalf'—a kind of representation to the deities 'by proxy' which is perfectly acceptable. Instead of carrying out the arduous and time-consuming duties of keeping the balance with the spirits that surround them with daily gifts of beautifully woven leaf trays of flowers and food themselves, they can afford to buy the materials and pay someone else to do the work.

Is there any less virtue in this? (You might ask!) In Bali, no blame is placed, as long as family commitments are fulfilled. The women who sit for hours on end preparing the many different shapes and sizes of delicate offerings with patience and love are thought to benefit personally from their 'bakti', as their acts of devotion will bring them good karma. I know my mother thinks so, and perhaps that is why she is so serene and jolly in her old age.

I wonder if this was what my father was talking about all those years ago when he held up the importance of 'family honour' as a reason to force me to marry a man I barely knew. He thought that all my mother's hard-earned honour and respect from her service to the Gods and ancestors was being thrown away because her daughter had invited a man home to sleep in her room. And right now he was probably concerned that I was going to shame the family again, after all my sister's hard work in the village, by leaving my husband, the father of my son.

I'm sure he would rather preserve the status quo of my current marriage, no matter what the consequences could be to me, than bring shame on the family again.

My last days with Jack

It was early December and the roads were full of tourist buses. I had just spent half a day in Sanur and driven all the way back to Ubud in peak traffic when I got a call from Jack asking me to pick him up in Kuta.

"You gotta be f***ing kidding me" I said, "that could mean another two hours driving each way with the state of the traffic at the moment. Four more hours on the road!"

But he sounded so lonely, sad and desperate, very depressed that no one wanted him, "Blah, blah…" So, to cut a long story short I agreed.

"Ok," I said, "on the condition that you are not allowed to be angry in our villa when you get here—you have to control yourself—no fighting." He agreed to my terms.

"Call me when you get to Sanur," he said, "so I can catch a taxi from Elvanda's to Carrefour." He obviously didn't want her to know I was the one picking him up.

My son Dharma and I set off together to get him. As we were running late due to heavy traffic we called him at least ten times as we were passing through Sanur, but each time his phone was still engaged. We arrived at the shopping centre, but there was no sign of Jack and his phone was still busy. Carrefour was closing at 9.45pm, so I sent Jack a message. "If you aren't here in 10 min I will leave."

Just as I was driving my car out of the car park to head home without him, I saw him enter, riding pillion with an *ojek* motorbike taxi-driver. I waved, and pulled over and waited for him in the car.

"I was on a 'long-call' with my girlfriend" he said, instead of apologizing for not picking up the phone. I thought the way he said it implied that he was too busy having fun with her to rush. Words were on the tip of my tongue. "That's what you get for dating a call-girl, Jack, next time it could be a close-call," but I held them back, remembering my son was sitting in the back of the car.

"How selfish can anyone get?" I thought to myself. What the hell is wrong with me coming all this way to pick this smug idiot up?"

I pictured my friend Annie telling me that I should just leave him there in Kuta.

"You have a life to worry about," she would say. I could hear Annie's voice loud and clear in my head telling me "You are an idiot, sister." My weakness of being too nice to the wrong people generally results in regrets, and usually I have to taste the bitterness of my own medicine for it.

Jack had not been back in the villa for more than five minutes when he started his familiar rampage again, shouting and thumping things around and telling me it was a mistake he had asked me to pick him up. He started throwing things, slamming stuff down on the table, bashing his computer and—to make matters worse—tried to tell me to drive him back to Kuta.

"I don't think so..." I said, loud and clear.

I left him in the villa with Dharma, and went out, telling Dharma I would be back the next morning. Usually when he spent time alone with Dharma his anger would subside and he could calm down to his normal self. They would play video games together, swim in the pool and make jokes with each other. But this time when I got back from my parents' house the following day I found Jack sitting there looking miserable. Dharma had gone off to play games in his room by himself.

"I broke up with Elvanda," Jack said. "We have to pick my things up from her place." At that stage I was not sure if I was pleased or not to hear his news, but Dharma insisted we go with him and we set off once more to Kuta, on another errand of mercy, this time to pick up Jack's things.

When we got there and parked just down the road from Elvanda's place, Jack explained that he wanted to take Dharma in with him.

"He is very cute, even a very cruel Muslim would not hurt him," Jack said.

I was worried about this idea as I had no idea what he was up to, or how many cruel Muslims Elvanda could have guarding her place.

"What if things go wrong?" I asked him. But I know no

matter how mad Jack is he would not hurt our child. So I held my tongue and let it happen.

I stayed in the car with the back of my seat fully tilted so I could not be seen. Since I was in 'enemy' territory then probably it was not a good idea to show my face, I thought. I just kept lying there, pretended to be asleep, until I heard Jack and Dharma come back. When Jack got back in the car he asked me to keep my head down until we passed the house where Elvanda rented her room.

It was a while before I noticed that among his things was a fancy Chanel bag.

"What's that?" I asked him.

"That's the bag I bought for her on Rodeo Drive when we were looking for Prada shoes," he said. "It took us four hours long to find a pair of women's shoes that would fit her."

"Oh yeah, so what else did you get?" I spoke softly, to keep the anger out of my voice.

"Then we went to buy a dress and we had the same problem," he said. "Most of the dresses didn't fit as her body is not the average size and shape of a woman."

"Ha ha!" I thought, but I kept it to myself.

"So in the end we went and bought this Chanel Bag right at the entrance of the store."

"Wow, that must have been fun," I said, my sarcasm lost on him.

"You wouldn't believe it… we were welcomed with a glass of champagne and they treated us like a King and

Queen."

I could see that Jack was reliving the feeling of being a big man, so needed and so rich.

"The bank called me to see whether it was really me who was buying all this stuff," he went on. "Just confirming... so many unusual expensive purchases... they said."

"And so they bloody well should have, they must have thought you were out of your mind!" I said. I was about to say more but then I caught my son's eye in the rear vision mirror and bit my tongue. The poor boy looked pale and tense. I didn't need to rub it in. It was obvious enough that his father had been prepared to go to any length to woo the 'travesty' to love him. I kept my mouth firmly closed.

Mending a Broken Heart

Never in my wildest dreams had I actually imagined myself watching my own husband crying. Sitting quietly in a chair opposite him I watched tears running down his face as he hurriedly messaged Elvanda on his Samsung tablet. He was listening to songs on Youtube, and then pasting them on Facebook. It was his birthday, and he was listening to songs like Metallica's *I want to destroy you*, and others, even more vicious. I've never been a fan of Metallica but I chose to give him an audience, as it seemed to be what he wanted and needed at that time.

"She has broken my heart," he said, "playing with my emotions." He continued to press and swype his toys.

Of course we all knew by now that Elvanda was a professional hooker. It was her job and livelihood to make Jack fall in love and then get all his money, use him as an ATM. I had to pinch myself hard to keep from breaking out laughing. How could he fantasize that such a farce of a romantic comedy could be any more than just that?

Indeed drugs do affect our minds in very strange ways, but in this case it was not funny at all and his behavior was causing sorrow for all of us. It had been months now that we had no idea whether Jack was coming or going.

Life seemed to have taken a horrible twist, and I had

little faith at that stage that it would improve. My husband and friend—the person I thought was my soul mate—was telling me that he didn't know whether he wanted to stay or to go. What was I supposed to do? I felt that I had no choice under the circumstances other than just to let him go and let it be.

Just recently we had looked at a new villa to live in. It seemed very comfortable and we were planning to share it. I had been thinking of ways in which we could live together, but stay apart.

"You can live downstairs and I will take the top floor with the boys," I told him. It would allow the boys and I to each have our own rooms with balconies and he could have the whole bottom floor. The villa was very conveniently arranged with an office, storeroom, swimming pool, dining room, lounge and so on… and if he decided he didn't want to stay there I could always rent it out as a bed & breakfast or find someone else to lodge with me. "Here goes," I thought as we moved in, in spite of all my doubts.

In retrospect it was completely my fault to let him walk all over me. I had always been there for him, forgiving and accepting. Perhaps my father's words had more effect on me than I realized. After all, I'm supposed to be a sensitive wife and give Jack comfort and understanding, even if he keeps on listening to a song that reminds him of a happy time when he was high in a nightclub with his personal sex fantasy.

Between a Rock and a Hard Place

In his messed-up head Jack continues to romanticize his liaison and to my dismay he wants to share the ups and downs of this new relationship with me. He thinks of it as a true love story, he tells me—a fairytale. Now he is crying again, his heart broken, he cannot live without her… I'm regretting having allowed him to be my flatmate.

The day after we moved into our new villa he got a phone call and a long conversation ensued, so I assumed that they were going to get back together again. I was keeping very quiet about it, and staying away from him as much as possible, but he caught me at the bottom of the stairs and abruptly turned against me.

"You are a bad person," he said. "You're to blame for everything. You lied to me!"

I had no clue what he was going on about, and was more interested in stopping him from yelling at the top of his lungs, to not disturb the neighbors, so I was taken by surprise when all of a sudden he physically attacked me and knocked me off balance. I fell to the floor, but I quickly got up and scrambled out of doors to the patio where I knew I had a diving knife. He followed me out of the room and went to punch me. This time I was determined to fight back.

"He mustn't know how scared I am," I thought, and turned to face him, waving my knife at him, spitting out the words "Don't you dare touch me!" But he grabbed me and pushed. I had forgotten how tall and strong he is—at least 6 feet tall. I only managed one little stab at his arm before he dragged me off balance and I fell to the ground with a thump. From that position he easily gained control over me, slamming my head on the rock path by the pool. He kept on punching me in the arms, ribs, head, shoulders, wherever he could find a ready spot. By then I could not move and everything had gone dark.

When I regained consciousness he was carrying me, towards my bed and I seemed to be covered in dirt.

"Stay with me…" he was saying. "Don't leave me—I need you to stay alive, or I'll be in trouble with the police."

I felt like I was dying and I knew that he was not sorry. It was obvious he didn't care. All he wanted was to get back together with his lover in Jakarta and to take her to live in Australia. I had heard them skyping the night before. I kept my eyes closed.

He went on, his voice getting stronger and more resentful.

"You deserved this beating for not obeying my request to be a good and sensitive friend. But don't worry, I will go to Australia and you might never see me again."

My poor little boy was distraught. He had run to hold me as soon as Jack had dumped me on the bed, and had heard every word that his father was saying. He reassured me through his tears in whispers in my ear.

"Don't worry Mum, I won't be angry with you if you decide not to let daddy into our home anymore."

I didn't want my boys to hate me for deciding that Jack could not come to our villa anymore, so I was relieved by Dharma's words. Perhaps the boys could help me to make up my mind; as I saw things now, it was no longer a matter of choice.

Finally, Jack left me alone, departing the villa in a hurry, leaving me in a semi-conscious state. I drifted into sleep and when I woke up my brother-in-law, alerted to my situation by my housekeeper, was there to take me to the doctor. I had concussion and head injuries that caused nausea whenever I moved. My right arm was black and blue, my ribs hurt and my knees were covered in grazes.

But I was alive, and more worried about the effect this last clash with Jack had on my little ten-year old than about my own physical state. He seemed very withdrawn.

Dharma alone had witnessed his parents fighting and seen how his father hated his mother. Viewing his father being so abusive towards me could scar him for the rest of his life. I'm overwhelmed with worry about what this will have done to him.

Enough is enough. Now it's all over! No turning back. My door is closed for Jack.

Something to remember

For the Christmas break, as the children had been invited to visit their respective paternal grandparents, I decided to take a little walk down memory lane and explore my new life as a single woman.

The day I arrived back in Australia at my old hometown—well I did live there for almost twenty years, practically all my adult life—there was a special reason for my unaccustomed nervousness. Not only was I arriving back as a single woman, I had also been in touch with my old friend Ben who I had always admired, and he sounded like he wanted to see me right away.

I had chatted with him before leaving, on email, and we had agreed to meet at 7p.m. at the most atmospheric restaurant in town, an up-market place that offered fine dining by the beach. Then he had emailed me back, and suggested we put it forward to 5p.m. so we would have more time to chat and relax, or perhaps take a little walk on the beach, and have a few cocktails before dinner.

My friend who I was staying with had also arranged to meet her friends at a trendy local pub that afternoon—it used to be our local surf house bar by the beach when I formerly lived there and had recently become the 'in' place to go. So, I went with her in the afternoon and had a few too many glasses of champagne to calm my nerves before I met my date.

I had just endured a very long trip from paradise the night before. It was impossible to sleep during our six and a half hour flight from Bali to Sydney, and before that I had a two-hour trip to the airport before check in, plus three hours of queuing, checking-in and waiting before boarding. Upon arrival in Australia at 7.15 a.m., my sons and I had gone through Immigration, picked up our luggage and then queued again for customs clearance. By the time we finally got out of the airport we were exhausted, but it was time to catch the train into town to meet their grandparents.

The journey to Central Coast usually takes two hours, but on that particular morning it took three hours due to railway track repair work. We finally got transferred on the last leg, about twenty minutes away from town, by bus. It was an awful trip as we had to wait in the heat for another bus. The two buses in front of us were already full and they didn't have enough baggage capacity.

I was totally exhausted by the time my friend picked me up at 12 p.m. at the train station, but didn't feel up to calling off my date, besides I had been looking forward to it for many days and nights. I had lunch with my friend and an hour's rest. Then I showered and headed out with my friend to her champagne party, my dinner date my top priority for the night. I wanted to see if I could enjoy myself and forget about my husband, his abuse and rejection, just for one night.

Ben had suggested we meet at his work studio, as Christmas was his busiest season and he was working long hours as a professional illustrator. He was just finishing off for the night when I walked in the door, so he gave me a welcome hug, took me by the hand, and we stepped across the road and upstairs to his apartment. He looked even more like Daniel Craig, the James Bond actor in Skyfall, than I remembered.

"I need to change before we go out," he said. The minute we got through the door of his one-bedroom apartment we collided. It was as if our two bodies had become one and the clothes somehow melted off us as we danced. It was pure and joyful sex, no time for thought, no time for words. In spite of shyness, feelings of inadequacy and not being accustomed to being touched by a stranger. Although I had known Ben for a long time we had never been intimate in the past. Our lovemaking felt completely natural and minutes after it was over I fell into a deep sleep. He woke me up at 7.15 p.m. Apparently, I had been sleeping so peacefully he had already called the restaurant to move our dinner booking forward and give me a little extra time to rest.

"I was tempted to sketch you during your sleep," he said, "but I thought you might be offended, so instead I have been watching you sleeping and memorizing each part of your body." I blushed, pulling the sheet up to cover my body and feeling just as shy as if he had painted a full portrait.

"You're so sexy, so beautiful," he said, and he couldn't stop cuddling and kissing me.

We went off on our dinner date, and I still remember every detail of every course clearly, as if it is imprinted on my brain. Starting with a delicious entrée: he had a lamb filet with couscous and I had local river oysters in Kilpatrick sauce. For my main course I chose Atlantic salmon and he a Scotch fillet, medium rare. It looked so good I couldn't help but ask him for a bite. To accompany this he had a South Australian Merlot and I a white Pinot Grigio. Dinner was perfectly served; we were easily satisfied customers tonight.

We went back to his apartment with a plan to watch *Eat, Pray, Love* so I could show him some Ubud scenery from home, with Julia Roberts in it. But the DVD was playing up so he put on a jazz CD and we chilled out. My jetlag was setting in, and my eyes felt incredibly heavy. He offered me a massage, and asked me to lie down on a sheet on the floor of his bedroom in front of a mirror. Moments later he started rubbing some aromatic massage oil into my back. I was feeling so good with his soft touch, and then he gently eased his body flat on top of my back, and started sliding up and down—it felt sensational as he gently entered my body. He continued to massage my neck, my back and every part of my body trembled with pleasure. I had never experienced such delicious and truly exotic lovemaking. He grabbed my hair while moving hard inside me, still teasing my most erotic spots till I became so excited I thought I would explode from sheer joy. My mind was trembling on the verge of this discovery, and I felt truly loved.

I felt as if Jack's imprint had been wiped from my memory.

Life as a fatal fantasy

I had been back in Bali for two weeks. It was January 2013 and I had settled happily into the routine of life, taking my son to school in the morning and picking him up in the afternoon, doing as much work as I could to further my villa and other projects in between. Then Jack showed up, demanding to move into the downstairs room.

After some arguing I relented, telling myself it was for Dharma, as I knew he had been missing his father a lot.

"You can stay as long as you don't get angry and don't do any drugs," I told him. "And don't forget I am your flat-mate from now on, nothing more, nothing less."

I was still concerned about his drug abuse, as I had figured that was what made him so unhinged and violent. Recreational drugs had never been a part of our family life—as far as I knew—until we moved back to Bali to live. We liked to enjoy the usual pleasure-enhancing substances—a few glasses of beer or wine, to loosen up at a function, coffee to give a much-needed boost in the morning, but I was not prepared to hear, (gasp), that my estranged husband was now into inhaling 'ice' in clubs these days—or so he started to tell me now he had moved in downstairs. Drugs and sex now seemed to be his favorite topic of conversation.

"There are a lot of people out there who love to get high. I've been regularly taking drugs in clubs since I started going out with 'the girls' in Kuta," he informed me, confirming my suspicions.

"To this day I am still completely incapable of naturally feeling as happy as ecstasy is able to make me," he went on. "It's difficult to put into words the pure bliss and serenity that a good roll of ice can make you feel. That being said, once you do it, life is never the same again."

"It's not just you who will never be the same," I muttered under my breath. "None of us will."

"It feels amazing," he said. "Kissing, right there in the club, with pumped-up techno music vibrating through my body—even the hugs feel good." And then he added, "It didn't even matter when I realized she was a lady-boy."

I couldn't bear to listen to him raving on as if I had no feelings, as if I was a complete stranger, and not the wife who had shared his every intimacy for more than a decade of our lives. Even though we were no longer together in that way, I still felt sick whenever he went on about it. There was just one question I wanted to ask.

"What about the... you know... the male organs down below?" I asked him.

"No problem," he said—he didn't even care when he felt the size of his partner's arousal. "I felt completely uninhibited, and open to all kinds of kinky sex scenarios."

e other effect the drugs seemed to have had on him

was his lack of inhibition or guilt in openly sharing his experiences with me. He showed no sign of remorse at all or concern for any affect his words could have on my feelings, or that I would be imagining my husband doing all kinds of strange and immoral things while I stayed home with my children on weekends.

I felt sure the drugs he described to me must be illegal. And they weren't socially acceptable as far as I was concerned. They most certainly posed health risks and if he was caught he could end up in jail. I felt sure, although many drugs are shrouded in mystery and misconception, despite the fact that a lot of people still opt to take them, he must be on a dangerous path to destruction, with no concern whatsoever as to what could happen to his family.

In order to understand the attraction, risks and effects of the drugs he went on about, I decided to find out more about the infamous euphoria inducing 'rave-drug' of his choice, MDMA, also known as Ecstasy, E, the love drug, Adam, XTC, or X. My ex-husband—now my new flat-mate—couldn't stop talking about this drug each time he returned from his Kuta weekends. He spoke about it as if he were describing a lover.

I found out on Google.com that his favorite drug of choice, Ecstasy, described as 3,4-methylenedioxy-methamphetamine), causes 'dissociation'. I had to look that word up in the dictionary, but it certainly made sense when I read that 'to dissociate' means *'to become disconnected, separate in thought or in fact, declare oneself unconnected with a person, an organization or activity."*

Apparently in vulnerable individuals it could lead to *"causing a person's mind to develop more than one centre of consciousness."* It could even *"cause a pathological coexistence of two or more distinct personalities in the same person."* Just reading this made me come out in a cold sweat. It had dawned upon me that the Concise Oxford Dictionary was describing my husband's behavior with remarkable accuracy.

There was no doubt that he was in the "vulnerable individual" category, I decided. Or was he just a simple liar, like most Balinese men I knew who liked to cheat on their wives, including my father? I could just imagine Jack out there cockily telling all the prostitutes in Kuta that he was a single man, who had already divorced his wife, not unlike the Kuta 'cowboys' who feigned bachelorhood even when they already had grey hair and grandchildren.

It wasn't long before my worst fears were confirmed. I ran into an Aussie hairdresser who worked in Seminyak, and while colouring my hair she told me she used to live next door to the place where the 'trannys' hang out. The number of clean-cut, good looking foreign men who passed in and out of their door had amazed her. She told me she had been shocked one day to meet Jack there, as she thought she recognized him as my husband, although s he had a brother?

"He mustn't have recognized me," she said, "he told me that he was single when I asked after the family, and when I asked him if he had a brother here on the island he told me his brother was not in Bali.

"Yeah," I told her, "he considers himself single, even though he wants to come home to us and pretend we are a normal family after his weekend trips in Kuta."

A number of things about Jack's behaviour had started falling into place. What I had read on the Google search engines and the Oxford Dictionary summarized his condition so neatly, I could now understand a little more about the drugs he was taking and their side effects. It seemed that all of Jack's puzzling behavioral patterns that I had so struggled to comprehend as reactions to my own behaviour were simply the common symptoms of a regular drug-taker. The symptoms matched perfectly; once he switched back into his 'other personality' he really thought he was still a part of the 'normal family' life he was returning to after the weekend.

It was so sickening to realize that all his lies and abusive behavior could simply be due to the side effects of drugs on a man who already had a history of depression. Plus his doctor had warned me back in Australia that the anti-retroviral drugs he was on were likely to heighten the effects of stimulants of any kind.

For too long I had been blaming myself.

Perhaps I had worked too hard all those years and

not paid enough attention to what was happening to my partner? Perhaps I hadn't tried hard enough to be a good wife? The self-doubt had harrowed me and left me wallowing in a painful state of low self-esteem, which caused me to be plagued by lack of confidence. I had started considering plastic surgery, liposuction, or whatever other extreme measures might be necessary to get him to feel attracted to me again, as I felt so ugly.

The next phase that 'vulnerable' personalities enter if they continue with their drug abuse—I read on Google Search—*is possible schizophrenia or even a psychotic episode, in which the user may become extremely dangerous to others.*

I already knew that on his 'downs' Jack no longer felt any emotional connection with me at all. If he had dissociated from his family through his regular use of ecstasy, then he was probably already entering the dangerous stage described online—we could be in line for a *psychotic episode*, which sounded extremely scary.

I couldn't ignore it any longer. I had to get away from him with my little boy to a safer place, a place where he could never find me. But shouldn't I alert the police and the Australian embassy first? He could be dangerous, and I wanted to make sure there were no further victims.

No, I decided. The police wouldn't do anything to protect me, and the embassy probably wouldn't even believe my story.

Now he is alone downstairs...and angry

Today I wrote in my diary... *I think my ex-husband's angel, if indeed he ever had one, has turned on him since he has chosen to dwell on the dark side, the place where his destructive childhood experiences always seemed to be leading him. He has never dealt with the scars of childhood, and the issues always come back to haunt him. He seems to be heading down a crazy path of self-destruction.*

"Who does that bloody bitch think she is!" He was screaming and swearing because some other prostitute—not the one he had set up in Jakarta in style—but another one from Kuta, was asking him for money.

"I imagine by now that word has got around on the street that you are a soft touch with the street girls," I told him from the top of the stairs.

Then one of our neighbors peered in through the front door.

"Please don't make so much noise, your foul language is disturbing the neighborhood," she said.

"I'm sorry, I have been telling him, but he's not willing to listen," I told the irate looking woman.

"F..k off!" Jack piped up from the kitchen.

"Your husband's language is not acceptable," she shouted up to me, ignoring him. "We have children and we don't want them to be exposed to it." She went back out and slammed the front door behind her.

I tried to pass the message on later in the day, when he had just eaten a big breakfast and seemed to have calmed down, but he wouldn't listen.

"Perhaps you will only learn when you have lost everything," I concluded. "It seems there is no going back."

Our ten-year-old was in tears, he had been in his room at the time and he felt so embarrassed by his father's behavior, especially as our neighbors are friends with his classmate's parents.

Then Jack told us he was about to make a very important conference call at 11a.m. Of course the electricity went off just before he could connect and didn't come back on until 3p.m.— which in Australia is already 6p.m. and after office hours—yet another excuse for more anger and shouting.

"What's the point?" I told him. "You will succeed at nothing as long as you treat other people badly."

* * *

I have come to believe that the only way to heal our soul and move on is to learn from our mistakes. We need to be honest to those who genuinely love us. It is important to free ourselves from lying to one another, so we must clean ourselves from negative thoughts and to do this it helps if we understand that we all have our own personal protectors to call on. They have been with us since we were in the womb, our spiritual siblings, and they remain there for us when there is no one else to turn to.

My mother and other Balinese women call these siblings *semeton* in high Balinese or *nyame* if speaking to someone of *Sudra* caste. Perhaps we will not be able to see if they are there at the exact moment we ask for help but at least we have the comfort of knowing that we're not alone.

"Take an offering of food and *canang* and place it on the stone by the door," mum used to tell me whenever I had an accident or was feeling miserable, "call your siblings to be with you and protect you."

In Bali we believe that the place to connect with our unseen spirit guides is marked by a rock that has been placed on top of the spot where our placenta was buried on the day we were born. That rock marks the place where our unseen siblings will visit and come looking for us. When I was a baby my mum always put an offering every day on that rock, asking my siblings to guard and protect me from evil, illness and bad people. When I was learning to walk, each time I had a fall my mother used to rub the rock three times to make me feel better.

"You are blessed to have this place to connect with your siblings," my mum told me. "You must remember that we are not alone, we just need to call them. They will always come to protect us."

I decided to take an offering home and place it in the same place that I had often visited to place offerings from the time I was little, to thank my siblings for being here for me.

The next time I went to the village I took some fruits and flowers especially for my siblings and placed them on a small woven tray with some freshly cooked rice and food from the kitchen and left them in the same place in the garden. I placed a stick of incense beside it and wafted the fragrance three times with my hand as my mother had taught me to do all those years ago.

A feeling of peace descended upon me, and the tightness in my head and shoulders seemed to loosen. I felt a weight had been lifted from my heavy heart.

After having left them behind so many years ago, now, in my time of need, I felt my spiritual sisters had reunited with me. I said a little prayer in my heart that they would forgive me for my neglect. I needed them to watch me, guard me, tell me to stop being sad and to bring me a cool breeze at night so I can let go of the events of each day, no matter how traumatic they might be, so I could fall asleep and wake up to a new day with a smile on my face each morning.

The road to despair

It was already February 2013 and the boys were dreading their father's next visit. Jack and I had shared so much love over the years we had been together that we all found it hard to believe the estrangement had happened between us. Our relationship had been through lots of difficult times in the past, but I guess we have always appeared to be a very loving couple in other people's eyes, even our children.

In the past six months, since I found out he has been having an affair with a transgender, we have become alienated. I alternate between anger and forgiveness, but my anger cannot be buried. It is eating away at me, like a hungry worm.

Not only has he spent more than a hundred thousand dollars of our family savings on this creature, now he tells me that having sex with her is the fulfillment of a fantasy he has nurtured for many years, long before he knew me.

It frightens me to see what has happened to him and I wonder if he is still interested in me at all. He hasn't appreciated me sexually for nearly a year, but all along I simply assumed that was because of his high stress levels. Being HIV positive had hardly dented his libido in the first place. It was only since he started this new liaison that he always managed to find an excuse to avoid sex with me; either he was too tired from work or not feeling well, or whatever—I was not very happy about that as I was only 40 and he 41. I couldn't understand why he didn't seem interested in making love to me anymore.

I wondered if it was a result of the party drugs that they took in the nightclubs where the lady-boys hang out. Apparently those drugs enhance sex immensely, but I was not prepared to go to that extreme.

Just the fact that Jack indulged was enough to really worry me, as in Indonesia taking illegal substances is an offence punishable by death. Just two days ago when we discussed it I reminded him how dangerous it was.

"You are risking your life every time you go to those clubs and take drugs—the police raid them regularly."

"Don't worry," he said, "the clubs are very generous to the police, and the girls are paying for protection by the Laskar Bala—they're the local militia—the police don't mess with them," he said. "But I'm past it now, it takes too long for me to get back to normal after a night out on that stuff. I love you guys, and I promise you I'm going to stay away from that world from now on."

I know he is lying, as he is still totally enamoured with the *waria*, emailing, skyping, calling and messaging her.

I don't know what to think anymore; I am kept confused by his continued professions of 'love' for the boys and me.

I imagine he is only clinging to our family as he still feels insecure in his down times. I can't tell the difference any more between the truth and lies in the stories he keeps telling me and I don't even want to know. I've started feeling bad about myself again.

Jack's continual bad moods, angry tirades and violence have worn me down. I'm worried how I will manage to complete our villa project if he continues to throw our money around. He no longer hides from me the fact that he has been spending heaps on partying and drugs, purchasing expensive clothes and plane tickets back and forth to Jakarta in hot pursuit.

"It's the lifestyle, hon," he tells me, "it's important to keep up the image."

I wonder—who am I to him now? I can't see a future together as the 'sister' and minder of this shallow guy, no matter how good he was to me in the past. That was not a role I had ever imagined to play in my life.

I have never met a grown Balinese man who professed any interest in bisexuality, although they all love to talk about sex. I don't think that the average adult person here even knows that it is a possibility, except perhaps for in the early experimental stage where children play sexual games quite naturally with each other. Physically, if he's interested in the 'feminine' role, then he has that in me. But I can't play the 'male' role sexually; I find it completely unattractive and repellant.

I wondered if it was my 'male' energy and strength, from being brought up by such a tough father that made me appealing to Jack in the beginning. He was such a shy man back then.

Once, in a late night conversation after having drunk too much, he had referred to being abused as a child by an elder man.

"It was on my way home from school. He used to wait for me in the park and force me to do things." Jack had never shared the details with me. Could that experience as a child set him up for a lifetime of confusion?

I had a gut feeling that he wouldn't make friends with someone unless he personally met them in the course of his normal life. How could he help it then, if that someone, who happened to have the sexual characteristics he confessed to have had years-old fantasies for, pops up? So now he looks at the past—his life with me—as a big mistake?

I needed to do some serious thinking and I knew I had no choice other than to let him go. It was the only way to know where I stood. In this situation, I could no longer go on trying to please him, giving in to every whim. It was endangering my life and damaging my children. Time for me to draw a line in the sand.

I wanted him on my own terms, exclusively, baggage or not, and I wasn't willing to share him with anyone else. I didn't think it could be possible any more since Elvanda came into his life.

My reaction to Jack's suggestion that he and I could live in a polygamous relationship with Elvanda was one of absolute horror.

"You've got to be kidding! Never! Not in my life!" I objected.

"Lots of Balinese do it," he told me, "why can't you?"

I had to admit, in the world I grew up in it is very common for Balinese men to have more than one wife— even my grandfather had two. But this was different.

Anyway, in my experience polygamous relationships are generally very hard for the women involved. On the surface it would appear to work quite well in some families as it's handy to have more women in the household to do the work, but I know of many instances where the relationship ended in difficulties. It generally had a severe impact—mentally, physically and financially on the family.

My cousin's dad had three wives. Wife number two didn't produce any offspring so she left her husband when he was getting married to wife number three and went back to her own village as a single woman. She didn't see the need to stay in her husband's compound any longer and was not going to compromise her life and love as she could predict that the future would be bleak. Although she had become a real mother to some of her stepchildren, she still didn't see any point in staying, especially as her husband was quite violent towards her whenever she questioned his behavior and attitude.

It was always a tradition amongst Balinese royalty to have many wives. That was one of the ways in which the royals consolidated their power over huge areas of land and made alliances to expand their kingdoms. In contemporary times a number of wealthy men, some of them from high caste families, have been famous for the number of wives they keep… a lot of hard work was required if the husband is to support each wife and their children equally. The most successful of these men are able to own several houses and provide a different home for each wife and her children, as well as fulfilling their financial needs. Some men even give each wife an entitlement to their family rice paddies to ensure there will be enough to feed them in generations to come.

Women in these polygamous relationships often have no choice but to make the sacrifice of giving permission to their husband to acquire a younger wife due to difficult circumstances. It commonly happens if the woman is terminally ill and unable to perform her wifely duties, or in the case she has failed to produce a boy to continue the family line. Bali has a patriarchal tradition where girls marry into their husband's family so they do not inherit anything from their birth parents, and are not expected to carry out duties in their own family ancestral temples after marriage.

Village customs differ from place to place in Bali,

and there are different levels of acceptance of polygamy, depending upon local customary lore, or *awig-awig*, a village rulebook that is passed down through the generations and is rarely changed, as it requires the agreement of every individual community member.

My schoolteacher from primary school days is in a polygamous relationship with her husband; she is wife number two. She has two girls and a boy whilst her *madu*—a term which means 'honey', used to describe the 'other' wife—only produced one girl. I don't know why Balinese women would call their rivals by such an endearing name; there is no way I would call my contender 'honey'! My teacher's husband tends to favour her as she is younger, has a career and earns money for the family. She has also produced a boy for him.

I had an intimate view into my teacher's family life as I often went to her house for extra tutoring after school, and in return I helped her to clean her house and look after the children. She was very kind-hearted and genuinely in love with her husband and she was always really good to the first wife and her daughter. Indeed, mostly they seemed to be living in harmony, but there were times when she spoke to me about her dilemma

"Why did I have to fall in love with a man I have to share with another woman?" She would let herself go with me. "I often cry when I am on my own, I feel so emotionally drained by my situation."

No doubt she has regrets—with her good looks and career as a teacher she could have easily chosen one of the many single men from our village.

My own situation was different of course, but I couldn't help comparing. Here I was, my husband Jack offering to live half with me and half with Elvanda. I rejected that idea unconditionally—it was too confusing to even think of—I could not imagine sharing my husband with another woman, let alone with a lady-boy prostitute. I felt that even daring to ask me to do so was insulting my dignity. It was as if there were no rules for Jack. He felt he could do whatever he liked to me and expected me to remain by his side without any consideration that I have my own view of what is right and wrong.

There are so many compromises to be made even in the usual polygamic relationship, without introducing the complexity of different sexuality. The man with more than one wife gets a big ego boost in Balinese society, being able to boast about his ability to satisfy more than one woman. There is no doubt he would feel like a big man in front of his friends. They will all be jealous of him having sex with a different woman each night without having to feel ashamed, as his marriage is legal and the community accepts it—I wonder what they would think of this!

There could be advantages and financial gain for some women who are clever at manipulative games, playing off one wife against another to make sure that their wealthy husband favours them. Inheritance is an important consideration—the woman who produces the first boy in that relationship will get the most wealth for her son. The prettiest wife or the best one in bed would have more chances to play with her husband's emotions. While those other wives who find themselves in a lesser category will be tempted to have affairs with other men outside the marriage—after all they can easily put the blame on the husband for his lack of attention.

I have heard of many such marriages that ended up very badly, with one of the wives picking fights non-stop with the others. In some cases they even try to kill each other. There are also tales of murder where all the wives got together, killed the husband and divided his assets equally amongst themselves and their children. This is extreme, but I do believe it could happen.

"I'm not even willing to think about it—even if it were another woman you had fallen in love with I would tell you the same," I informed my husband. "If you are actually in love with another human being in a different sexual category to me, I believe that is firm enough evidence that you no longer love me, and for that matter, you will probably no longer be interested in any of my gender, from now on."

"It's possible to love more than one person at once," he protested.

If only it were so easy for me to stop loving him.

But I have made up my mind. I only want a partner in life who can wholly and truly love me alone. I will not share my bed with anyone else and I will not be happy to share my husband.

Several times I have thought of running away to another foreign country. It would be so tempting to start a new life, but with two growing up sons there's no possibility of that anymore.

I was hoping that my life would look rather different by the end of 2013, as I have been through a challenging metamorphosis and I am still dreaming that I will come through this with some brilliant new wings. If I survive my own turbulence, perhaps I can find a way to help others in a similar situation.

The Power of Words

Unfortunately, we can never take back our words, they are like a glob of spit that has fallen onto the ground and disappears into the dust, but the germs keep on spreading and multiplying. Such is the power of the spoken word… once uttered, it can become like a curse or a blessing. But in my case the potential for it to become a curse has proven to be much more probable.

I recall my schoolteacher, when I was sitting in my hot and dusty schoolroom as a child trying to teach us about *Tri Kaya Parisuda*, the three things mankind must do to find a true path to peace and purity in life. At that time it was beyond my comprehension.

"How could thinking pure thoughts—*Manacika*, speaking the truth—*Wacika*, and being honest in one's actions—*Kayika*, affect our lives?" I thought.

"Of these three things," he told us, "*Wacika* is perhaps the most dangerous to neglect, as our words have a life of their own. They sprout roots, grow branches and bear fruit."

Now I remembered I had done a terrible thing. It was just after our last huge fight, when my ex-husband had seemed intent upon killing me by slamming my head on the rocky path next to the swimming pool at the villa, punching and kicking every part of my body until it was black and blue. I was stretched out on the wet ground barely conscious—that was the moment I cursed him.

"Something bad will happen to your hands and feet," I spat the words at him in desperation and anger. "You will never be able to hit me or kick me again."

It hadn't taken long for my curse to take effect, even though he is back in Australia. For the last two weeks now, whenever I have spoken to him on skype, or received his emails, he has complained about sharp pains in his fingers and ankles. His doctor in Australia has advised him to get scans and blood tests done to determine further diagnosis and find out if he needs surgery. The doctor is almost certain that my ex-husband is suffering from rheumatoid arthritis.

When I picked him up from Bali International Airport at the weekend I was shocked to see that he couldn't even lift a bag from the boot of our car without screaming in pain. He is staying with us for now in the apartment downstairs. Each morning over the last couple of days, I saw him taking painkillers as well as his usual antiretroviral HIV medication. That added up to around 10 tablets at one time, all during morning coffee.

Perhaps I should feel happy or relieved, but the inner guilt of having said those words at a time when I could no longer see a way to save myself from his attacks is making me miserable. It might not be my fault that he is ill… it could be a result of all the medication he has been taking, plus the party drugs and unhealthy lifestyle, nothing to do with my having cursed him. But I still have a niggling fear, deep inside me, that I could have been the one who caused him this pain, and perhaps I would be the one to earn bad karma from this evil act of mine.

Karma is a bitch! Cursing is a bitch! Is it possible to 'speak no evil'? My personal history tells me that the power of my words and my intent is something out of my control. Am I trapped in this cycle of violent cause and action? The results of my actions and my words have already frightened me too many times. Each time Jack has done something bad or lied to me there has always been an accident or something bad waiting for him just around the corner.

I explained it to him but he wasn't impressed.

"Are you trying to threaten me?" he said.

"Not at all, I don't need to," I told him, "if I give you enough rope you will hang yourself! Remember the time you went off to China with your Chinese secretary? You said you needed her help as an interpreter. You looked so guilty when her ring fell out of your clothes onto our bedroom floor, I could tell you must have been having an affair. That was the time you crashed our one-week-old car! My instinct told me you must have been up to something bad."

"You're a witch," he told me, "a Balinese witch!"

"Yeah sure," I said, "and I can turn myself into a monkey too!"

"Well why can't you make me a potion to keep me home then?" Jack was in his usual joking mode. It was hard to have a serious discussion with him—that's how he avoided issues—by making jokes and passing things off as humour."

"That's not how it works," I told him. "We all have to pay our own karma. You had been doing bad things to me for a while. Even after our holiday in China, when you vowed you would be faithful to me and never rent a prostitute, you couldn't keep your word."

"I kept my word to the letter," he replied smugly. "I didn't hire 'one'—I hired two Chinese prostitutes on the same day—we had a threesome!"

"Yeah, and you caught the worse disease imaginable. That's your karma, not mine, although you've tried so often to share it with me."

It was indeed a lifetime sentence—there is no cure for HIV yet, and the anti-retroviral drugs were not pleasant. Fortunately Jack had to inform me, it was against the law in Australia not to, as a man in his profession clearly knew. He could face a prison sentence if I was to catch it from him. Luckily as a lawyer he was very aware of that.

And then he had lied to me back in June last year when his car broke down at the busiest intersection in Bali, the tortuous *simpang siur* roundabout, which had earned its name by frequently leading people astray and into traffic chaos. If I look back I figure that's the place where Jack got lost in Bali. He had a flat tire right there in the middle of the swirling traffic, and didn't know what to do.

That was the time Jack first called his friend in Kuta for help. He had met her some time ago, along with the man she professed was her partner. Her mobile number was just waiting for him to press. Of course she knew how to sort it out—she was able to take Jack off for a little rest and recreation. He didn't even realize she was not a real woman at the time. At the time she had the perfect cover of an Australian partner and a one and a half year old child who looked as if he was half Indonesian and half Australian.

"Can you even remember how many times you have lied to me?" I asked him. "And how you have paid for it?"

He had the grace to look a bit sheepish, but his training as a lawyer led him astray. His answer was as glib as ever.

"What you consider to be a lie, might just be an omission on my behalf to keep you informed," he said.

Each time Jack lied to me something odd happened to him; even when he transferred money into his account for some dishonest purpose it somehow ended up in my account or our joint saving account.

"My angels are certainly working overtime to protect me and my children," I thought at the time.

And how many times had he told me he had broken up with Elvanda? But of course I always found out afterwards that must also have been a lie, as he still transferred money to her and I heard him talking to her in endearing terms on skype from the next room.

Now, all I have are regrets and Jack is still suffering from the pain in the joints of his hands and feet. I hoped and prayed that it would not be in vain and he could no longer vent his anger physically.

Finding my way

I woke up this morning aching all over perhaps due to my restless sleep. I could feel the stress throughout my body, and I thought I had better get moving and do some exercise, or I might catch the flu. I pushed my blanket away and dragged myself out of my comfy bed, headed downstairs to my kitchen and managed to make myself a cup of aromatic Bali coffee. To my disappointment when I went back upstairs and headed to my balcony my glass coffee table and seat were covered with drops of water from the rain. No big deal, its just water, I figured, so I brushed it lightly and sat there anyway.

The sound of the rain drizzling down was so peaceful, a rhythmic patter of ground tapping that started with regular beats and intervals, then was suddenly followed by a gust of wind. The wind hit our tall bamboo hedge so violently and it continued to blow, getting stronger and stronger, till the bamboo tips almost touched the ground but it was strong enough to spring back up again. I wondered at the resilience of nature. The coconut tree leaves looked like they were waving their arms at me and I could see a tiny squirrel climbing from leaf to leaf, trying to find a hidey hole in between the coconuts for shelter. I felt the wind hitting my chest, the coolness in the air—it seemed nothing could comfort my cold heart and longing for somebody right now. Even if deep down I knew that sunshine always comes after the rain.

"In the meantime," I told myself, "I will sit here, drinking my warm coffee, trying to write down my thoughts and being creative as if there is nothing else I would rather do on this miserable rainy morning." I realized now how much my writing had helped me to be steady, to observe myself, my situation and the world around me, keeping it all in perspective.

My powers of observation were heightened. I could smell the fresh earth, damp with rainwater, and now the ducks were quacking in the rice paddies next to our villa. They sounded happy that it was raining and the water level on the rice paddy was so high. The fields looked like a row of swimming pools all in a line, all with green borders. Rain is good for the ducks and also good for the earth, for that I am thankful.

My little boy is ill with a sore throat and his body temperature is rather high, so I'm keeping an eye on him at home today. I'm planning to steam a bunch of asparagus I picked up from a supermarket in town yesterday. I also have lots of fresh vegetables to make soup for us for lunch. The thought of eating healthy and warm food gives me comfort. Today will be a nice day, being at home, resting with my boy. Just the two of us.

I still have a tingle of discomfort, knowing that my

situation is very complicated with my ex-husband Jack. I keep telling myself "Just move on, Madé, don't let all these negative thoughts bother you anymore." I need to enjoy each day and each moment.

There is no sign of sunshine yet, and the arching bamboo poles are waving again, they are almost reaching my feet. I'm still sitting in a small corner of this balcony so I can be protected from the rain as I watch it dripping down from the roof, dancing away ready to touch the earth. I stretch my neck left and right, start to breath regularly closing and opening my eyes, feeling the air and focusing on the sounds of nature. I can hear a priest's bell ringing from somewhere in the neighborhood. Someone must be doing some sort of chanting to prepare for meditation. A car passing on the road sounds like it is crashing into a huge puddle of water. The rain is getting harder and starting to wet my computer screen. I'm getting myself ready to move to another spot but not sure what is the best spot to find contentment in being alone.

"Oh I know"—I spoke to myself out loud. "I will move to my downstairs coffee table by the pool." A good spot, protected from the wind by huge glass windows. Impossible for the rainwater to splash my computer there. I'm planning to write some more today.

Not so bad at all… When I finally got all my stuff moved to the coffee table downstairs, I sat down and the first thing I saw was two water fountain statues, their spouts splashing like a myriad of sparkling crystals, into the swimming pool. It is absolutely gorgeous in the morning light and even more peaceful than my balcony. The rain is still falling heavily on the grass, dripping from the roof and hitting the ferns and palm trees.

"It's a concerto!" I decide, and sit back to watch and listen.

Best of all, Jack is not here to spoil my moment of peace. Just to remember his name now brings a stir of discomfort to my stomach and creates a tingle in my body like an ant bite—not too painful but it itches, and I can't help wanting to scratch it from time to time. I don't understand nature sometimes. It seems intent on giving us a reason to feel pain; perhaps if we know how to feel we will be more aware, and next time appreciate things more when that pain has passed.

I can hear a sound of a motorbike heading towards our villa complex; it must be the gardener on his way to work, as it is almost 9 a.m. At this moment I truly appreciate all of God's gifts. I feel so lucky to have been able to improve my destiny in life through education. Blessed that I'm not my gardener on rainy days like today. I can sit here and write down my random thoughts of the day, I don't have to go anywhere, well except for perhaps one meeting, but I can put that off too if I'm not ready.

So for now I will continue to write, enjoying sounds of the rain hitting the ground and sitting here in peace. In my deep contemplation I know everything is going to be all right in the end. "If it is not all right, then it is not the end"—I recall my favorite quote from the film *Best Exotic Marigold Hotel.*

I feel grateful that my sibling guardians are continuing to protect me in times of need, when there is no one available to support me, and no one within reach to hug me at night. They will accompany me in my loneliness; wipe my tears in times of sorrow. For that, I will not forget to acknowledge my gratefulness with an offering on the stone at the entrance to the pavilion where I was born when I go home to the village next. And I will thank my mother for all her years of placing offerings, taking care that my siblings didn't feel deserted.

I recall that desperate moment when my life nearly slipped away, when I entered that parallel world between light and dark on the day I tried to end my own life, how my guardians had come to bring me back to life, whispering that I needed to fight once more, not for me but for my children.

I guess life is about choices. We can choose to be happy or sad. We can pick and choose the people we want to spend our days with, the people who will influence our lives. I choose to be me; I choose to be alone for now and to learn to love myself again. Sure, loneliness always hits me badly at night, and the longing to be touched by a loving man, to be hugged and comforted. There is nothing to compare to being flattered with kind words, or feeling my skin touching another's. I miss those nights so much. It is not possible for me to welcome anyone new into my life for now until I'm content and fully recovered. I need time to pick up the pieces of my life once more, and put it back together.

My focus for now is my ten-year old boy who is suffering from the exposure to his parents' fighting and separation. He is sad every day, remembering all the battles when we were together. He doesn't expect us to live together again, he said that he understands that's not possible.

Yesterday he told his class teacher "I simply don't want my parents to fight with each other ever again. Not in front of me." Then he went to the appointed room she has made available for him whenever he feels like crying.

I knew he is upset with both of us; he loves both of us and he wants to spend time with both of us equally.

It is almost impossible for me to even face Jack—I have no desire to contact him considering all of his violent behavior and his lack of remorse for what he has done to me over the years. But for the sake of my child I will try my best to keep in touch with him so at least from time to time I can tell my son what he is up to or where he is. I don't think it will be an easy task but at least for now I need my little boy to be happy. I have to consider his wellbeing, and he needs to be focused and improve at school. I will do anything I can to help him to find stability at school and at home. I have arranged to meet a psychologist in hope that with counselling my son will eventually learn to manage his anger and resentments towards us. Both Jack and I came from violent childhood backgrounds, and I suspect that neither of us has resolved our personal damage until now. Perhaps I can do something better for my son, and break the vicious circle of patriarchal violence, so his karma will be better than mine.

Changing my tactics

When Jack asked me if he could stay with us at our villa during the July school holidays of 2013 for three weeks, I agreed, thinking I could use this opportunity to experiment.

From the moment he arrived, I intentionally changed my tactics and tried to do everything in the opposite way to what I had done in the past. I wanted to see if it was my behavior that had caused so many dramas between us. I started by simply trying my best to live in the 'here and now' and avoid challenging him with any questions about the past. I endeavored to not to get angry or show any resentment towards him, hiding all my pain as if I was tucking it away neatly under a mattress. Then I paid attention to the results. I created a measuring scale for this purpose, marking our relationship as a top priority, and my effectiveness in all other areas of my life, including the achievement of quality of life for my son and I, on the same scale.

To my surprise, during the following three weeks that Jack was with us, we had no arguments or screaming matches, just a handful of ironic conversations that proved if I stay calm, remain nice and sympathetic, I would be better rewarded. "Of course," I thought. "Marriage requires sacrifice! My mother had always told me that. But why does it feel as if there is no end to the giving?"

At that time I figured if I could return marriage to its rightful place in my priority list, it could quickly change from something that needed continual maintenance and sacrifice, into one of our greatest assets, affecting every other layer of our lives.

One question still remained at the back of my mind. It just wouldn't go away.

"Can we ever repair our trust?"

If he didn't show any inclination to change then it was not likely. I would probably never trust him again.

Then during a long car trip to my land in the southwest part of Bali I talked openly to my brother in-law, who often drove my car for me in his spare time. For the first time I shared with him my real situation with my husband. I described to him how I felt about Jack's behavior and what I had been doing to avoid fights with him simply to maintain a peaceful atmosphere for my son and myself, not to mention the surrounding neighbors.

"I feel I will only able to re-build my trust if in the future Jack shows some positive changes in his behavior," I told him.

"I never thought I could trust you, or my own family again—not after you betrayed my trust with my land papers, and ripped me off at the bank. But because you all showed me how bad you felt about it, and I could see you were trying to help me, I have been able to forgive you all."

"It's up to you, then," my brother in-law told me. "I just feel sorry that everyone you love has done you wrong and betrayed you—including me."

"Holding a grudge is heavy," I told him. "It was making me miserable."

"I am inspired by how forgiving you are," he went on. "I didn't imagine anyone could have such a kind heart. And your parents were so happy to have you and Jack visit them during his three weeks stay in Bali. They heard from the villa staff that you hadn't been fighting this time."

I wondered if it would be a worthy sacrifice to try and forget about my own pain, just keep on pretending that I was happy so that everyone around me could feel happy. Perhaps eventually I would start to feel happy too? "Fake it till we make it!" How many times had I heard that saying? Maybe in that way I could find the power to turn the curse around?

As you can see, dear reader, I don't give up easily, and I'm still doing my best to be optimistic, in the hope that one day Jack will recognize my love and the sacrifices I have made for him.

It's a Jungle out there....

Jack is now telling me "Gender is no longer the most important thing in relationships. Our personal attributes are more important than our physical bodies or sexual preferences. You are still living in the dark ages!"

Well, I had thought that I was quite an open-minded person, but indeed, I am challenged to consider the vast number of sexual possibilities open to us today, with an ever-expanding list of different gender mixes to choose from, and sexual acts to explore, as demonstrated by *Fifty Shades of Grey,* the trilogy that I read Charlie Hunnam was about to play a role in. The reviews say it has been 'steaming up bedrooms' and 'saving marriages' around the world, in spite of its dubious literary merit.

If only we are able to forget what we were taught by our parents and teachers, shrug off our inhibitions, and distance ourselves from the community around us, perhaps we will one day evolve into a different kind of species altogether.

"So if its not just about sex, and love is more important, then it doesn't matter if we are woman, man, she-male or he-female? I wonder if ordinary men will get a run in—I am sure they will no longer look at women in the same way," I told Jack, "and women might just turn out to prefer women altogether—at least we understand each other's needs."

My Jack was already claiming to have become a liberated metro-sexual after his encounters with Asian gay guys in Sydney and she-male hookers in Kuta, Bali, so I had to put him straight, if you will pardon the pun.

"Jack you are no more metro-sexual than I am," I told him. "A metro-sexual is a straight guy who is happy to explore his "feminine side" which can be anything from taking pride in clothes, having manicures or facials etc. I looked it up. You are much more wacky."

He looked a bit miffed that I presumed to know more about it than he did.

"Bisexual doesn't even cover it," I told him. "I reckon you would probably be better classified as 'pansexual'— like the ancient Greek God, Pan. He even did it with a goat. *Pansexual* means 'gender blind' as in: gender doesn't matter."

"Well I'm a bit more fussy than that!" Jack protested "I do draw the line at goats, at least. What I mean is that there is no longer any distinction between woman and man, no specific rules apply any more," he said. "Anyone can make love to anyone else, regardless of gender."

"Exactly. It sounds like Roman times—didn't all that debauchery lead to the collapse of an empire?" I asked him. "I do agree that the world is becoming more accepting to different choices of gender in relationships. Although that's out there, in the big cities and the international hot spots, not back here in Bali, well, not yet in my village, that's for sure."

"Not even amongst Balinese witches?" he asked me, winking. "I reckon they get up to all kinds of tricks!"

It always made me wonder how we could have these long and animated discussions whenever Jack was in a good mood. He was such a different person when things were going his way.

I had agreed to let him stay with me again, on the grounds that he remained downstairs at the villa, away from me, and controlled his bad moods.

"Otherwise," I had told him, "I'm out of here, and I'm not leaving any forwarding address." The subtle balance of power had reversed between us along with a series of events that culminated in bad fortune for Jack when his bank account was hacked by an intimate group of gay friends in Sydney. He suspected Elvanda was involved. They had barely left him enough money to pay for his ticket back to Bali. He had to ask his boss for an advance on his wages, or so he told me. I hardly knew what to believe these days when Jack spoke about money, the stories seemed to get more and more convoluted.

But he was all fired up now, and grabbing a couple more cold beers from the fridge, so I knew he wanted to carry on with our discussion.

"After all," I prodded him, "it is no longer necessary for a man to marry a woman or even to make love to a woman.

Think of all the options: men with men, women with women, men with a lesbian partner, men with a transsexual partner, and women with a transsexual partner—it seems to me this could be nature's call for evolution."

"What kind of evolution do you mean?" Now he was following my train of thought.

"In this era there is no need to think about regeneration, creation of other human beings—the world is already over-populated. All that matters now is sexual desire between one another and the exploration of human beings' most vulnerable states of mind."

"Well, it may be a confused era of sexuality, but out of chaos comes creativity," Jack answered. "In these times the best paying job will be as a sexual psychotherapist or liberated tantric guru—exploring the 'pure joy' of sex between humans without the limitations of gender."

"In that case, human beings will probably become extinct in the long run, the writing is on the wall."

"You may be right," he agreed, "there is a huge increase in the number of transsexuals in every big city in the world. They are joining forces and pushing for their rights and gaining acceptance. Take Sydney and Jakarta for example—you don't have to look far to find special clubs and entertainment designed for metro-sexual life right on display, right in front of your eyes."

"Yeah, but that is the entertainment industry," I told him. "You are looking in the wrong places for love. Those are places where love is for sale, and the kinkier it is the higher the price. Those people who have made a career out of their exotic sexuality are not necessary happy either. Of course they feel better if they stick together."

"At least they are out there," said Jack, "whatever would we do without them!" He started to look lovesick again, his eyes staring off into the distance, a forlorn look on his face. I knew at any minute he would be rushing back to his room to skype his 'Honey'.

I tried to get his attention back.

"What really worries me is all those frustrated people of repressed sexuality out there who live like criminals in our societies with no better outlet than to abuse children and butcher their lovers out of confused self-hate," I told him. "There are heaps of cases like that in Java, the police are forever digging up dead bodies; it's absolutely tragic. That wouldn't happen if society was more accepting."

But it was too late to catch his attention; he was already on his way back to his room, leaving me to ponder.

Back to the basics—why are we here after all? Are we here on this planet simply to fulfill our desires for sex or did nature create men and women as sexual creatures so they would be driven to have more babies? What would have happened to Adam and Eve if Adam had been sexually attracted to another Adam, Eve to another Eve, or even Adam-Eve with Adam, Eve-Adam with Adam, Adam-Eve with Eve, Eve-Adam with Eve? There were too many possibilities to even imagine. Would such human complexities of sexual preferences have made any difference to the history of mankind? Or had they always existed? I couldn't stop pondering the matter.

What are 'moral codes' based upon anyway, especially those taught by a patriarchal society led by predominantly heterosexual men?

How could 'other' sexuality be morally wrong when it occurs in such a relatively large number of our population? Perhaps nature is trying to tell us something? Is mankind getting closer to becoming extinct? Nature has the power to destroy and re-create, beyond any human comprehension—in our Hindu pantheon of Gods we attribute this power to Siva.

Not even governments with all their laws have any power to control this impending gender revolution—they only look silly when they try. Transsexuals are so popular in the entertainment industry. If more of us decided not to procreate, and adopted children instead, it would at least give some relief to the starving millions on our over-populated planet. A human transition towards accepting different sexuality globally could be nature's way of positively correcting mankind's excesses, as with erupting mountains, floods, hurricanes and tsunami. But I am beginning to sound like a Doomsday prophet!

What drives human nature to change? Is it simply a natural process of evolution? Or have we always been a rather variegated bunch, our differences less obvious as long as the minority is severely repressed by the heterosexual majority?

Jack hit the target when he told me "I would still love you even if you had a horn growing out of your belly." I thought about that for a long time.

"Perhaps he does love me after all," I thought.

He fell in love with a similar type to me when he met his she-male—he even admitted to having found some traces of me in her, some similarities in our strength, our aggression and our dominating personalities. His transsexual is a very confident person, s(he) really knows exactly what s(he) is—a man with boobs and the instincts of a woman. She knows exactly what a vulnerable man like Jack desires.

By now Jack had told so many stories about me to his she-male that I imagined she was trying to imitate me to keep Jack in the 'crocodile hole'. Her favorite nickname for Jack was *Berondong Tua*, the 'old man with childish ways'—taken from the popular Indonesian *dangdut* song about the old man who continually wanted younger lovers, and was always poking himself into a crocodile hole.

I knew that each time we had a fight Jack would run off to his *waria* and confess—burbling like a brook about what he didn't like about me and those things he regretted loving. No doubt he was welcomed with open arms and comforted. He always got what he wanted. In this case he got a fake me with all the fantasies drugs could enhance to top it up, and heaps of fun out clubbing—all at a price, mind you.

Of course Jack doesn't really need me. He needs to open up and discover the person he has long buried inside, the character that exploded from time to time with such anger, whatever sexual preferences that person might have. He had to come to grips with it. I guessed that would only happen in time, as some people have to learn the hard way. We both had a lot more in common than he realized.

However, right now he was clearly being taken advantage of, and I didn't like that, as it was impinging upon the rights of our little family. He thought of the she-male as his real friend and his lover—someone genuinely able to understand him and to offer so much fun—yet similar to his wife in lots of ways. He thought he was getting a bonus: a double whammy.

"Time to cut your losses," I felt like telling him. But this time I remained silent. It was time for him to find his own way. It felt like taking another step backwards with Jack back on my doorstep when I least wanted to see him. I had no choice but to deal with him again.

"Perhaps his lover needs a few more skills and a bit of intellect to imitate me," I told myself smugly. "Surely the real thing is always better than the fake."

Jack's psychiatrist at BMMC hospital, Dr. Tang, had told me it wouldn't last more than 9 months. Fantasy and drugs can cover up a person's faults for quite some time, but I thought at the time I would be a hard act to follow.

Surely my Masters Degree in International Business, my experience of managing our law firm in Australia and running my own Balinese restaurant in Australia, were qualities hard to match. But then again, I was a Balinese woman with a childhood of hardship, and still conservative to a certain degree. It would take a clever she-male prostitute to be able to imitate Madé intellectually, but when it came to kinky sexuality, with all her experience in back-street life, Elvanda would surely be streets ahead.

To be honest, I was very impressed Jack's relationship with her had lasted for almost a year. Even when Elvanda feigned interest in business, while making request after request for expensive gifts, money, land, car and so on. I had figured it would take a ton of ecstasy to alter Jack's mind and blind him permanently into accepting more fake attributes in return for this needy relationship. For sure she could be sneaky and empty his wallet each time he was on drugs, which Jack might not even remember, but that would never be enough to satisfy her.

It seemed she had already over-stepped her boundaries. Unsuccessful efforts of hacking into Jack's bank account, most likely in cohorts with a gay Thai guy in Sydney who Jack had flatted with, had put a stop into further funds being channelled into Elvanda's account for now.

Has Jack finally woken up? Only time will tell.

He has spent most of his time sleeping for the last two days since he's been back in the villa downstairs, either exhausted from working too hard, or simply coming down from a high overdose of something. It could be some illegal substance he was using to help himself relax or simply an overly high consumption of caffeine to help him to focus enough to complete his work in Sydney before coming back to Bali. Whatever it is, something has severely taxed his system. He has a permanent blurry hangover look, and seems to need to sleep day and night.

What the hell am I doing letting him visit us again?

I think I must have my own problems with addiction. I may be addicted to the adrenalin rush I get from the emotional topsy-turvy of our relationship; I do think I probably miss Jack simply for that! My life has been so boring and so in order without Jack to keep me off balance, and I am getting tired waiting for Mr. Right who is in scarce supply in this yoga, meditation and healing centre thanks to Elizabeth Gilbert for bringing all the desperate single mums of America to Ubud looking for love. She may have called her novel *Eat Pray Love* but in reality they are finding they have to Eat, Pay and Leave—probably feeling rather disappointed at the outcome. I don't want to become one of those women either.

Jack can be a very nasty person when he is under pressure with work, or under the influence of drugs, and he often gets violent when his needs aren't met but in his 'normal' human moments he isn't a particularly bad human being or even a minimally good one. He is simply a human with all the usual, and perhaps a few extra, frailties—a very funny fellow human in fact. He is the only one I know who answers all my accusations with jokes and smart-ass comments, and manages to use his smart lawyer ways to avoid feeling any guilt.

The violent way he has broken up our family, damaged our children's future lives, destroyed all of our mental wellbeing and knocked down every boundary we ever established in our marriage—these things I am not prepared to forgive or forget. I have always been able to forgive everyone's bad behavior, but for sure I will be on shaky ground if I ever decide to accept this man back in my life as a lover or part of our 'happy' family.

It would require too much work on everyone's part. He remains just as insensitive, feels no shame for what he has done throwing money that his family will need at the feet of his lover. His latest extravaganza was her birthday party for which he boasted he had paid for entirely, including the drugs, all the drinks, entrance fees and rent of private rooms in clubs in Jakarta.

Then a week later there was a 'life event' notice on Elvanda's Facebook page that they were engaged. No doubt that would also involve an expensive engagement ring, a party and more drugs, as according to Jack's latest disclosures, Elvanda is a drug addict, as are most of her working-girl friends. Jack described it as an 'occupational hazard.'

Disconnected, one way or another

Something weird just happened... Jack has been trying to call our son without any luck as whenever he calls Dharma's phone he gets a recorded message saying it is the wrong number. He then tried to call my phone but the same thing happened. So he sent me an email telling me what had happened.

"Did you block my phone?" he said.

"No," I replied in an email, "I hadn't even thought of doing that, although in retrospect it's a good idea."

Then I kept on trying to send my reply to his email, but each time I typed my message and hit the 'send' button a message came up on Hotmail saying my request could not be processed, it was either an error in connection or something wrong with Hotmail. And then my attempted reply disappeared. I tried to type in and send my reply for a second, third and fourth time and the same thing happened each time.

Other new emails had appeared on my inbox, so I replied to the one I had received from my editor friend, telling me she thought my "Rendition" must be nearly over. That email went out without any issue and when I checked it was already in my 'sent' box. Then I replied to another one—no problem.

"Ok, now let me try to reply to Jack again," I thought. But once again I had the same problem. Not only that, when I checked my message lists on my phone there was nothing in there from Jack, every message from him had disappeared without a trace, whereas all the conversations from other people are still on my phone going back to around six months ago.

Both my cell phone and my computer seemed to have made up their minds without me.

"Is the universe telling me something?" I asked myself. "Is this supposed to be a signal? Do I have to cut off communication with Jack from now on?" It felt good to be away from his demands, although I still missed his companionship. We used to always talk so much, about anything and everything, and we always joked together. It was only in recent years that we had grown so far apart.

"You must be careful what you wish for" my friend told me. "If you wish for something to happen it very often will."

I thought of all those times I had wished he was dead, although I hadn't really meant it. Now it felt as if he was already dead to me.

"Words have many meanings, depending upon how we use them," my friend went on. "So be careful what you say. Or even think. Sometimes we don't consider the full implications of the message we put out there."

Ever since Jack had gone off on his last trip, saying

he didn't know when he would see us again, I had been hoping not to hear from him.

Does this mean he won't be able to contact us again? What else does it mean? He cannot contact me now and I don't seem to be able to get through to him either. He is in Jakarta with his new partner Elvanda, or at least that was where he told me he was going, on his way out from our villa in Ubud at 10 a.m. on Monday morning. I didn't really care any more.

I asked him to take our son to school at 8 a.m. before he went to the airport, as I thought it would be a good idea if they can spend a little time together. Jack had been ignoring him since he got back.

* * *

I didn't hear from him for at least a couple of months, when all of a sudden there was an email asking for a loan of 4000 Australian dollars. Jack explained at length that he was so broke, his boss hasn't paid his wages yet—he had cleaned out his account to send money to Jakarta for a business management course for Elvanda without thinking he would run out. Right now he was in Sydney and could barely afford food or petrol.

"If you don't transfer that money to me by Friday, then I will simply die by the weekend" he said.

Of course I replied right away.

"Why don't you borrow money from all your 'genuine' gay friends, or your she-male girlfriend, instead of me?" I said.

I didn't make any transfer. By the weekend there was a barrage of emails from him.

"You are a horrible person," he said. "Clearly you are not one of my friends when the chips are down, blah, blah, blah…" I kept on ignoring the emails.

Then on Sunday night I was on Skype – Jack had seen that I was online and he messaged me to ask me to accept his video call. I refused… so he sent another message.

"I am in my office," he said. "I have 23 doxylamine tablets and 27 sominex tablets and 2 bottles of wine– enough to kill myself. I am absolutely broke, I have no more friends. I am living in my boss's office as I can't afford accommodation or food."

Before I answered his message I quickly googled all the brands of tablets and sleeping pills he had mentioned, and read some blogs to find out whether sleeping tablets combined with alcohol really can kill someone on the spot.

The answer was there in black and white. It was pretty clear and easy to read.

"*NOPE!*" one blogger said. "*Sleeping pills won't work. Your body naturally vomits the crap out after you pass out. So you will most likely wake up in a puddle of your own puke. How do I know? Because I tried it! I took two entire boxes of extra strength sleeping pills with alcohol, Whiskey to be precise. I slept for three days, I kid you not... three freakin days! Anyways, I woke up in a puddle of my own puke. It was freakin nasty. I got a new bed and new sheets and everything. PLUS I was mad as heck at not succeeding."*

Well, that was a relief. After reading a few other similar blogs I was feeling confident that he wouldn't be able to kill himself, even if he took all those tablets with two bottles of red wine. I hoped he would make himself sick!

I went back to answer him on skype and said to Jack: "Go on then brave boy, do it!"

Then he told me to turn on my video call. He had turned off the speaker, so I wouldn't hear a thing.

"I just want to share this moment with you," he messaged.

"Lucky me!" I replied. I kept my video camera off, and turned his on. Then I watched him taking sleeping pills and washing them down with red wine, even though my body was shaking as my head was thinking "What if..."

Another typed message came through from Jack.

"I'm feeling the rush now, I think the effect is starting to kick in."

I was feeling very nervous. Although I felt sure he was calling my bluff I could not continue to watch this video of him sleeping on his desk. I turned off my Skype, as it was late at night, and tried to go to sleep.

I kept telling myself "Jack is not dead!"

When I woke up in the morning, just to be sure, I made a phone call to his office and asked the receptionist if I could speak to him.

"Jack is in a meeting with someone" the receptionist said.

"I'm his wife, it's urgent! I need to speak to Jack about our son," I said, and then she put me through to his phone line.

As soon as he picked up the phone I hung up. At least I knew he was not dead. It had simply been another game to trap me into giving him sympathy.

I realize now that his emotional blackmail is no longer working with me. Hopefully he has no further power to influence my state of mind. I had been so down I had risked my own life, but his 'death' had been a total sham. His life was consumed by game playing, such dangerous games I no longer wanted to participate in.

Since then I have started to imagine that he is dead, at least to me, and in my darkest moments I wish he was dead for real. At least it would make this rendition easier and I could bury my regrets.

6

Life after Death...

Writing a new story

There is life after death, I know, because I have experienced it. As well as one rather infamous near-death experience of my own making, and another parody of the process generously provided by Jack and viewed reluctantly by yours truly online, I have been through all those little deaths: the killing of my self-respect, my pride, my love, and my will to live. I feel lucky to be a survivor, and especially to have survived with my humour intact. In fact humour is perhaps one of the secrets of my survival.

Sometimes I look back upon my life and I laugh— could I ever have dreamed, as a little girl peeling peanuts for the infamous witch Dadong Tublin, that people in my family and village might not accept me, or my choices in life? Was it the black magic of her peanuts, those peanuts that put my aching hunger to rest as a little girl, that had made me so different, such an outsider? Could it be my adventures with her fellow exile, Dadong Tinggal, playing in the place of death where nobody dared to go, that had twisted my fate so that I should have no choice but to experience the darker side of life as an outsider? Or was it simply my bravado as a child, my refusal to be subdued by a father's beatings and militaristic discipline that set me up for these ongoing renditions of my soul?

Why was it always those I loved who hurt me? Who lied to me and treated me with disrespect? Did they sense the chink in my armour? Were they attracted to the weak point in my defense—my discontent, my ambition, my longing to be someone else more beautiful and powerful than myself? Too many questions to answer, still.

I must be careful, I realise, now I have the power of my own future in my hands, to find a balance. Not that I can possibly avoid the pain of loving too much, it's just that I do not wish to allow dark and negative feelings into my heart again, and to do that I need to focus on bringing bright and positive healing energies into my life.

I am determined to write on, to write new stories, as many as possible, till the fogs clear and the mystery of my strange path in life becomes exposed. Armed with my experiences, both good and bad, I would like to write a new story in my life for the future, one full of laughter, joy and light.

As a starting point I have started writing children's stories, about my old friends, the two Dadong's Tublin and Tublen, and Dadong Tinggal. Doing this brings back all my memories of those days as a child, when those brave and independent women, both exiles in their own way, were my allies in a world where girls and women were of little value.

My first story is about Dadong Tublin, and her reasons for living alone. By now most people in the village have forgotten what happened to her as a young girl, when she was shapely and beautiful, but she had told me her story in those long afternoons of shelling peanuts as a child. Perhaps that is why I was so drawn to her—she was such a good storyteller.

I settled down to write one morning recently when I woke up feeling resentful again and unsatisfied with my lonely existence. Indra had not come back from Australia, and Dharma was still at school. I miss my boys but I am determined to be productive, in one way or another, and I had completed everything else on my long list when I took out my notepad and started remembering the past.

I had two very important stories to tell, so I sat down and started to write in my new blue diary:

The Story of Tublin

Tublin was a very special girl. Whenever she passed down the village street, the butterflies and birds flew about her, and instead of barking at her the dogs all wagged their tails. It seemed the sun came out whenever she smiled, even if she was always dressed the same old faded batik sarong

What's she got to smile about? asked all the neighbours. They knew that Tublin was one of two sisters, Tublin and Tublen, orphans who had lost their father when the fighting men in the village had gone to help the Raja at Kesiman fight the Dutch invasion in 1906—their mother never recovered from the shock. She had gone quite mad.

After that Tublin and Tublen didn't have anyone to take care of them, and even though they had been the most well liked girls in the village, everybody shunned them. So Tublin roamed the village, usually at dusk when nobody was around, while her sister Tublen remained home to look after their ailing mother.

Tublin took over her father's responsibility for feeding the family and she used to follow the women to glean rice grains from the fields after the harvest, and catch baby eels in the river. On sunny days she would go out at midday, when all the villagers were resting from the hot sun, put some sticky sap on a long twig and catch dragon flies along the side of the road. Wherever she went she gathered dry twigs and logs for firewood, tying them together and hoisting them up to carry home on her head.

The villagers became used to seeing her in the strangest places at the strangest times, as it was not easy for a young girl to gather enough food to feed herself, her mother, her sister and her dog.

Sometimes they would see her at sunset on a distant hill, gathering leaves from a tree, and another time in the river, feeling around in the gurgling river for freshwater shrimps under the full moon.

Although she remained such a familiar sight in the village, Tublin stayed away from people, crossing the road and hurrying homewards to avoid their questioning looks if she saw anyone coming.

*It was rumoured that she had stopped talking altogether,
even to her mother and her sister, but she always talked to her
dog, the faithful companion that followed her on her foraging
far afield each day in search of twigs to keep the home fire
burning, and roots, leaves, berries and nuts to cook on it...*

I put my pen down to rest for a while, thinking of
how resourceful my elderly friend must have been in her
troubled youth, first to feed what was left of her family
on whatever she could find in the fields and forest that
bordered our village, and then eventually to survive on
her own after her mother died, and her sister went off and
eloped with a young man in the village.

My grandfather had told me some stories of how she
was shunned by the villagers, and I now filled in the gaps
of his stories with my imagination, remembering some of
the things she had told me when we sat amidst the piles of
peanuts she had harvested in her back yard.

There were only two people she ever spoke to as far
as I remembered, her niece and me—we were in the same
class together at school, and we used to go to Dadong's
place together to help shell her peanuts. I loved to watch
Dadong Tublin sitting on the floor next to me, pounding
spices and roots with her mortar and pestle; that was my
first introduction to the mysteries of Balinese cuisine.

My interest in her cooking was mostly based on a
permanently hungry ache in my tummy, but after a while I

discovered that she was a master of the art of making tasty food from the simplest of ingredients. She had shown me how to apply her magical transformation with the simple addition of several different aromatic gingers, and when I tried her banana flower in coconut milk I could have sworn I was eating the most delicious chicken I hade ever tasted, although there was absolutely no meat in it. My other favorites were her steamed vegetable '*urap*' made with *daun tabia bun*, the upper leaves of a spicy creeper that grew wild high up in trees in the forest, and her honey-bee '*lawar*' of grubs from the honey-comb she picked.

"Where did you find this?" I would ask her with admiration, as she was an elderly woman by then, and I could not imagine her scaling the high trees where the honey-bees nested. But she would just chuckle and wink at me, and go on with her work. Perhaps that was why I believed the villagers when they said she could fly.

I always wondered if she knew that all the neighbors thought she was a practicing witch, and watched her carefully for signs of her witchery, but she seemed to me too far removed from the mundane world of other people to be bothered with their suspicions.

Perhaps my writing would give me a similar gift, I thought, as it enabled my mind to explore places that were undisturbed by the base elements of human nastiness, as if I were a fly on the wall, observing the antics of those who loved to criticize and condemn.

Reclaiming my Soul

Now I have closed the book upon my relationship with Jack I feel empowered at last to make plans for the future.

But first, perhaps I need to apologize to you, dear reader, if you are still with me that is, if you have survived being bored or offended by Jack and his shenanigans.

I now know that he is a different creature, not the one that I fell in love with and married, a man who is driven by his urge to discover and recognize the other parts of himself through his sexual adventures, much as a chrysalis endures transformation into a butterfly, which beats its beautiful wings for such a short and dangerous life-span.

Although I still look back upon our good times together with nostalgia, I see no possibility that we could return to those times when with my boldness, my broad shoulders and masculine stance, I was his preferred partner. Just as I had striven to change into someone more feminine and alluring, the Jack I knew was a creature whose transformation was not yet complete. Neither Jack nor I can predict where his adventures will lead him, and there is not even any certainty he will survive the journey.

Looking back on my story now it is transferred to black and white words on paper, it is hard to imagine how I have managed to put myself through the hoops and hurdles of life with my relationships, but I now realize that I am undergoing my own transformation. I have never been afraid of taboos enforced by my family and community, although at times I fought them bitterly. Perhaps my unbridled enthusiasm and ambition to achieve my dreams have led me onto paths that those more patient and discerning would have avoided. Nevertheless, it is these experiences that have let me to a greater height of awareness when it comes to understanding human beings, our weaknesses and our desires, and I feel fortunate to have discovered through my difficult times that each painful experience has contributed to my own personal evolution.

Not only have we (both of us, dear Reader) escaped from my mental and emotional Renditions. I have also managed to return to that other shore, the beautiful tropical island that I left to seek my fortune. Now I realise, no matter how often I leave my home in Bali, it will always be here for me, full of childhood memories and stories that are written on my soul, perhaps my most valuable inheritance.

I no longer see any reason to be cynical or dismissive of my home. So what if my village is transformed on the surface into a centre of "obat" and healing? After all, it was originally named for this very function. Neither do I resent that it is hyped up as a place of spiritual healing for those who can afford it.... including the rich and famous.

They too must deal with their karma in life, those times they have been angry and negative, those lives they have stolen or condemned with their actions and words.

Now I am learning to listen to the words, the words I say, the words I write and the words I hear.

Perhaps that is why I can hear the voice of my Ksatrya ancestors more clearly now in my imagination. "Life is a battle," they tell me. "We must be strong, and we must have principles to guide us, and be prepared to sacrifice our souls."

I know now that I can leave Jack to his own karma, and rely upon the positivity of aligning all forces for good offering me something more in my life than the sheer pressure of success in the worlds of money and career. My mother's gentle wisdom has awakened my spirit and I feel so happy to be able to spend time with my family, and explore my own future here, and place my son within reach of their love. I forgive my family for their deceit and lies towards me and from now on I will put everything behind me.

Bali has become a dream place for so many people to live in, but I can see now that happiness is not guaranteed by place. Happiness derives from our own striving, and if in living here the price we pay is to support our living culture while helping it adapt to the pressures of modern life, we must continue to nurture our Gods and our ancestors. I am ready and willing, even if I have to go back to Australia, or further afield to USA to support my family in hard times.

Bali has always been a place where artists and creative people have felt at home. There is something warm and forgiving about the tropics, for those who have come from less temperate countries, and a generosity of spirit and stimulation of the senses that is quite unique to our island home.

Far from being a 'paradise' as romanticized in tourism brochures—with a past of evil kings and slavery, we Balinese have long accepted that good and bad are inseparable companions. That is why we are forever making mystical ceremonies to clear our space of evil and putting offerings out for our invisible deities and ancestors to encourage them to stay with us and put pressure on the scales in favour of good. Even when we are growing up, we have to undergo life-cycle ceremonies to help subdue the bad influences within ourselves, to be aware of our weaknesses and strengthen our good qualities, and at times like Balinese New Year we create ceremonies and parades to drive out the evil spirits that accumulate in our back yards each year.

* * *

I have decided I want to focus on building good karma. During my father's youth so many expatriate artists became famous in Bali, after being welcomed to Ubud as strangers. A number of them stayed on and shared their good fortune with the community. People like Walter Spies and Rudolf Bonnet, who are often credited for the modernization of traditional Balinese painting, Arie Smit with his 'Young Artists' style, and Antonio Blanco whose Blanco Renaissance Museum chronicles his personal growth as an artist. Accepted by the community at large, and benefiting from their idyllic surroundings, these artists were able to share their art and materials with their struggling Balinese colleagues in difficult times, and many great Balinese artists and artists' communities emerged from that connection over time.

Now we have a different kind of expatriate settling in Ubud, young people on the cutting edge of business and environmental concern, the kind of person I aspire to be. I have recently been spending time at the 'Hub-in-Ubud', Hubud for short, a community co-working space in Ubud that offers a place to work and network, for more flexibility and entrepreneurship in our work lives. I like it—the Hubud team wants to support the launch of my "social enterprise, my freelance career" and my "best self."

I never dreamed I would find a 'Holistic' School here in my hometown for my child, either. Nor did I imagine there would be a Fitness Centre for working out just around the corner, and a Yoga Barn offering yoga lessons and retreats just down the road from the hamlet where I live. Never in my life before have I been surrounded by so many tempting opportunities to work on myself, my physical health, to find my own peace and balance.

Not only are there now doors to knock on that offer spiritual healing and meditation classes, there are also clinics that offer new ways of healing and paths to beauty that are less intrusive than western medicine, and right here in my home village I can find masseurs who practice therapeutic treatments of both Balinese and Western origin, as well as many different kinds of meditation classes to heal my torn and battered soul.

If only I could be sure that I was safe from Jack, and find a way of living here in peace where he could no longer reach or attack me, I would be in paradise, living here with my son, creating my new businesses, and making new friends from all around the world. But there was no guarantee that he would not show up at any time, although I tried to pretend that would not happen, and did my best to distract myself by enjoying the many opportunities to meet new people and enjoy new experiences, new ways of being healthy and appreciating life.

Especially when it comes to food in Ubud, we are spoilt for choice as we don't just have some of the most famous Babi Guling *warungs* selling my favorite traditional Balinese roast suckling pig with all the spices, we now also have the latest in contemporary Balinese cuisine and for the vegetarians and health conscious there are vegan restaurants with metres-long salad bars, and the healthy juices and 'Zen' foods of Jl. Hanoman.

I think of my childhood, when we could hardly find enough food to eat and the gap between the different castes and classes within our community was so great. I realise that this new generation is already vastly luckier than we were, not just in terms of material wealth, but also in educational choices. My generation grew up hungry, without choice. This generation of Balinese children will be different. They have access to the world with a click of their fingers on their smart phones and other devices. Opportunities are available that were never there before.

My friend Desak has started a children's library in the village, with all kinds of multilingual books and stories that will help the local children to learn to read, to appreciate languages and learning. Eventually we will get some computers for the children to use as well. I will arrange some weekend activities for cross-cultural debates, and my son's foreign classmates can get together and make friends with the local children on the weekends and share their experiences—they will all benefit from having less fear of the unknown.

Perhaps I can tell my precious stories of the two sisters Dadong Tublin and Tublen. My stories of Dadong Tinggal, who loved to sing all night. My new children's books will soon be ready for publishing.

One day there will be an eccentric Dadong Madé

in their village who will show them her photo album of memories from the big land of the Kangaroo down-under and tell stories about skiing on tall mountains covered in snow. When they tell her they are going to fly, she will believe them!

I digress, dear reader, as I sit in my favorite weekend hideaway hotel overlooking the caldera of Mt. Batur, the place where I love to write, looking out over the volcano and its crater lake as the sun peeps through clouds that pour over the ridge and wrap the lake in a fluffy blanket. From where I sit now, life looks full of opportunities, and I imagine that the tiny cactus that once struggled for survival on the lava fields below is now in full bloom.

I want to write about all those I have known, those I have loved and lost, and I want to write about my latest experiences, discovering children in Bali who still live in a state of poverty and hardship not much different to my own childhood. The changes in Bali over all these years when I have been away have not been kind to everyone, it seems.

I want to write about the different choices we all have in life and love, forgiveness and acceptance. To remind my readers that we must open our minds to the changes that happen to us all during our journey in life: nothing stays the same. Difference is not evil, it is nature's way of ensuring survival. No human being should be limited in choice when it comes to marriage, personal sexual preferences, religion or politics, and how we wish to live our lives.

But my cellphone is ringing... I glance at the number. Oh no! It is Jack! He must be back, and he is trying to track me down! I turn my phone on to silent and let it ring. There is no hurry to deal with him now, let him deal with his own problems, his own karma.

Therein lies another story.

Epilogue

When I started writing this book, driven by a number of cataclysmic events in my life that had left me gasping, I was wondering what dreadful karma had been incurred in my past lives by my ancestors or myself to wreak such havoc on my life and that of my children. I had no idea where it would take me.

I had been cleaning out the garage, ready to move back to Bali, when I found a box of old diaries, and started reading them. The temptation to pick up a half-empty one and keep writing was too much for me, and I began filling my late nights and early mornings by jotting down my thoughts.

Then I met Sarita Newson at the 2012 Ubud Writers & Readers Festival, and after reading some of my work she agreed to help me edit and compile my stories into a fictional memoir. With her assistance I overcame my fear of writing in English, my adopted second language. When I started working on the first rewrites of my personal diaries I discovered that in putting the events of my life and those of my friends and family on paper there was a certain process of catharsis to be gained... Events that had seemed so traumatic in the past, when rendered in ink on paper somehow developed more clarity.

In order to protect the privacy of my family and other people in my memoir, I have changed the names of people and places.

The more I wrote about the life of Madé Angel, the more I realised that I had been denying the damaging impact upon my own daily life and also to my children's lives of my long-term marriage to a violent and selfish man. I had discovered many women who were having to deal with similar issues. Married men and women I knew in both Australia and Indonesia are struggling to find their sexual identity, and the devastating effects of drug abuse were wreaking havoc. Not to mention the effects of partners or parents becoming HIV positive, something impacting upon more than 7000 families in Bali alone.

Slowly but surely my story expanded to include the trials and tribulations of a number of my friends and aquaintances, most of them trying to keep their families intact. By including their stories my own moved firmly out of the arena of memoir and into the world of fiction.

How long, I wonder, can we live with a fellow human being and love him or her, without really knowing the real person? We all change and grow as we mature, but is there any guarantee what direction those changes will take?

I woke up one morning, after re-living my own years of personal trials, haunted by bad memories, and I wanted to jump ship. I felt threatened by a downward spiral of bad fortunes and violence. I needed to re-examine those years of my life, to find a way to understand the changes and to learn to let go with compassion. I expressed this in my writing, and in completing the story I discovered there was much more to learn. There are still choices to be made, and I also know now I will have to make compromises, but I also know that my life is no longer going to be limited to this story alone, and this knowledge gives me courage to persevere.

In this way my writing has empowered me, enabling me to accept that my husband was not the same person I had loved for so long. He was not what he seemed on the surface, and perhaps I would never know the real person that lurked in the shadows of his own confusion. He was on his own personal journey of discovery, one that my children and I could not share.

I decided to go back to my childhood to try and find clues regarding my own choices in life, hoping we could patch up our relationship with compromise. In order to get back to my roots I returned to Bali. After nearly twenty years of living away from home I no longer felt Balinese, and could barely understand my family and the villagers where we lived, or their blind devotion to spiritual and social matters. Many of my old school friends seemed to still live in the abject poverty that I had escaped. I also found an interesting multi-cultural international community had parked itself on my doorstep.

Adjusting back to life in Bali, I filled the gaps of my experience through sharing stories with friends and family, and in doing so rediscovered aspects of my Balinese heritage that comforted me and gave me the strength to continue growing and understand the human dilemma. I realized we are complex and evolving creatures—there is no way in which we can all conform to popular norms.

I discovered forgiveness, although I know it takes time. Forgiving myself is the hardest part, but I am working on it.

Now I wish to dedicate this story to fellow travellers in life, especially women, Balinese or other, in the hope that you too will find your strength within. If life does not serve you your heart's desire, keep your mind's eye wide open.

Desak Yoni, Bali, 2013